ROGUES

AND WILD FIRE

CREATIVE CENTRAL PRESENTS

ROGUES AND WILD FIRE

A SPECULATIVE ROMANCE ANTHOLOGY

Balance of Seven

To those who hear stories in their hearts

and wish only to share them.

Your stories chose you for a reason.

You both are worthy.

CONTENTS

LETTER FROM DEBBIE BURNS

Dearest Adventurer (a.k.a. Awesome Reader),

Hello and welcome! I think I can speak for both Balance of Seven (the publisher) and myself when I say WE ARE SO HAPPY YOU ARE HERE!

I'm Deb, founder of Creative Central—a space for lady fiction writers who want community and belonging, not just another writing group. We're all about keeping it positive and supportive as we help each other and ourselves fulfill our Soul Songs to write books and get them into the hands of readers who will love them!

Thank you for being one of those readers and for helping these authors reach another milestone on the journey toward their big dreams. You are who we write for. You are who we dream of. You are the one we hope our words will captivate, entrance, and inspire. So, thank you, thank you, thank you for saying yes to this anthology!

Rogues and Wild Fire actually started as a simple exercise in storytelling. We'd just finished the Character Deep Dive, a workshop series designed to help the members of Creative Central to write characters readers remember. Our topic on the final day was "Impact on Others."

What impact, or *influence,* does this character have on others? Do they cause other people to feel awkward, ashamed, bigger, or smaller? When they enter a room do people want to leave, stay, make fun of them, or join their party?

And that's when I brought up Strider (a.k.a. Aragorn) from *Lord of the Rings* (the film). His presence is *felt* from the moment he enters the screen. We *know* he is impressive, feared, respected, loved, hated based on how *others* react to him throughout the trilogy.

We love him because the *characters* love him.

And it's not Viggo Mortensen we love, it's *Aragorn.* That's when the words dropped from my mouth . . .

"He makes dirt look good!"

Oh. My. Gosh! The whole group lost it! And from that one comment (and agreement from the ladies) came the idea for a quick and dirty (pun intended) challenge we called the Dirty Ranger Romance.

Could we all write a romance short story in *one* month with a "dirty ranger" as the focal point?

And that, my friends, is how *Rogues and Wild Fire* was born. From a little bit of dirt and a *whole* lot of *impact*!

Thank you again for supporting our authors and helping their Big Dreams come true! We couldn't do it without you.

Loves & hugs,

Debbie Burns
Head Unicorn at
www.DebbieBurns.me
Founder, Creative Central
+ Fiction Expedition

THE RANGER AND THE GREENWITCH

CELOSIA CRANE

My eyes didn't want to open. My head was fuzzy. Putting thoughts together shouldn't have been that hard.

Then the smell hit me. Cold and damp, it smelled of mildew, with a faint whiff of death.

I blinked hard. My vision cleared. The room was dark, with only a patch of light on the floor from a small barred window in the door. My shoulders ached. My wrists were screaming.

I remembered.

I was in Piatra, and I was a prisoner.

A scream built up inside my chest, but a gag prevented it from escaping. My heart thundered in my chest as I struggled against the ropes.

How many days had it been since the attack on Tala? Two? Or was it three? I couldn't be sure. They had drugged me with something on a cloth, forcing me to breathe it in until I fell unconscious. When I had awakened, the rocking of a cart was all I had known, until one wheel struck a rock, throwing me against the pile of plunder. I had screamed against the gag as, cursing, the driver had stopped the cart. My vision had cleared for a second, and I had stared into narrowed angry eyes. Then the cloth had been slapped across my face and the smell, wet and unpleasant, had cut through my senses. I had fought as much as I could, twisting my head away, but they had kept the cloth tightly over my face, and I had known no more.

Wiggling, I managed to sit up. Resting my head against the cold stones, I closed my eyes as tears pricked at my eyelids.

The attack had happened so quickly. Willem had fallen guarding the main gate, pierced through with four arrows. The soldiers had torn out of the trees, their faces savagely streaked with black, twisted in hatred.

Then *he* had arrived—dressed in all black, his face a black mask, and his helmet covered with a black fur pelt. His eyes had burned with a fire I felt down to my very core.

And I had known then that they had come for me alone.

I had shuddered at his touch. I had known in that instant the hatred that burned deep inside of that man. It was like a fever, infecting his entire being. And he had come to claim me.

Diavol, the Witch Hunter of Piatra.

Heavy booted footsteps coming down the corridor brought my attention back to my surroundings. The first thing I saw through the small window set within the door was the light of a smoking torch, and then I heard the sound of metal jingling, like someone lifting a ring of keys. The scrape of metal turning in the lock followed.

The door opened slowly. I could feel my lungs burning in my chest as I struggled to breathe around the gag. Behind my back, my hands trembled in their bonds as a man stepped through the door, stopping two feet from where I sat on a bench. I knew it was him, even without the pitch. A dark-brown beard covered his chin, and his brown eyes glittered in the torchlight.

"Sorin, release her bonds. We will need her to be able to walk." In this tight space, even without physically touching him, I could feel the hatred. It poured off him in waves. Its darkness spread throughout the tiny cell, rippling like eddies at the river's edge.

Sorin stepped forward, blade outstretched. My gaze fixed on the blade, and I fought back another scream. He grabbed me by the shoulder and threw me down against the bench. The knife tore through the rope that bound my hands before he grabbed my ankles and did the same.

Pins and needles shot through my hands and feet as Sorin stepped back, sheathing his blade. I tore the gag from my mouth, addressing the leader.

"Why have you taken me? What have I ever done to deserve Diavol's hatred?" The words sounded thick and garbled in my ears. With impatient hands, I shoved my curly rust-colored hair back from my face.

"You exist. You and your kind." He turned his head, his lip curled in disgust. "*Magi!* You infect the world like a plague. And like a plague, you must be cleansed." His eyes almost glowed in the dim light as he glowered at me. "Through fire, you must be made pure once more. That is the only way to scorch the evil from your blood." He turned and began walking toward the door.

Glancing backward over his shoulder, he sneered. "I wouldn't get too comfortable. You won't be staying here long." His laugh echoed off the stone walls. My stomach lurched and contracted tightly at the sound.

"The pyre is already set. We but wait for the full moon to rise." Walking out the door, Diavol sent one final remark back over his shoulder. "I have work to do among my people. But do not fear; I shall be back for you." His laugh started to trail away as he moved down the hall. "Tonight you shall burn."

Malice dripped from the words as he walked away. It danced along my spine, making my body shudder. I heard the scraping of the key as it turned in the lock, imprisoning me once again.

They had left me the torch. Its smoke carried with it the distinct scent of sulfur, clogging my nose with the smell of bad eggs. Sitting on the bench, I pulled my boots off and massaged my ankles. My wrists bore red welts and blisters from my struggles against the ropes. Beyond that I was unhurt.

I stood slowly, uncertain if my legs would hold me. The smell of the torch took me right back to the scent of burning thatch and the screams of my people. It shuddered through me. I sank down against the wall, my shoulders shaking as sobs tore through me. My chest hurt and my ribs burned as I wept for the innocent dead.

When the tears had passed, I brushed my hair out of my face once more. The light from the torch lit it as it brushed in front of my gaze, illuminating the rich reds and coppers. I pushed myself up to a standing position again, feeling the numbness in my hands and feet.

I slapped my thighs. My hands felt bloated and nerveless. As I did, the palm of my left hand brushed my medicine bag, which hung from my belt. Grasping at my hip, behind the medicine bag, I felt for my sheath. I wrapped my palm around the pommel and drew my belt knife.

The torch light glinted off the blade as my fingers gripped the hilt. I smiled for the first time. *They didn't check to see if I was armed.*

Diavol's words returned, ringing in my mind. I clutched the knife in my hand. *At least I can take one of them with me.* Icy hands gripped my stomach now as I fought the terror rising inside me. My stomach jerked, and I swallowed hard against the bile. I refused to defile myself in that manner.

Footsteps approached rapidly. The sound and cadence indicated a flight of stone steps.

I froze.

"Who are you?" the guard outside my cell demanded.

There was no answer, except for a sickening thunk and a slight moan. Then came the harsh jangle of metal keys. Metal scraped against the lock again as a key was tried.

Forcing myself to my feet, I clutched my knife tightly. Whoever was coming through that door, I would defend myself from them to the best of my ability. I wouldn't let myself be taken lightly.

My hand shook as whoever was out there cursed at the keys, fitting another one to the lock on my door. This one turned slowly, grating against wood and metal until the door slowly eased forward.

I crouched behind the door.

A tall man with wolf pelts across his shoulders stepped into the room, his face hidden within a deep hood. Taking a deep breath, I leaped.

He spun toward me and caught my hand, plucking the knife from it. "I appreciate your desire to protect yourself, Dejah Raad. But I'd much rather you use it against the enemy."

Lifting his other hand, he pushed his hood back, exposing light-brown hair and intense blue eyes. "And I am not your enemy."

"Calder Magnus?" Heat leaped in my stomach as I met his gaze.

Shaking his hair back off his face, Calder released my wrist and handed me back my knife, hilt first. At the first brush of our fingers, the heat in my stomach surged through my body. Our gazes locked, held. I saw intensity in his gaze and felt an answering heat rise up my neck slowly.

He was a man on a mission. Turning, he glanced about the cell before turning back to me. His focus was clear in his shoulders and how he held himself. Alert. Ready to give battle.

"Follow me, quickly. Diavol is busy whipping the townsfolk into a witch-burning frenzy. If we don't leave now, they will catch us for sure." He waited only for me to sheathe my knife before turning and leading the way out of the cell and up a twisting flight of stairs.

We climbed two stories before we came to a window opening that was wider than an arrow slit. Propped in the corner of the window was a grappling hook. Calder turned to me. "Climb on my back. Put your arms around my neck and wrap your legs around my waist. We'll moved faster that way." Turning and crouching down to give me greater ease, he waited.

I stepped forward, heat climbing up my neck at the thought of being pressed so firmly against him, with only layers of wool and leather between us. But I could hear the chanting now, and it drove all other thoughts from my brain.

Quickly, I did as he had asked, wrapping my legs around his waist, using my feet to secure myself. Grabbing my thighs, he adjusted my position before turning and backing out the window. "Hold on tightly." His voice was a low whisper as he descended the rope. I closed my eyes and tightened my grasp. Pressing my face into the wolf fur, I breathed in his scent.

He was here. I breathed in deeply, tightening my arms about his neck. If he had left when he was supposed to, would I still be in that cell? Would aid have come in time?

Calder had chosen a solitary life, roaming the forests with a small band of men and protecting our borders with his life. He returned to the village only once a month now to report to his cousin Alain, our chieftain. He stayed a few days, usually, before leaving again. And it had been during these visits that I had often found him sitting outside my home. Just as I had the night before the attack.

Calder had seemed unwilling to talk to most of the villagers on the occasions he returned to the timber fortress of Tala. But he had spoken to me.

I cherished those conversations. I longed for the companionship that had disappeared from my life with the deaths of my mother and younger brother. Our conversations had become the basis for our unlikely alliance. Two outcasts, perhaps, recognizing each other.

Still, though Calder had singled me out, I had a long memory, and I remembered what had driven him into the forest all those years ago.

And Deidre, the woman he had mourned.

I had cooked dinner for him that night, and we had talked into the dark hours. The next morning, I had stood at my cottage door, watching him as the gates opened. I had seen him tense, his hands flying to draw his sword and axe as the Piatran warriors came storming into Tala.

I felt the slight impact as his feet struck the rocky ground now. Loosening my grip, I slipped from his back. I stepped backward and watched as he whipped the rope up hard and the grappling hook came free, tumbling down beside us.

"We shall have to move quickly." He turned to look at me. "You are not hurt badly?"

The darkness that covered the land hid his face from me, but I still felt the ferocity of his gaze. I shook my head. "I have some minor bruises and rope burns around my wrists. Beyond that, I am whole."

He nodded, making quick work of coiling the rope. "Let's go. We need as much distance as possible between us and them before your disappearance is discovered. The full moon will be both help and hindrance to us tonight." He held out a hand toward me. I grasped it, and we took off into the deep cover of the trees.

Dawn's approach began slowly, the faintest lightening of the horizon. My legs ached and my eyes burned. So far, we had only heard men. That one blessing, at least, we had been given. They had not brought the dogs.

I wanted nothing more than to sit down and rest, but the thought of our pursuers was never far away. We could not stop to rest. We dared not stop.

Ahead of me, Calder pressed on. His fur-covered shoulders became more visible with the gradual lightening of the sky. We were following an old deer trail, faint and disused, when he turned his head and met my gaze. Stepping closer, I could see the color of his eyes; day was rapidly approaching.

"We need to find somewhere to hide," he whispered. "We need to rest."

Ahead of us, the ground sloped downward. We were leaving the higher foothills now and descending into an old forest. The forest I was familiar with. The forest that Kyllikki favored.

At the thought of the demigod, I raised a hand and clutched my amber amulet. We were back in his territory.

Following the deer trail, we moved forward until we came to a narrow box canyon that ventured back, ending in a boulder fall. Calder stepped forward, his gaze examining the walls. They rose gently, their tops covered with old forest growth. Moss and lichen clung to them, ferns growing from cracks. In normal circumstances, I would have felt very much at home here.

Stepping forward, I lifted a hand and placed it on the rock wall, feeling the coolness of the stone beneath my palm. Calder was looking carefully around the back of the valley, where the boulder fall cut it off. I turned my head and saw a fallen tree near the boulder fall.

The boulders had knocked it over. Its trunk, which lay along the valley floor, was raised by the root mass at one end. Through the gap, I saw what I was looking for. A faint trail led underneath the tree, back into the wall of the canyon.

"Calder." I spoke his name on a whispered breath, but he heard me and turned around to see what I had found. I gestured toward the spot, and he swiftly joined me, crouching down to examine it. Dim light filtered in through the canopy now, giving us enough light to see a large hollow. It was dry, with crumbling leaf litter, and hidden enough for our purposes. Calder nodded, a smile creasing his cheeks as he gestured for me to enter first.

His smile did funny things to me. The proud approval in his glance had warmed me, but the smile unstitched me. I could feel my stomach trembling as I crawled on my knees into the den.

Calder followed behind me. Using a branch, he rubbed out the signs of our passage before turning and gazing around the small space. It wasn't a cavern, really—more an undercut of the cliff wall that the tree had obligingly fallen against.

Unbuckling his belt, he laid his sword between us and the opening. Pulling out bread and cheese, he cut thick slices of each and handed them to me silently. I took them without comment, my stomach talking loudly as I did so.

"Did they not feed you?" He spoke in a low whisper as he pulled his waterskin from the belt.

I shook my head, too busy chewing bread and cheese to speak. In the silence that surrounded us, I devoured the sustenance he provided and drank the water greedily.

His eyes watched me constantly. I felt the heat in them, the awareness that tickled up the back of my neck, sending goosebumps over my scalp.

I had come to cherish his visits in the village, eagerly anticipating them as I felt increasingly isolated from the other villagers. Never had I imagined us in this situation, though.

"We should rest."

I looked up to see him wiping the crumbs of his own food off his hands. Nodding, I turned my body and lay down on the ground, pulling my cloak tightly around me.

I closed my eyes and felt Calder stretch his body out along mine. My breath caught in my chest as his hand brushed my arm. He settled beside me, his chest against my back. Squeezing my eyes shut, I felt his hand brushing hair off my shoulder and gently tracing the skin of my neck. We had pushed hard and long, though, and I was exhausted. Now, here in this dim hiding place with the heat of his body helping to warm mine, I closed my eyes and drifted to sleep.

I woke suddenly. I felt the pressure of tears as they built behind my eyes. A sense of panic swelled in my chest.

Then Calder shifted slightly behind me, his arm slipping around my waist, pulling me back against his chest, and I relaxed. We were safe for the time being.

He murmured something beneath his breath, burying his face in the hair at the back of my neck. His broad hand spread across my stomach, pressing me into his embrace.

In the stillness, my heart beat like a drum, my tears forgotten. I had been like a starving woman at a feast table when he had begun to visit me in the village. Over the course of a year, I had lost my mother and brother and then watched as the village slowly turned on me. Fear had run rampant with the witch hunts ripping through the mountain villages. Only Calder and Chief Alain had remained on my side.

And for months during the long evenings Calder had spent in my home, I had longed for this. For him. I closed my eyes as tremors ran across my skin. I didn't want him to stop. For once, I wanted to hold onto this dream.

His breath stirred, rushing across the join of my neck and shoulder. His lips pressed against my skin, the hair of his beard and moustache making me tremble.

His touch was firm and gentle. His hand moved slowly, caressing as it wandered across my midriff, slipping higher. His light touch caused my breath to catch in my throat as his fingers lingered along my neck.

I rolled onto my back and met his half-opened, slumberous gaze. His head dipped and then paused for a second, his gaze lifting once more to mine.

As his lips took possession of mine, I knew without a doubt that he was fully awake. This was no dream.

Shifting suddenly, he leaned over me, his eyes blazing down into mine. I held his gaze, my breath frozen in my chest. We didn't speak, and the silence enveloped us in its embrace.

I lost myself in the fervor of his gaze. Almost as if time had frozen, I drowned in his eyes. With a slight groan, he closed the distance between us, taking my lips in a passionate kiss.

Outside, a branch cracked. We both froze. Another branch snapped, and there came the sound of men tramping through dry leaves. Calder lifted a finger to his lips, meeting my gaze.

Raising my hand to the amulet that hung about my throat, I wrapped my hand around it and closed my eyes. The sun shining upon Calder's wolf pelts had given me an idea.

Kyllikki, help me! We are under attack. Hide us. Let them see only what I want them to see. There was the faintest echo in my mind, and I relaxed. He had heard me.

Calder's hand was at his belt, drawing his long hunting knife. I felt his slow movements, the coiled tension in his body. Ready to spring. To attack. To defend me.

With Kyllikki's power supplementing my own, I pictured wolves. I squeezed my eyes shut, envisioning two wolves curled up in their den, sleeping. One with tawny brown hair, the other a russet ginger.

Outside our hideaway, the footsteps slowed. Then stopped.

Even the slightest of movements seemed extremely loud as I

caught my breath and drew once again on the image of the two wolves. My whole body tensed with the focus. My ears heard every breath and the slight scraping that Calder's knife made as it was drawn free of its sheath.

"Shit, it's a wolf den." The whispered words were urgent. "Let's get out of here before they wake up."

"What do you mean?"

"I mean, there are wolves sleeping in there." One set of footsteps could be heard moving away. "I'm getting out of here." A low murmured conversation followed, the sound of men with opposing views, and then more feet joined in the retreat.

Neither Calder nor I moved. Slowly, the crunch of leaves faded into the distance, and we were surrounded once more by the silence of the forest.

Calder slowly sheathed his knife, looking down at my hand curiously. I still clutched the amulet.

He leaned down, until his mouth was by my ear. "What the hell just happened?" he asked, his words deliberate and quiet.

I closed my eyes, swallowing hard. "Kyllikki came to our aid." I felt a sudden shakiness as I waited for his response. Few in our village knew of my connection to the deity. Chieftain Alain alone understood the full portent of it.

"The demigod?" I nodded my head, opening my eyes to meet his astonished gaze. "He comes to your aid?"

"He has long been a companion and teacher of mine as I walk the woodlands."

Calder's brow relaxed as he reached out a finger and gently touched the stone. "I am very grateful, then."

The corner of his mouth twitched as he shook his head slightly. "You constantly surprise me, Dejah Raad. Always full of new ideas and knowledge." His finger slipped off the amulet, tracing my collarbone lightly. "Something I find quite enticing."

My breath caught oddly in my chest at the caress and even more at the smile. He had not turned away, as the rest of the village had. He had simply accepted.

I wet my lips as our gazes locked once more. His fingers trailed up my throat, gently tracing my jawbone to trail lightly across my lips. "You were ready to defend yourself against the worst. You kept pace with me through the forest last night. And now this. Are you enchanting me, little greenwitch?" He cocked his eyebrow as his lips twisted into a smile, displaying a dimple in his cheek.

I couldn't speak. The magic his fingers were working drove all thought from my mind. My breath quickened beneath his touch. Our gazes locked. His face softened, his lips relaxing into a gentle smile.

"I wouldn't care if you were." His hand slid along my cheek, cupping it in his sword-calloused palm as his mouth covered mine again. Something lurched within my chest as I wrapped my arms around his neck, tangling my fingers in his tawny mane.

I sat huddled against the trunk of a tree, watching Calder survey the riverbank. We had left our wolf den at dusk, slipping silently away into the forest once more. Our final hurdle, before we would be in familiar lands, lay before us now, its wide surface reflecting the brilliance of the full moon's light. There had been no sound of our pursuers, but neither Calder nor I believed they had given up the hunt.

The moonlight seemed to capture Calder in its beam. His fur-clad shoulders stood out with startling clarity. Hungrily, I watched him move along the bank.

Finally, he turned and walked back toward me. Slipping into the mottled shadow of the underbrush, he turned to me. "We must cross here. The rapids make it far too difficult elsewhere, in either direction. I'll make us a guide rope." His gaze held mine, as though trying to reassure me.

I nodded. I tried to smile, but early spring meant the waters would be icy cold. We could easily die of shock if we weren't careful. I watched him take out the grappling hook. Carefully coiling the rope beside him, he swung the hook in a circular motion until he had gathered enough momentum. When he released it, the grappling hook sailed out over the waters, landing with a thunk in a fallen tree on the far bank. Calder pulled on the rope to make certain it was secure before turning back toward me.

A faint clink of metal widened my eyes as he slowly unbuckled his belt. Efficiently removing his sword and dagger, Calder leaned them against the tree before untying his cloak and laying the weapons on it. Then he stood and stripped his shirt off.

Even in the moonlight, he was impressive. His movements were fluid, his chest only covered in a light dusting of hair. My eyes traced the lines of the tattoos that covered his right arm and side. Intricate whorls and patterns danced along his skin.

Feeling his eyes on me, I lifted my head. Our gazes locked. I recognized what he was doing. Understood it, even. But after what had occurred in the wolf den earlier, my whole body trembled at the heat in his gaze, anticipation tightening my gut.

Keeping his gaze firmly fixed on mine, he reached down and pulled off first one boot, then the other. His pants followed, leaving him wearing only a modesty cloth. I watched as he rolled all his clothing up into his cloak and tied it into a bundle.

I could feel my heart pounding. It was trying to break out of my chest, it was hammering so hard. I slowly untied my cloak and laid it on the ground. My hands went to the ties on the side of my dress, loosening them so I could draw it over my head. His gaze burned into my flesh the entire time.

Beneath my dress, I wore only a thin shift. Soon it would be plastered against my skin with the water of the river. I shivered with the heat of his gaze and the coolness of the night. Pulling off my boots, I added them to my bundle before tying the corners together. Twisting my hair into a coil on top of my head, I pulled a polished hair stick from my pouch and secured it.

Calder leaned down, his lips touching my ear. "You go first. I'll follow, watch our backs." My eyes closed involuntarily. "I'll make sure you don't wash away." His lips pressed suddenly to the skin just in front of my ear. "I don't want that to happen."

The conviction in his voice shook me, and I shivered a little as he handed me the rope. One hand balanced the bundle of clothing on my head, while the other gripped the rope tightly. Stepping down the bank, I gasped as my bare foot entered the water.

We had no other choice. I placed my other foot into the icy water. It was so cold, it burned. I sucked my stomach in as the waters swirled around first my calves, then my thighs, and finally my breasts. Using the rope to help propel me, I felt the ground carefully before each step forward. My whole body shook from the burn of the icy spring meltwater.

Behind me, I could hear Calder murmuring encouragement as he protected me, as he had done since coming through the door in the tower. Finally, the water level began dropping as we approached the farther bank. As I entered the shallower water, the night air hit my wet shift, causing my skin to contract anew. The cold drew my nipples into tight, hard points that rubbed painfully against my shift. As I climbed the bank, the heat of Calder's hand on my hip cut through the cold, wet fabric, giving me the stability I needed to reach the top of the embankment.

Standing there in the chill night air, I wrapped my arms around myself, shivering. The trees were thick here, providing us good cover from the moonlight. I followed Calder as he stepped away from the riverbank, into their welcoming darkness.

He quickly untied his bundle, throwing his cloak around his shoulders. I watched him, my mind stalling with cold as my body shivered. He stepped toward me, enveloping me in his embrace, pulling me into him, and wrapping the cloak around both of us.

"We need to warm ourselves and dry a little before we can continue." I felt his lips skimming my ear as his hot breath danced across my skin. I shook, but no longer from cold.

Beneath the cloak, my hands slipped around his chest, wrapping around his back. His skin was cool and still damp from the river. My fingers found the ridge of a scar and traced its jagged length gently.

Suddenly, Calder moved. My back was pressed against a tree, while the burning heat of him pressed against my front. I lifted my head to meet his eyes mere seconds before his mouth crashed down on mine. His hands, now freed from the cape, skimmed up my hips and sides, his palms brushing the sides of my breasts.

I gasped against his lips. His hands, large and calloused, traced my curves, pausing at my hips to pull my body more tightly against his.

This. I had never known anything like this. This raging fire, all consuming. It filled my body, driving out the cold.

Abruptly, he broke the kiss. Leaning his forehead against mine, our noses brushed and our breaths mingled. "We should probably dress. I find you far too tempting, clothed as you are now."

His hands skimmed the sides of my breasts again. His words hammered against my gut, making me shiver even when pressed so firmly against his body. I gasped softly. This close, I could feel a smile cross his face at my response. Suddenly, the pressure intensified. His palms cupped my breasts, his thumbs brushing against my nipples.

The warmth of his hands, mixed with the friction of the fabric, was almost more than I could handle. I reached across the small distance between us, sealing my lips to his in an urgent kiss. His arms, like molten bars of steel, wrapped around my back, holding me tightly against him.

A single howl rose on the night air, jerking us apart. An icy hand reached deep inside my chest. Calder swore. "They've brought out the dogs."

He released me so suddenly, I reeled back against the tree. I watched him for a second as he dressed rapidly. Then, turning to my own bundle, I followed suit. A second howl tore through the air, closer this time. I wrapped my cloak tightly around myself as a shudder tore through me, icy fingers trailing up my spine as yet another howl awakened fear.

Calder held out his hand. His warm firm grip helped anchor me. I lifted my head and met his gaze. Unable to keep my chin from trembling, I tried to smile.

Calder cupped my cheek. "They are still miles away." Stepping in, he pressed a kiss to my forehead. "You have been very brave. We're almost home now."

I nodded my head, breathed in deeply, and squeezed his hand. "Let's go."

I kept my gaze firmly on Calder's signals. So far, we had managed to escape Diavol. But now the hounds had our scent. The grappling hook and rope had given Diavol's men the marker for where we had left the river, an oversight that Calder was still cursing beneath his breath.

The forest was more ominous with the baying of the hounds in the background. Crouching down, I surveyed the land around us. A flock of birds suddenly took to the air, issuing startled, angry cries as they circled the canopy, before coming to rest in a new location.

Calder reached out a hand and stopped me. We paused, listening carefully to the sounds around us. The birds quieted and the forest stilled again. We slipped forward.

Calder grabbed my arm. We ducked down and found shelter in the hollow of a large, lightning-struck tree. We huddled close together in our improvised shelter. I lifted my eyes and met Calder's gaze. He smiled wistfully, lifting a hand to brush my cheek. I found a similar smile tugging at my lips.

We had spoken so little to each other, and yet I knew him better than any other man in Tala. He had sat in my little hut and given me companionship when the rest of the village shunned me. He had given me warmth and passion. And now, his arm draped around my shoulders, as though trying to comfort and reassure me. His hand brushed hair from my face, caressing my cheek.

After a time, Calder stilled. Rising slowly, he held out his hand. Stepping back into the forest, we moved slowly forward until we reached a large glade.

"You cross first; I'll cover you," Calder said quietly into my ear. Nodding, I drew my knife and stepped forward into the silent glade.

Reaching the far side, I sank down against the trunk of a large tree, my eyes sweeping the forest on either side of Calder. He leaped forward into the clearing. As he left the safety of the tree line, a shadow caught at the corner of my vision. A black helmet rose slowly above the brush to the left of Calder. The savage lines and grimacing lips were more than enough for me to identify him.

Diavol.

He had found us.

They must have pressed on through the night, returning with horses and dogs to a rendezvous point. *We'll never make it now.* I was frozen, watching the tableau unfold before me. Aware of the dogs howling as the rest of the soldiers began closing in on us.

Diavol lifted a bow, nocking an evil-looking arrow and sighting along its length, taking aim at Calder.

I gasped, my chest tightening painfully as I watched him draw the bowstring. I was helpless to prevent what I knew was about to happen. My throat clenched as tears filled my eyes.

My face drawn, I looked to Calder. His gaze held mine for a moment, and then he started to turn, glancing back over his shoulder. Time seemed to slow around us.

I blinked away tears as they fell down my cheeks. The arrow flew from the bow. It hit Calder in the back of the shoulder with enough force to throw him forward. The sound of it striking his flesh echoed in my ears.

He stumbled, his face ashen with pain. Then he steadied and rushed on, grabbing my hand as he passed by me. Rushing us farther into the forest.

I risked a glance at him. Seeing the black feathers that fletched the arrow shaft protruding from his back made my stomach turn. I watched his lips tighten against the pain.

The baying of the hounds was much closer now. And Diavol was just behind us.

Calder kept pulling us onward.

We crashed heavily through thick underbrush. Calder was fading rapidly. The arrow was still visible as it stuck out from his shoulder.

He tried to move forward through the heavy undergrowth, but his movements had become ponderous and clumsy.

The opposite of the man I knew.

"Over here," I whispered, seeing a familiar place where we could hide. The forest hills had grown around us until a series of ravines and palisades appeared in the deep canyon ahead of us. It was a place sacred to Kyllikki. We would be safe there.

We had to be. We couldn't go any farther.

Calder stumbled toward me, his face drained of color. It was ashen against his tawny hair.

As we reached the nearest small escarpment, Calder simply collapsed, crumpled into a heap on the ground.

This was it. Without help, we were done for. Diavol would have his victory.

I could hear the crunching of feet through the underbrush that signaled our pursuers were still very near.

Pulling out the amber amulet that Kyllikki had given me, I drew in a deep breath and clenched it tightly. *Kyllikki, help me, please! Calder is wounded, and the enemy is upon us! I cannot escape! If they capture us, we are dead!*

Tears slipped down my cheeks as I opened my eyes. Calder was still an unconscious heap at my feet. Lifting my head, I breathed a sigh of relief as Kyllikki stepped around one of the palisades, approaching us. He looked like a tree come to life and was lumbering toward us. Branches sprouted from his head and shoulders, shaking with each movement. In this moment, nothing had ever looked so beautiful.

He crouched next to Calder, his branch-like appendages examining the unconscious man. "That arrow needs to get out as soon as possible," he hissed. "It has poison on it."

"I feared as much, but we couldn't stop. They are still after us." I choked on a sob. "They brought dogs. They were going to burn me."

Kyllikki's face lit up in a feral grin that almost scared me. "No longer." He waved a hand behind himself, and a rock wall appeared, completely blocking the entrance to the canyon. "From the outside, they will see only a cliff. You will be safe here." Mossy cliffs rose up around us, and a stream ran among the palisades behind us. I would be able to find wood and medicinal plants growing in abundance here, I knew. A weight lifted from my shoulders, and I took a deep breath. We were safe. Kyllikki would help us.

He crouched over the prostrate warrior. "I'll see what I can do to fight off the poison." He glanced over at me. "But you shall have to use your herbs and skills to actually heal him. I can only do so much. Cursed iron." He growled.

"Thank you, Kyllikki." I swallowed hard against the lump in my throat. "He rescued me from the tower in Piatra."

Kyllikki's face contorted. "I had wondered why you had not been to see me these past few days."

He turned his gaze back down to Calder. Rubbing his hands together until they lost their branches and resembled human hands, he laid one near the place where the shaft pierced Calder's shoulder and the other on his left side, along his ribs. The gray tinge slowly left Calder's skin, and his breathing steadied as Kyllikki lifted his hands.

"There. I have done what I can. Though you will still have a battle on your hands." He grinned. "You will be safe here. I will keep them busy."

I nodded, my face twisting in anger as I thought of Diavol. "Their leader shot Calder. He wears a helmet wrapped in a black fur pelt and discolors his face with pitch. He is evil. He attacks Tala and other settlements, looking for witches—magi—to burn."

Kyllikki's eyes narrowed as he met my gaze. His face was no longer that of the friend I knew, but a hideous mask twisted with anger. Then, he was gone.

Calder murmured something, and I turned back to where he lay. I laid a hand on his back. The warmth of his skin was encouraging, but the skin around the wound still looked gray and angry.

"I'm sorry." I gripped the shaft of the arrow with my other hand. Bracing myself against him, I pulled hard and sharply on the arrow. He made a slight moan as the arrow came free but lay still. The wound bled sullenly.

I built a small fire from the litter and debris I found on the forest floor. "I'm sorry. I'm so sorry." My throat tightened as he flinched with the first puncture of my needle. With each stitch I winced, hating that I had to inflict even this small pain on him.

Kyllikki returned. "They will not bother you again, child. I have befuddled their minds and led them on a merry chase, setting their own dogs upon them. They know not why they are in the forest nor where they are."

He looked down at Calder. "Now you must focus on healing this man."

"He saved my life. The very least I can do is try to save his." I lifted a hand and brushed back my sandy-red curls as tears suddenly began to slip down my cheeks.

Kyllikki held out a handful of herbs. "I've brought you these. They will help when the fever sets in. I acquired their provisions, as well. They will help to make him more comfortable." With that, he disappeared, leaving me alone with my unconscious patient.

As night fell, Calder's skin heated up. He began to move restlessly on the small bed of boughs and furs that I had made. His body was raging with fever before it was fully dark. I quickly filled a pot with icy water from the stream that lay near us. Returning, I used a cloth to cool his forehead. His skin trembled beneath my touch.

Near the middle of the night, his eyes opened. They locked on me. Hard and bright, they danced in the firelight. He reached out a hand toward me. "Deidre. Come here."

His voice rumbled through the small enclosure, full of intimate knowledge. The words hit me like a hot knife, sliding sharply between my ribs before pain blossomed within me, even as his gaze had its own effect on my body, heat flushing my cheeks.

Sucking in a shuddering breath, I furiously blinked back tears. "I am not Deidre, Calder." I swallowed, trying to keep the tears from my voice. "That's the fever talking."

His hand grasped my wrist, pulling me toward him. His eyes

were narrowed, and in the firelight they glowed like sapphires. "You speak nonsense." I found myself draped across his chest, his arms locking me to him more effectively than any ropes.

"Calder, what are you doing?" Pain turned to panic. I struggled against his hold, my tears falling in earnest. This was wrong. I didn't want this.

"Please, Calder!" The pain tore through my chest as though something were breaking. "Please let me go. Please, Calder. I'm not Deidre." Tears threatened to overwhelm my words. They were a breath away. I swallowed against them. For a moment, I saw his eyes widen and knew that he had returned to full consciousness.

"I'm Dejah Raad," I whispered. My forehead dropped to his chest, tears streaming down my face. "Deidre is gone. I'm so sorry."

His arms relaxed, then fell limp to his sides. His eyes closed, and he slipped back into fevered unconsciousness.

I watched as Calder opened eyes free of fever. He moved slowly but sat up. Reaching over his shoulder, the fingers of his left hand traced the stitches I had placed. I watched him turn his head, suddenly afraid to meet his gaze. "You did this?"

I held out a wooden cup full of water. "What less could I have done? You saved my life." I smiled weakly. "Diavol would have killed me."

"When you were taken, Alain was desperate. You are invaluable."

"And that was why he sent you after me?" My voice trembled.

Calder leaned back against the rock face, a slow grin crossing his face. "Truthfully, I volunteered. I knew I could succeed where others wouldn't. That I could get to you faster alone."

I swallowed hard. "I am grateful you came." I shuddered. "It was like a nightmare."

The touch of his hand made me jump. Raising my head, I met his gaze. It was full of caring and concern. "I had to save you." He spoke in a low tone.

I had to blink away the tears that threatened. His thumb brushed rhythmically against the back of my hand.

"You are free of that place." He glanced around. "But where are we now?"

"We are well hidden, with some help from Kyllikki. You've been unconscious for three days, fighting the poisoned arrow that struck you as we ran."

"And Diavol?"

I closed my eyes. "He is still out there. Kyllikki drove them away from us, and we are safe for now. But he is still out there."

I watched him nod slowly as though processing the information. His expression turned thoughtful as he stared into the small cooking fire.

"Seeing you in that dungeon nearly destroyed me. I had thought Alain was being overly sentimental about your role in the village until that moment." For a long silent moment, he said nothing more.

"I see now that I was wrong." He sighed. "I didn't realize the truth about your connection to the land and to this forest. There have been magi in our village in the past. Very powerful ones. And I have heard the rumors and stories about the god of the forest. But I never connected them with any of the many powerful entities who roam our woods and plains. Much less to someone with gifts such as you possess."

"How could you have known? My gifts never came up during our conversations."

His chuckle surprised me. "I still can't believe you tried to come at me with your belt knife." His smile tore at me. "I admire your courage."

I looked away. The intimacy and camaraderie that had grown over the past few days now hung like a specter between us.

I stood up. "I will be back in a little while. I need to gather some more firewood and check my snares. You need to rest." Without meeting his gaze, I slipped away from the stone undercut where we sheltered.

I prepared the small rabbit my snare had provided for roasting.

My entire world had been turned upside down in the past few days. The strength of Calder's arms and the feel of being draped across his chest haunted me.

I desired him and I wanted to be with him, but I needed to know that he saw me and not the long-dead Deidre.

The smell of the game began to permeate our camp. Calder's eyes opened. I watched his gaze search until it found me. I felt the brute force of his concentration, his glittering, jewel-like eyes flashing across the fire, and again the heat began to climb my cheeks.

My hands trembled and fumbled with the simple meal preparations.

I handed him a slab of wood that held the roasted rabbit and some wild greens I had gathered. He touched my hand as he took it, his fingers stroking slowly against my own.

I started back, my gaze wide. What I saw in his eyes shot a hot blush into my cheeks. I took my own portion of rabbit and began to eat, trying to hide the tremors in my hands.

Outside, the sky darkened, thunder rumbled, and rain poured down. The ground beneath the outer wall of our shelter was wet with the suddenness of the precipitation. It puddled around my feet as I crouched on the far side of the fire.

"If you stay there, you will become wet through." Calder's words echoed through the space. Looking up, I met his gaze.

His aquamarine eyes were narrowed in intense concentration. "Come over here. The natural overhang will protect us." He held out a hand, compelling me.

We sat for a while in silence as the thunder rumbled and the rain poured. Pressure built slowly and inevitably in my chest.

"Tell me about Deidre."

I felt tension in his arm as it pressed against mine. "She was my first love. Beautiful and kind, her gentleness won me over. Idealistically, I thought our love would live forever. But then the wasting disease struck her. Took her away from me."

He no longer carried the pain of loss in his tone, but rather acceptance. "After her death, I fled to the forest. There, I had to stay alert to survive. I could not afford to waste time on human affection."

The pressure in my chest reached the point of pain and burst free. I raised my head and met his dazzling gaze. "And now?"

A smile split his face, warming his angular features. "Now, I feel alive again." He leaned toward me. "And I want to kiss you."

I swallowed hard as the pain of that night flushed through me. "What is wrong, Dejah?" His voice was soft. I almost flinched as he brushed his fingers across my jaw.

"That night . . ." I couldn't continue. My chin trembled as I fought back tears.

He drew me gently to him. "In my fever, I mistook you for Deidre. I'm sorry for the hurt that caused."

Placing his thumb beneath my chin, he forced me to meet his gaze. "Dejah, you are so different from Deidre. So full of fire and life. I have always looked forward to our conversations during my monthly visits. Your sharp wit made those trips worthwhile. Dueling words with you sharpened my desire for companionship again."

He brushed a thumb across my lips. "You inspire me to fight for a future again."

His arms locked around me, lifting and spinning me so that I straddled his lap. "So, I'll fight for you the only way I know how to right now." His lips crashed down onto mine.

Closing my eyes, I wrapped my arms around his neck and clung to him tightly. His lips released mine for a moment as he pulled back and met my gaze.

I closed my eyes, throwing my head back, as his lips skimmed down my neck. I felt the furs against my back as, suddenly, he was lying above me, balancing his weight on his forearms. Our gazes met and clung. Then, carefully lowering himself, his lips claimed mine once more.

His hands caressed me, cupping my breasts through my gown. I could feel him. His great size, his enormous strength. And yet also his gentleness. He was not rough, but his passion swept through me like a tidal wave, toppling any remaining defenses.

Pulling back, he rested his forehead against mine and remained there for a long moment. When he opened his eyes, I saw the torment in them.

And the desire.

"I want you," he said roughly. His breath heaved in his massive chest. "Here, in this secluded forest hideaway." He held my gaze. "Just you and me."

I heard in his words the longing for connection and belonging and the same acceptance I craved. I threaded my fingers through his tawny mane. "Just you and me," I assented.

He seemed to rear up above me then. His tunic was gone, and his fingers were busy with the lacing on my dress. I reached up and flattened my hands against his chest, tracing the lines of the tattoo that climbed his ribs. I felt his skin shudder slightly under my hands. I slowly spread my fingers, sliding them against his heated skin.

He paused to grab my hands and kiss them. "Stop casting your spells," he murmured with amused irritation. "I cannot seem to untie these laces."

Laughter burbled up in my chest. "Here, let me." He released my hands and watched with hungry eyes as I made quick work of the side laces of my gown. With a quick sweeping motion, he pulled it over my head, my shift quickly following.

He froze, staring down at me. "You are beautiful, Dejah Raad." His fingers traced my collarbone, dancing along my neck. The anticipation was incredible. I ran my hands up his arms and across his shoulders until I could pull his head down to my lips and kiss him.

His breath whispered against my lips. "You have bewitched me completely, little greenwitch." His hands danced along my ribs, making me squirm. They cupped my breasts as his lips worked their way slowly down my neck. "It is more magic than I ever thought to experience. And I wouldn't change it." His breath gusted against my skin. "Don't ever stop."

I awoke slowly, aware that I was cold. Turning my head, I looked around for Calder, but I was alone in our shelter.

I laid there, disoriented, unsure what had truly transpired and what had been a dream. As I moved, my cape slipped off my shoulder, exposing naked skin, and I knew. It hadn't been a dream.

Rolling over, I looked around the small space. I was truly alone. Doubt pulsed within me, and shame rose, heating my face. Then, once again, the ache returned. The familiar sense of abandonment filled my chest as tears rose in my throat. Pulling my legs against my stomach, I wrapped my arms around them and held on tight.

He had left me. Just like my family. Just like the villagers. Just like everyone I had ever cared about.

Clutching a fur to myself, I quickly pulled my stained, crumpled dress over my head with distaste. Standing up, I swiped at the tears that still leaked from my eyes. Stepping outside of our camping site, I felt as if I were standing naked in front of my enemies. I hadn't even left Kyllikki's protection.

I scanned the trees around the small clearing, my heart still hoping to see Calder. But it was an empty hope, and the ache in my chest built. There was no one there. I did not see even a squirrel or hare. I was truly alone.

Tears blurred my vision again as I grabbed onto a sapling to refrain from collapsing to the ground. A hot rush of despair filled me. Too much had occurred. I couldn't contain it any longer. My arms and legs trembled. I pressed my hand against my mouth, trying to keep the sounds muffled.

The snap of a twig had me spinning toward the sound, my adrenaline spiking. Calder was stepping into the clearing carrying an armload of wood. He set his bundle down and approached me, his brow furrowing.

He lifted a hand and brushed the tears from my cheek. "Did you think I had abandoned you?" I could hear the concern in his tone as it shook slightly.

I closed my eyes, his touch evoking echoes of delight, even as my breath shook. "I woke alone," was all I could manage before opening my eyes and meeting his. "I was afraid." *And ashamed.*

Calder muttered something under his breath as his other arm wrapped around me, pulling me close against his chest.

"You should never be afraid," he murmured, his thumb brushing my cheek gently. Leaning down, he laid his lips on my forehead in a gentle caress. "I will never leave you without saying goodbye."

I laid my head against his chest. Closing my eyes, I listened to the slow, steady beat of his heart. "What is supposed to happen now, Calder?"

Calder chuckled. "I don't know, Dejah." His laugh reverberated against my ear, causing me to look up into his face with a tentative smile.

I was met with a kiss—one that had me wrapping my arms around his neck and pressing close against his hard body as all my bones turned to marrow.

By the time he broke the kiss, Calder was breathing just as heavily as I was. "This is uncharted territory for me, Dejah." His voice shook.

My arms were still around his neck, so he dipped one arm down and swept me up against his chest. Carrying me, he walked back to the shelter.

Once inside, he set me down and framed my face with both hands. "All I know, Dejah Raad, is that you have inflamed me. I want you."

I felt my cheeks heating and tried hard to break free of his bright sapphire gaze. But he would not release my face. Instead, his thumb brushed against my lips, and I quivered in his hold.

"But for how long?" My voice was thin and fearful, even as it filled the space between us.

Calder stepped back and looked at me. I felt the heat wash over my cheeks again. So much depended on what he said next.

"Do you really care that much?" His voice was soft, filled with earnest entreaty.

My own shook, but I met his gaze. "I do." Emotion made my words thick. "It would kill me to return alone to the village. To have to continue in this lonely existence."

He stepped forward, placing his fingers on my chin. "Dejah . . ." He hesitated. "I live in the forest for weeks at a time."

I held my breath, waiting. His thumb brushed my lip. "Would you be willing to be separated for such a length of time?"

I met his gaze squarely, even as tears filled my eyes, threatening to overflow. "I would have you, Calder Magnus, for whatever period of time I could. But to lose you and have to see you about the village? To be nothing to you, as I am to everyone else? That would be a slow death."

Calder pulled me tightly into his arms as his lips ravaged mine. Pulling back, he pressed his forehead against mine, his breath gusting against my lips. "I have lived alone for so long," he murmured. "But now that I have found you, I no longer wish for that cold existence."

He pulled back and met my gaze, smiling the soft smile of last night. "You have warmed my cold existence, Dejah Raad. You healed my soul as well as my shoulder." There was certainty in his voice.

I smiled. "You've brought warmth back into my life as well."

He swept me up in his arms again, laying me down on our bed. He smiled. "My little greenwitch." Slowly, his body covered mine as my arms wove around his neck.

His lips met mine as I clung to him. "My ranger." The words were whispered against his lips as our breath merged. The future was still unknown, but in this moment, we were in our own world. Soon we would have to return to the village, where fear and suspicion left me needed but not wanted. And eventually, Calder and I would have to face Diavol and the poison he infected our world with.

But for now, everything was quiet and peaceful. The sound of the stream running over stones, gurgling and laughing, could be heard faintly in the distance as bird song echoed through the forest canopy. Calder rose above me, his face blocking out my fears as his lips covered mine in a deep and tender kiss.

BEWITCHING THE RANGER

PATRISHA HARRIGAN

ONE

"Can you see them?"

"Four in the cabin, one by the corral. The other, I'm not sure. What do you want us to do, Captain?"

Vince O'Connor swung his midnight-blue gaze across the homestead laid out below him. They'd been tracking this particular gang for the last month. Vince was anxious to get the job over and done with so he could go home and eat a proper meal. A fallen branch jabbing him in the ribs reminded him that he had not slept in a decent bed for that time as well, and the two comforts warred for priority in his thoughts. *Patience,* he reminded himself. If he rushed or misjudged one step, the prey he sought would run, and neither the bed nor the meal would be his anytime soon.

"We need to get around them, block any way they could possibly get out," he said, more to himself than to his men, but Russ—the lean man next to him—overheard.

"Might be tough, considering. But if we could post men just inside the facing tree line, it might work."

Vince turned and looked over the rangers kneeling behind him.

"Russ, take Clint, Tom, and Lefty. Make your way around and take positions with clear lines of sight. Take your time and keep out of sight as much as possible. I would love to eat a steak dinner and sleep in a real bed tonight."

The younger man grinned before motioning for his team to move out.

Vince tracked their movements, watching for the flash of light from Russ's pocket watch that signaled they were in position. Directing his own men, he drew his pistols and motioned the men to move closer.

"Joe McNeally! This is the Texas Rangers! Toss your iron out the windows and come out with your hands in the air! We have you surrounded, so don't try anything stupid!"

Out of the corner of his eye, he caught movement from behind the cabin. The man by the corral tried to run, but Lefty stopped him cold. More movement from the cabin drew Vince's eyes back. Pistols and a couple of rifles fell from the windows before a voice called out.

"Don't shoot, Ranger. We're comin' out!"

The door swung open and four men filed out. Vince signaled his men to come in and walked forward, eyes still scanning the area.

Vince stopped in front of a rather homely man of average height who bore a thick moustache and dull brown eyes. "Where's the other one?"

"What other one?" the man asked innocently. Vince's upper lip curled into a snarl as the hairs on the back of his neck stood on end.

"My report says there were six of you. There are five here, so cut the bullshit, McNeally. Where's the other one?"

"Oh, now I remember. He went to town for supplies. Should be back anytime now."

Something was wrong. McNeally was too calm. The skin on the back of Vince's neck was trying to crawl up over his scalp. Movement to his left caught his attention, and dread flowed through him.

"Ambu—"

The word never got out before his world went black.

Pain. That was the first thing that registered in Vince's hazy mind. He was lying on his side in a dim, warm room, and a low fire crackled in the fireplace on one wall. He blinked several times and shifted, groaning as the pain increased.

"I would stay as still as possible. It took a long time to stop the bleeding."

The voice coming to him was soft and almost dusty, as if the person speaking hadn't used it in a long time.

"Where am I?"

A dark shape came into view and crouched by the fire, adding wood until the flames drove the shadows deeper into the corners of the room. Vince was in a cabin; the thick log wall he was facing sported floor-to-ceiling shelves. Those shelves were packed near to groaning with bottles and crocks. Bundles of herbs hung from the rafters in varying states of preservation.

"Safe," the figure said, swinging a pot over the fire. Vince's gaze swept over the figure. A dark cloak covered it from head to foot, the hood obscuring all features. The voice had been so soft, he couldn't even tell if it was a man or a woman. He drew in a breath of annoyance, only to have it come out in a racking cough. In an instant, the figure was next to him, a cup of tea in its hand. Vince took a long drink once the cough had subsided, noticing a bit of blood on the rim as it was pulled away.

"You'll find that patience will be much to your benefit right now, Ranger. Especially if you want to avenge your men."

"My men," he repeated softly. Trying not to jerk, he lifted his head as far as he could. "Did they make it out?"

There were a few seconds of silence.

"No," came the simple answer. Vince's eyes closed as a new pain spread through his chest. He had been responsible for those men, and he'd failed them. How was it that he had lived, while those good men had been shot down like dogs? His eyes opened, and he looked at the cloaked figure.

"Who are you? How did I get here? And why am I even alive when my men aren't?"

The hood tilted a bit to one side.

"Is who I am really important? I heard the gunshots and went to see what happened and found you barely clinging to life. Taking one of the horses I happened upon, I built a travois and brought you here." One shoulder lifted in a shrug. "And I suppose it was not your day to die."

Vince's brow furrowed. There wasn't a lot of emotion in the voice coming from within the hood. All the answers had been rather short and matter of fact. He took a slow breath.

"How can I thank you if I don't know how to address you?" he asked. The hood tilted the other way, and Vincent couldn't help comparing the movement to a puppy hearing a new sound. "If you want, I can start. My name is Vincent O'Connor. My friends call me Vince."

"Vincent O'Connor—a good strong name."

Annoyance was starting to build, and he pressed his lips together to keep from snapping.

"Now this is where you tell me your name," he urged, managing to stay polite.

The hood lowered a bit closer to him, and he caught the shadow of a rounded chin.

"Good. There is fire left in you, yet you are learning patience." Setting the cup down, small work-roughened hands emerged from the cloak and rose to the hood. The thick material fell back, releasing a mass of rich walnut-brown hair. Braids twined from above the woman's ears to gather at the back of her head, keeping her hair from falling into her face. Oddly, the braid above her left ear was white, the pure white of new snow. She hesitated several seconds before her eyes came up to meet his. His own dark eyes widened as he stared into orbs that should have belonged to two different people. Her right eye was a clear emerald green, as warm as a summer meadow, while her left was an intense pale blue, as cold as winter ice. Seeing his reaction, she turned her head away and stood, moving back to the fire to refresh the cup of tea.

"My name is Orla Milne," she said, the emotion gone again from her voice. Vince could see that he had upset her in some way.

"Thank you, Orla, for saving my life. And I'm sorry if I have offended you in any way. It was not my intention to upset you; it is just that I have never seen eyes like yours."

"Not many have." She took a long spoon and stirred the pot above the fire. "Your reaction was very mild compared to some."

His gaze lingered on her for several seconds.

"I remember hearing stories in town about a woman who lives alone in the woods."

She straightened and looked over her shoulder at him, her blue eye flashing.

"And which stories have you heard? That I am a witch who lures children to their deaths? A demon that cavorts with the Devil on the full moon?"

"Versions of both, told by ignorant old biddies. I doubt a witch or a demon would rescue a dying man out of the goodness of her heart."

Orla sighed, and her shoulders slumped a bit.

"I'm sorry for my outburst. I go to town so rarely because of the reactions I get. People cross themselves when they see me. Children have thrown rocks at me . . ." She stopped and pressed her lips together. Vince smiled softly.

"It's okay. You don't have to explain."

Scratching at the door took Orla away from the fire. Vince heard the door open and close, followed by a rumbling sound. Orla's soft voice reached him, along with her returning footsteps. As she came back into his line of sight, the biggest bobcat in creation padded along beside her. The creature gazed up at Orla, adoration in its golden eyes. Those eyes turned to Vince and he froze. The big cat crouched and stalked toward him, stopping only to lift its paws to the edge of the bed and touch its nose to Vince's. Whiskers tickled his face as the creature sniffed at him thoroughly. Lowering back to its haunches, the cat sneezed and proceeded to clean its paws. Orla raised a dark brow.

"He likes you. That's good, seeing as you've kept him out of his home for the last week."

"Is that how long I've been here?" His throat tightened a bit. His shoulder and hip were beginning to ache from his prone position. "What happened to my men?"

"I got a message to the sheriff for him to come for the bodies. My main concern was to keep you alive."

"And thank you again for that. You must be a fine doctor."

A snort came from Orla.

"I'm not a doctor. What I know can never be taught in a school."

"Then how—"

"My mother was a healer," Orla interrupted firmly. "As was my grandmother and her mother before her, going back several hundred years."

He waited for her to explain further. When she remained silent, he changed the subject.

"Your bobcat is beautiful. How did he come to live with you?"

Orla looked down at the cat.

"I rescued him. His mother was killed by a trapper. I found him near-starved and nursed him back to health." She scratched him under the chin, and his purring got louder. "Now he won't leave."

"He seems like good company. What's his name?"

A small smile pulled at the corners of her mouth.

"His name is Aksel. He does help keep my feet warm on cold nights. Even brings home the occasional rabbit or bird to add to supper. So I guess he pulls his own weight pretty well." Her eyes turned back to Vince. "There will be more of my companions showing up from time to time. They shouldn't be more than curious about you, so don't be afraid."

"If they're as vicious as he is, I think I can manage," Vince replied with a smile. He shifted, and that smile turned to a grimace.

Orla crossed the room and knelt at his back. Her fingers were gentle as she examined his injuries. His head turned as far as he could manage to look at her. "I was shot in the back?"

"Twice," she said with a nod. "Three times from the front and once in the thigh. Luckily, I was able to get the bullets out clean. Most men wouldn't have survived so many injuries, so I guess the gods still have plans for you. I know it will hurt, but I think they'll stay closed while we get you upright. I have extra padding to prop you up so as not to put too much pressure on your back. Willing to give it a try?"

"Absolutely. My arm is going numb," he replied, curious about her comment about "gods." Following her directions, he rolled onto his back. Orla took his arm and drew it across her shoulders. The scent that reached him was not what he was expecting. She smelled of sweet herbs and wood smoke, and the hair that brushed his cheek was soft. It was extremely pleasant.

"I will take all the weight I can," Orla said. "Brace your other arm on the frame, and when I say go, push yourself up. Ready? Go!"

Vince grit his teeth and pushed. Pain shot through his body, and a loud groan escaped him as he rose to a sitting position. He couldn't help but lean on Orla as his breath came out in short pants. After he had managed to slow his breathing, he pulled away.

"Sorry, Orla," he grunted. "That hurt a hell of a lot more than I thought it would."

She checked the bandages on his back before adjusting the padding behind him and helping him ease back onto it.

"No need to apologize." She examined the wounds on his torso. "You're bleeding again. I'll get my kit and get it stopped."

Noticing her tension, he frowned as she moved away. She pulled down two small crocks and then gathered clean cotton, linen, and a large pitcher of water. Returning to the bed, she removed the soiled bandage and then cleaned and recovered the wound.

"What do you use to stop the bleeding?" Vince asked, watching her closely. She hesitated for a second before answering.

"A plantain and yarrow poultice. The bleeding isn't that bad, and the poultice will help fight infection." Dipping her fingers into the larger of the two crocks, she smeared a thick fluid along the edges of the linen and pressed it against his flesh. When she pulled her hands away, it remained, sealed snugly. Vince looked at the old bandage, then the new.

"That's clever. What is it?"

"Pitch. It glues the bandage in place instead of having to rely on wrapping. Less chance of shifting, and it keeps the wound cleaner. It's a bit of a hassle to clean up, but worth it."

"Our doctor could learn a thing or two from you, it seems."

Orla snorted. "As if he would listen. Nature gives us everything we need to heal. People seem to be losing sight of that." She scrubbed her hands and stood. "Supper will be ready shortly. You're probably hungry."

"Starving."

TWO

Orla paused from her work and leaned on her digging stick, her forehead resting on her folded hands. A huge raven hopped down to the branch closest to her and clicked his beak, a low warble coming from his chest. She raised her eyes to him and smiled softly, knowing he could sense her current mood.

"I'm all right, Euan. Just trying to sort out a few things."

Her mind wandered back over the two weeks Vince had been under her roof. The first week had mainly consisted of changing his bandages and watching for fever as he lay unconscious. The last week had been increasingly more difficult, at least emotionally. Her eyes drifted shut at the memory of his arm around her shoulders and his face against her neck after she had helped him sit up in bed.

She should have moved him back against the pillows immediately. The position he'd had her in had been quite awkward, but the feel of another human being against her had sent emotions through her she'd thought she had locked away. Squeezing her eyes more tightly shut, she tried to close the door again.

"Oh, my sweet autumn rose. You shouldn't make statements you know aren't true."

The memory of her mother came to Orla so vividly, it caused her a physical jolt. They had been in this very spot, harvesting dandelion roots for tea. While they had been in town the day before, several boys had taunted Orla mercilessly, throwing rocks and bringing her to tears.

"I'm serious, Mama. I am never getting married. There is not a boy in the world that will look past these eyes and see I'm not a witch."

Her mother had chuckled at her tirade, frustrating Orla further.

"My darling, those fools are nothing but what you just described: boys. Spoiled children who find pleasure in tormenting things that scare them. Now, when the right *man* comes along, he will see nothing but the fine woman you are. And he will come, darling, when you least expect it. He will turn your world upside down and make you feel like you could fly to the moon and back."

"Like Papa?" Orla had asked. Her mother had sat back on her heels and smiled dreamily, her eyes closed.

"Yes, like your papa." One wintry-blue eye had opened to gaze at her daughter. "A word of advice, though, Orla. When your man does come into your life, don't fight it like I did. I was cheated out of more than a year of wedded bliss with your father because of my family's caution. I don't want that to happen to you."

Orla had knelt next to her mother and kissed her cheek.

"All right, Mama. I promise not to give up on letting the right man find me. I just hope I will be young enough to enjoy it."

Her mother had chuckled and wrapped her arms around Orla's shoulders for a hug.

"Good enough. Now let's get home. Your papa will be home by dark, and we still need to get supper ready."

Orla lifted her head from her knees. She blinked several times and looked around her, wondering when she had sat against the oak tree towering over her. Euan was flitting from branch to branch, cawing nervously before settling onto her shoulder. She pulled his head to her cheek to quiet him.

"I'm sorry, Euan. I wasn't expecting that." She released him and leaned her head back against the tree. She reached up to rub her face and found it wet with tears. "It's been a long time since I've let memories of my mother through. I guess it just hurt too much to remember."

Thunder rolled in the distance, distracting her from the pain. She couldn't help but smile before shooing Euan off her shoulder so she could rise and gather her basket. She loved storms. They always made her feel free. The wildness and unpredictability, the fierceness of Mother Nature washing her world clean. In this case, she could consider it a rebirth, rekindling the hope that she could have a happy life with a man that loved her and a herd of children to dote upon and teach. The prospect sent a warmth through her unlike anything she had ever felt. Her spirit felt lighter than ever as she pulled her digging stick from the soft earth and turned toward home.

"Let's get back, Euan. Vince is probably getting hungry."

THREE

"Do you ever miss being around other people?" Vince asked.

Orla looked up from her gardening, streaks of dirt on her cheeks.

"I miss my mother. She was all I really needed. If you remember me mentioning, I never received a warm welcome in town." She sighed. "People fear what they don't understand, Vince—always have, always will. They don't understand me, what I do, or how I live, so it is easier to fear me. And I don't mind so much anymore. I have my animals to keep me company, and I can grow almost everything I need here. What more could I want?"

Vince stretched gingerly. Two more weeks had passed since he had woken up in Orla's cabin. His wounds were all but healed, but they still pained him if he made any sudden moves. Orla took him for walks in the mornings to help him gain his strength back, and then he would sit and watch her work. She had patched his shirt the best she could, but it was still stained with his blood.

A raucous cawing had him looking up. Euan dropped down and perched on the garden fence, eyeing him suspiciously. Vince pulled out a crust of bread he had saved from breakfast and tossed it to the bird. Spreading his wings wide, the raven shrieked at him before snatching the bread and flying off.

"He still doesn't like me," Vince commented. Orla chuckled, a soothing sound that caressed Vince's ears.

"Euan is the jealous type," she explained. "He wasn't the first animal I rescued, but he thinks he should be the only. Don't pay him any mind."

Vince leaned back on his bench and looked around the tidy garden. It was a peaceful place, filled with the hum of honey bees and the scent of flowers and herbs. It was indeed peaceful and a bit lonely.

"Did you ever want to have a family?" Vince asked softly. Orla froze midharvest, a carrot still half-buried. A moment passed before she continued, her movements stiff and her manner wary.

"What man would have me?" she asked shortly. "I'm a witch, remember? Not the most attractive trait in a wife."

"I don't know," Vince countered. "I'm seeing the benefits. You shouldn't sell yourself so short, Orla; you are a fine woman."

Orla added her vegetables to a large basket and stood, her back rigid. Vince wasn't sure what to make of the swift change in her mood.

"What about you, Ranger? Did you ever want a family?" she asked, turning the question back on him. Vince frowned.

"My line of work doesn't leave much room for a family. Not many women would be keen on being alone for weeks or months on end while I'm out on the trail, and I don't think it would be fair to expect it of them."

"Then the only difference between us is that I was outcast from society and you chose not to be a part of it. A bit sad if you think about it."

"Why is that?" Vince asked. Orla turned, basket in hand, and gazed at him.

"We are two people who just want to help others. You nearly paid with your life to keep people safe, yet you have no one to mourn you if you die. And I have much to offer others, yet they fear me."

Vince laid his head back and watched the clouds drift by. What she had said about him had hit its mark. He did choose not to be part of society. He didn't even have any real friends. He liked the men he worked with, would die for them if need be, but he had no desire to spend time with them outside of work.

As Orla passed him to take her bounty into the cabin, he reached out and covered one of her hands with his, stopping her. "You're right; it is sad. But I guess bad situations can bring good people together."

She looked down at him. "I guess so," she agreed softly. Her eyes were drawn to the sky as thunder rumbled. "Looks like we may get another storm."

Vince noted a bit of excitement in her voice as she mentioned the storm.

"You enjoy storms?" he asked. Orla nodded.

"They are as beautiful as they are destructive. I should lay in more wood for the fire before the rain starts."

Vince pushed himself up, managing to keep his hand on hers.

"I'll help." He gave her a lopsided grin. "At least as much as I can."

She returned the grin. "It's about time you started pulling your weight around here."

Vince watched Orla as the storm rolled in. Her demeanor changed completely from the woman he had known for the last few weeks. She was relaxed and quick to smile, and she teased him often. Once they'd finished laying in the supplies, she stood on the porch and watched the lightning streak across the darkened sky. The wind picked up and whipped her dark hair around her face, and she smiled and turned her face into it. Vince stared at her, mesmerized. He imagined any other woman gathering what they could and hiding in the house, cringing at every crack of thunder. Orla welcomed the storm like an old friend she hadn't seen in a while. It was fascinating and sent urges through him that had been silent for a long time.

The first spattering of rain hit her face, and she shivered and giggled. She leaned out from the porch, into the rain, letting it wash the dirt of her garden from her face before she stepped off completely. Her light dress was immediately soaked, and it clung to her body as she held her arms out and turned, laughing merrily.

That sound drew Vince to her like a moth to a flame, his feet moving as if by their own accord. He tipped his head back as he joined her, letting the rain pummel away at him. He released everything—his regrets, his guilt, his fears, and his pain—and let the rain rinse it all away. A deep chuckle escaped him as water ran down his back, and he began to understand why Orla enjoyed storms so much.

Looking down, he saw her smiling up at him, eyes shining and cheeks pinkened by the chill. Unable to help himself, he lifted his hands to cup her face gently as he lowered his head, his lips pressing against hers softly. There was no resistance; Orla leaned into him, her hands coming up to grasp the front of his shirt.

Her lips were cool from the rain and soft against his. One of his hands slid down her neck and shoulder to loop around her, drawing her closer. Orla gasped against his lips, and he took advantage of the slight opening, his tongue darting out to trace her lips. She released his shirt to slide her arms around his neck, fingers sliding into his rain-soaked hair. His lips released hers and moved over her cheek, across her ear, and down to her neck. Her head dropped back, and her breathing grew shallow.

Vince trailed his hands down to her rear, cupping the cheeks firmly and pressing her hips against him. His hardness pressed into her belly, and Orla groaned as her fingers tightened in his hair. With a grunt of effort, he lifted her, sliding one arm under her rear to support her. Only stumbling once, he managed to get them both inside out of the rain. He released her only to strip off his wet shirt and then kissed her again, his ardor raging like the storm outside.

Orla met his kiss with an urgency of her own, her fingers clumsy as she fumbled with the buttons on her own shirt. Once free of the wet fabric, she reached for his belt as he reached for her skirt. The rest of her clothing fell away easily, but his trousers took a bit of work before he could step out of them.

Lifting her again, he wrapped her legs around his waist and continued the few steps to his bed. He never broke contact as he lowered her to the mattress, trailing kisses down her neck and chest. She arched against him as his mouth settled over a breast, drawing the nipple in to tease with his tongue.

He let his right hand slide down her belly between them to the moist warmth pressed against his groin. She shuddered as his fingers slipped through the folds of her sex and entered her. She was hot and slick, and he wasted no time replacing his finger with his shaft. In the back of his mind he knew he should take it slow, but neither of them was in any state to rein in their urges. Their coupling was feverish. Orla clung to him until she reached her climax with a cry. Vince stiffened, reaching his own peak with a groan mere seconds later. He sagged atop her, his breathing ragged.

He enjoyed the position for a bit before rising up to find Orla asleep beneath him. With a chuckle, he rolled over to lie next to her and gathered her against him, falling instantly asleep.

FOUR

He woke up alone. Leaning up in bed, he looked around the room for Orla. She was nowhere to be found, but his clothes had been folded and set on the foot of the bed. Dressing quickly, he stepped out the door to scan the garden.

He found her where her garden met the forest, sitting on a fallen log with Aksel draped over her lap.

"Good morning," Vince greeted softly. She stiffened but didn't turn around.

"Good morning," she replied, her voice quiet. "Did you find your breakfast?"

"No, actually. I wanted to find you first."

"Why?"

Vince's brow furrowed. This wasn't quite the reaction he had been expecting from her.

"Are you all right?" he asked, concern shading his tone.

"As well as can be expected." Her tone was rather flat.

"You're angry with me?" he guessed.

Her shoulders dropped a bit. "I'm angry at myself for letting last night happen. It shouldn't have, and I'm sorry."

"I suppose, with the storm, we did get a bit carried away, but what is there to be sorry about? We didn't do anything wrong."

Orla sighed and her posture relaxed.

"How do you feel this morning? Any pain?"

"A bit," Vince confessed, stretching his shoulders. "I keep wondering if I'll ever be back to my old self."

Orla turned her head, her blue eye glinting in the morning light peaking over the trees.

"Strength wise, yes. You should be just fine. Spirit wise, I'm not so sure. You washed a lot away last night, but I'm afraid some of your guilt may still linger. Which is normal in a situation like yours. Until you find who killed your men and put their souls to rest, the guilt will most likely remain. And you will carry their spirits with you for the rest of your life."

Vince moved around the log to sit next to Orla. His brow furrowed in thought as he studied her face.

"I have never heard anyone speak like you do. Most priests would tell me to turn the other cheek and that my men's souls are already at rest. That revenge is not something to pursue."

Orla laughed, the rest of her tension disappearing.

"I was raised in a very different way, Vince. I don't mean to offend, but your god holds no power over me. I was raised as were all my ancestors: a pagan. I am a soulless heathen in your god's eyes. And I need no savior because I don't need to be saved." She waved an arm over her garden and the woods beyond. "This is my church, my haven. I find my greatest peace here among nature. People ask for miracles, yet they can't see the miracles all around them. It makes no sense to me."

Aksel yawned and stretched, a claw hooking Vince's sleeve in an invitation to pet him. Vince obliged and was rewarded with loud purring. Vince gazed into the forest thoughtfully for several minutes. He could feel the lump of guilt deep in his chest, small yet heavy. But overshadowing that was the deep burn for vengeance. His job was far from over, and he owed it to his men to find the ones responsible and bring them to justice.

"You're right," he said finally. Her head turned and she studied him.

"About what?"

"Everything. I still regret the loss of my men, I doubt I'll be able to fully get over that. But the need to bring their murderers to justice is overpowering everything. Seven men died because I missed something."

Orla's brow furrowed suddenly. "I found only six dead rangers at the farm, Vince. Not seven."

A cold wave of dread battled his rage for control.

"Are you sure?" His voice was a gravelly rumble. Orla nodded. He surged to his feet and began pacing, causing Aksel to start and hiss. Orla stared at Vince, her eyes wide as she tried to settle the cat.

"You think it was a deliberate betrayal," she commented finally. Vince stopped, his hands flexing into fists.

"It has to be. I limit the people I discuss my plans with, and I never discuss them outside a sheriff's office. Who else would have known?"

"Then the next logical step is to find the missing ranger."

Vince ran his hands over his face and up through his hair. "I need to get to town. The sheriff has to have a list of the men who were killed."

Orla set Aksel on his feet and rose, turning to the house.

"I'll gather some supplies for your trip. It will take you most of the day to get to town."

Vince watched her walk to the house and disappear inside, a new knot tightening in his chest. Following, he found her wrapping a loaf of bread and wedges of cheese in waxed linen.

"Come with me."

Orla froze. "I'm not sure that's a good idea. I wouldn't want to cause you any trouble."

"What trouble could you possibly cause?" he asked. She threw him a look that seemed to imply he was dense. "Point taken. The truth is, Orla, I need you to come with me. First, because I have no idea where I'm going. And second, I need someone to center me. I can't let my anger take hold of me, or I'll make another mistake. Please, Orla? Come with me."

She remained silent as she packed the supplies into a sturdy bag.

"I suppose if you get yourself shot again, you would need someone to patch you up." She paused and looked out the small window over her garden. "The place should be okay for a while if I'm not here, and Aksel can fend for himself. If you can be patient enough to leave in the morning, then yes, Vince, I will go with you."

He slid his large hands over her shoulders and pressed his cheek against her hair.

"Thank you. What can I do to help?"

She leaned back against him, her hands rising to rest gently over his.

"The tack can use a once over. The tack from the horse I caught when I found you should be fine, but I haven't used my saddle in so long, I'm worried about dry rot. Unless you think I should take the wagon?"

"I'd like to move as light and fast as possible. Can we pack what we need into saddlebags?"

"Most of it. I do have a set of panniers and a mule. He's not as young as he once was, but he's still spry. He should be able to keep up. That will relieve the horses of some weight."

He squeezed her shoulders lightly and pulled away.

"Sounds like we have a plan. I'll go check the tack and look over the horses. I'll be back shortly."

She nodded, continuing to pack.

FIVE

The next morning dawned cool, and a heavy mist had settled in over the meadows. Orla finished packing the mule and secured the flaps on the panniers. She rested her cheek against the mule's neck and stroked his long ears as he nibbled at her cloak.

"Not changing your mind, are you?" Vince asked from behind her. She smiled softly.

"Not yet. We'd better head out before I do. I don't want to spend any more time in town than I absolutely have to."

Vince ran his fingers down her cheek. "Thank you again for agreeing to come with me. I'll try to be quick in town. Let's get going."

Once they'd mounted their horses, Orla wrapped the mule's lead around her saddle horn and led Vince out of her yard. She was quiet for a long while, watching the trees pass by. Vince pushed his horse to come alongside hers.

"Would you tell me about your parents?" he asked, causing her to start. She smiled.

"They met much like we did. My father was a range hand for one of the local ranchers. While he was out checking the cattle one day, his horse went down in a wash, breaking my father's leg. My mother found him barely conscious. She nursed him back to health, and he fell madly in love with her."

Vince chuckled. "Did she love him?"

"Not at first. Her parents were leery of him because of how they lived, and those suspicions rubbed off on Mama. It took time, but he was a very charming man. My grandparents came to love him as well. They were very happy together."

"What happened to them?"

"Daddy died in a flash flood about seven years ago. Mama was devastated. She lived two more years until her broken heart finally killed her. I was nineteen."

"I'm sorry. It must have been hard living without your parents."

"It was, at first, but I had everything Mama taught me, and I had the property. Aksel, Euan, and my other companions drifted in over the years to keep me company."

A ruckus overhead had them both looking up. Orla sighed and shook her head when she spotted Euan.

Vince chuckled. "I was wondering if he would follow. Can't have you traveling alone with a man he doesn't approve of."

"I hope he has enough sense to stay out of sight when we reach town. I'm going to cause enough of a stir. I haven't been to town in more than six months."

"They'll get over it. If they can't accept you for who you are, then that's their loss." He reached over and took her hand. "Never be afraid to be yourself."

Orla smiled softly. "Thank you."

The sun was high when they reached the edge of town. Orla pulled her horse to a stop and looked down the bustling main street. Gilmer had grown since the last time she had been there. Wagons loaded with goods filled the street, and children skipped along next to parents who tugged them out of the way of passing horses.

"We can go around if it will make you more comfortable," Vince said. She shook her head.

"No, I'll be fine. Just taking in how much the town has grown since I was here last." She nudged her horse with her heels to continue into town. "Before long, you won't be able to throw a stone without hitting someone."

"They call it progress," Vince commented dryly. "And usually, more progress means more trouble."

They were passing by the dry goods store when a young girl started jumping up and down and pointing at them.

"Look, Mama! It's the witch!"

Orla stiffened but didn't look toward the girl. She did hear the mother reprimand the girl as they rode by.

"Jenny, it's not polite to point. Now come along."

"Interesting that she reprimands the child for pointing and not name-calling." Vince spoke loud enough that the woman overheard him. She turned red and hurried her daughter down the street. Orla gave him a small smile.

"Thank you. I usually just ignore them."

"The lesson she was teaching her daughter was unacceptable. I just wanted to bring that to her attention. No harm done, though I may have bruised her pride."

"A small price to pay."

They stopped their horses in front of the small sheriff's office. Vince dismounted and handed his reins up to Orla.

"I shouldn't be long. Unless you want to come in with me?"

Orla shook her head. "I'll be fine out here, and I can keep an eye on the horses."

Vince nodded. He stepped up onto the boardwalk and into the office.

The sheriff's office was clean but worn, the floorboards creaking with each step. He walked up to the desk, where a broad, slightly overweight man sat reclined in a chair, his feet up on the desk and his hat pulled down low over his face.

"Well, this looks like a good use of the town's money," Vince commented loudly. The big man at the desk started, his boots hitting the floor with a loud thunk. Pushing his hat back, the sheriff's green eyes scanned the man in front of him.

"Vince? Vince O'Connor? Is that you?"

Vince grinned slightly and held out his hand. "Good to see you again, Bill. I see you're keeping busy."

Bill gripped the outstretched hand a bit hesitantly, his eyes still examining Vince.

"Everyone thought you were dead. When we didn't find your body, we assumed McNeally had dragged you off somewhere to rot."

Vince dropped Bill's hand and pulled open his duster, showing him the bloodstains. "I very nearly was. Would have been if Orla hadn't taken me in and saved my ass."

"Orla?" Bill's brow furrowed. "Who's that?"

Vince motioned to the window. Bill walked over and looked out at the woman sitting on the hitching post, her feet swinging slowly.

"The witch? She saved your life?"

Vince rolled his eyes.

"Not you too. I figured you would be smarter than that. If the gift of healing is witchcraft, then she is a damn fine witch. Which brings me to why I'm here. After Orla brought me back from death's doorstep, she told me there were only seven rangers at the farm McNeally was holed up in, including me. There were eight of us there that day. I need to know who was missing. We were betrayed by one of our own, and I need to find him and make him pay."

Bill blinked, no doubt at the venom in Vince's last statement. "Then you'll need to go talk to the undertaker. He would have been the one to record the names when their bodies were claimed."

Vince let out a sigh. "Thanks, Bill. I really appreciate it."

"No prob—"

A scream from the street interrupted Bill. Both men raced out to see what the commotion was. A woman sat on the boardwalk in front of the dry goods store, a limp figure lying over her lap. Nearby, Orla stood toe to toe with a large man.

"What's going on here?" Bill boomed over the crowd as they approached. The large man glared over Orla's head.

"My daughter can't breathe, Sheriff!" the woman wailed. "And we can't find the doctor!"

"He's out of town today," Bill said kindly. He turned to the man and Orla. "What is going on here?"

"I'm blocking this witch from touching my daughter," the man growled. "For all I know, she's the cause."

Orla looked between Vince and the sheriff. "I can help, Sheriff!" she said fiercely. "The longer they wait, the more likely their daughter is to die."

"You're not going near my little girl, hag!" the man roared. Orla blinked in surprise as the sheriff took the man by the shoulder and pulled him aside.

"Simmer down, Carl," he said. "Why would she hurt your daughter and then try to help. You're being irrational."

Orla felt Vince's hand slide over her shoulder in comfort as he moved to her side. She shifted from foot to foot, watching the little girl struggling for breath.

"Please," Orla implored. "I can help her, but I have to do it now."

"Give her a chance, Carl," the sheriff said.

She saw Carl's hands curled into fists, but he nodded. "If she dies, so will you, witch," he growled.

Ignoring him, Orla sprang into action. "Vince, I need coals from the blacksmith, or something else I can use to make smoke."

"Done," Vince said and rushed off. Orla took the girl from her mother and examined her.

"Does this happen often?" Orla asked. The mother shook her head.

"Only on occasion. Normally after she exerts herself too much."

Orla nodded. "What's her name?"

"Carla, after her papa."

Orla gave her a reassuring smile. Vince returned with a metal dipper full of blazing coals.

"I need your help, Vince," she said softly. "I'm going to have to make a tent of my cloak so she can inhale the smoke."

"I'm here. Whatever you need, let's do it."

Orla rolled Carla onto her side. With Vince's help, she arranged her cloak to enclose Carla's head. Sliding the dipper of coals into the tent, Orla blew on them until they were cherry red and sprinkled a generous fistful of dried herbs over them. She adjusted Carla's head directly into the smoke, then closed her in. Vince held the cloak closed while Orla rubbed Carla's back, singing softly.

It seemed like an eternity before Orla felt Carla take in a deep breath. Orla sighed in relief and smiled up at Vince.

"We can take the cloak off. Just don't breathe in the smoke; it's a bit disorienting."

Vince nodded and pulled the cloak away. Carla looked up at Orla and blinked, her pupils wide and dark.

"What happened?" she asked, her voice a bit hoarse.

"You were having trouble breathing. I made it better," Orla explained softly. Carla blinked again.

"Your eyes are weird. Why aren't they the same color?"

"When they made me, they couldn't decide on blue or green eyes, so they gave me both."

"I'm tired, and hungry. Where's my mama?"

"She's here." Orla waved to the anxious woman standing behind her.

"I'm here, baby. Oh, thank God you're all right."

Orla turned the girl over to her mother and stood, draping her cloak over her arm.

"She'll be a bit disoriented for a few hours, but by tomorrow she'll be back to her old self."

"How can I ever thank you?" the woman asked. Orla raised a hand.

"No need. I'm grateful you allowed me to help. There is a tea I can make for Carla to help prevent these attacks. If you are interested?"

"I think you have helped enough," Carl broke in, pulling his wife and daughter away. Despite their objections, he led them down the street. Orla sighed and crossed the street back to the horses.

As they reached the horses, Vince heard Orla mutter, "Well, two out of three isn't bad, I guess." Vince rested his arms on her saddle and looked down at her.

"It's a start. That's all you need. The whole crowd saw you save that girl."

"But if you will notice, I am still getting suspicious looks from most of that crowd."

Vince looked up and saw that she was right. Small groups of people were casting glances at them and whispering. He sighed and ran a hand tiredly over his face.

"I guess you can't please everyone. We need to go visit the undertaker. Bill said he would have a list of the rangers that were brought in."

"Good. I need to get away from here. They're making me uncomfortable."

She never looked back at the crowd as she mounted her horse. Vince wasn't so tolerant; he gave the crowd disgusted looks as he moved his horse between them and Orla. She smiled gratefully, and her shoulders relaxed a bit.

A tall, lean man in a dark suit looked up as they pulled their horses to a stop at the rail in front of his small shop. Caskets of varying sizes lined one outside wall, and slabs of stone piled up against the other.

"Ranger O'Connor? Back from the dead, I see," he said. Vince frowned as he stepped to the ground.

"Yes, and it was a long road, Mr. Weber. I need a favor."

"Of course. What can I do for you and your . . . friend?"

Vince ignored the distaste in the undertaker's voice. "I need the names of the rangers who were brought in after the McNeally ambush."

"Of course, Ranger. Won't you come in? Your friend can wait out here."

Orla frowned, her eyes narrow. "Fine with me," she said shortly. "Too many restless spirits here anyway."

Vince raised an eyebrow but said nothing as he followed Mr. Weber into his shop.

"You keep unholy company, Ranger."

Vince folded his arms across his chest and watched the lean man flip through the pages of a thick ledger.

"Thank you for your concern, but it is neither needed nor wanted. I'm here for one thing; I'd appreciate it if we could focus on that."

Mr. Weber scowled but continued his search. Finding the page he needed, he turned the book for Vince to see.

"These are the names of the men I provided services for."

Vince's eyes roamed the page, then snapped back up to the undertaker.

"You're sure?" he growled. Mr. Weber nodded.

"They were identified by your commanding officer. You have found what you needed?"

Vince gave him a curt nod and turned on a heel to exit the building. Mr. Weber followed him out, stopping short when his eyes landed on Orla. Euan was sitting on her shoulder as she stroked his ebony feathers. Vince watched the bird turn his head to Mr. Weber and caw loudly, his wings flaring wide. Vince nearly laughed as Mr. Weber's pasty complexion paled further. Orla tapped Euan's beak in a mild reprimand before she turned her horse away.

"That woman will lead you straight to Hell, Ranger. I would get as far away from her as I could, to save your soul."

Vince stepped into a stirrup and swung up into his saddle.

"I understand your intentions are good, Mr. Weber, but the road to Hell is paved with them. I would take a good look at your own soul if your going to condemn a person based solely on rumors and speculation. Aren't we all made in God's image? Or am I mistaken?"

He set his heels to his mount, leaving Mr. Weber gaping behind him. As he reached Orla's side, she grinned at him sheepishly.

"Sorry, but I can't stand that man. Most of the people here are just ignorant, but he's a complete ass. While most of the townspeople just make me uncomfortable, his mannerisms are so cold and unfeeling. I'm not sure if it's due to his profession, but I feel that he's a genuinely heartless person." She glanced back at the cemetery. "He refused to bury my father in the cemetery because of his marriage to my mother."

"I agree whole heartily; he is a complete ass." Vince looked over at Euan. "That was quite a sight, though. Did he react on his own?"

Orla nodded. "Ravens are smart. My grandpapa told me once

that you can teach them to talk; I've just never tried with Euan." Her eyes swung over to Vince. "Did you find what you needed?"

Vince's face darkened. "I did."

"So where do we go now?"

"Where it all started."

"How do you know he'll still be there?"

"He'll be there. How could I have been so stupid?"

Orla watched Vince pace back and forth in front of her fireplace. He had been quiet the whole trip back to her cabin, his thoughts obviously in turmoil. She hadn't pushed, knowing he would share when he was ready.

"How could you have known, Vince?"

He stopped and stabbed his fingers through his hair.

"I should have seen it, Orla. He knew too much—about the farm they were hiding at, the way to get there, everything. He even avoided going into town to keep from being recognized. And I was so fixated on catching McNeally that I missed it completely."

"So what are you going to do? Ride in there and face them all single-handedly? You'll die for sure."

"Then what do you suggest? If he goes to town, he'll find out I'm alive and looking for him."

"How would you feel about turning into a ghost?" she asked. His gaze lifted to hers, one brow raised.

"I don't follow."

"I am a witch, Vince," Orla said haughtily. "We have been known to summon the dead. Why couldn't I bring your ghost back to haunt your killer?"

Vince was still for a minute, and then he grinned.

"What would we have to do?"

"It will take a few days of planning. We need to find out their movements first, and then we can have some fun with them. By the time we're done, they'll be tripping over each other to turn themselves in."

Six

"I'm not sure I'm comfortable with you going in there." Vince frowned as they looked over the farm. Orla set a hand on his arm, her fingers massaging gently.

"I'll be fine. This shouldn't take but a few minutes. Stay out of sight. If something does happen, I'm very handy with a knife." She pointed. "There's the berry patch I'm aiming for. I'll stay along the tree line; you shadow me. Where the berries are, they are sure to see me, which is what we want. I'll signal you when to make your move."

Without waiting for a reply, she started down the slight rise to the berry patch. Vince never let her out of his sight as he ghosted parallel to her, keeping in the shadows of the trees. Adjusting her hood, Orla began picking flower heads.

"Who do you suppose that is, Joe?"

Joe McNeally looked out the window at the cloaked figure standing next to a thicket of elderberries.

"Not sure, Russ," Joe replied. "Why don't you go find out since you're so curious. Ask 'em why they're trespassin' on our land while you're at it."

The younger man rolled his eyes as he exited the house, combing his pale hair back with his fingers before setting his wide-brimmed hat atop his head. The cloudlike flower heads of the elderberry plants swayed in the slight breeze. Every now and then, a cluster disappeared into the hood before floating down into the basket. He approached the figure warily, his posture tense until he heard soft humming. He relaxed and continued forward, stopping only when he stepped on a large branch. The snap caused the figure to stiffen. Slowly, it turned toward Russ, and he caught a glimpse of a rounded chin and full lips.

"Oh, my," the figure said softly. "You startled me. I hadn't realized anyone had moved in since Old Man Mathews passed away."

Russ smiled. "It wasn't my intention to startle you, Miss, so I apologize. I was just curious about who was raiding the berry patch."

The woman smiled and lowered her head.

"I didn't mean to trespass. My name is Orla Milne. I needed more elder flowers for a tincture I'm making and have already harvested more than I'm comfortable with around my place. I remembered my mother telling me about this patch and came to see if there was enough to finish the recipe."

Russ's smile widened, and he tipped his hat to her.

"I'm Russ Richards. You live around here?"

"Yes, I'm about a mile west of here." She cocked her head. "Did you know Mr. Mathews?"

Russ nodded.

"He was our uncle, on our mother's side. We inherited the place after he passed and moved in about a year ago." He looked her over. "I was told the neighbor to our west was a witch or some such hogwash."

Orla shrugged.

"I prefer to be called a healer, but most people call me witch. I'm sure my appearance doesn't help, either."

Russ gave her a lopsided grin.

"How bad could it be? Your voice is pretty." He leaned down, trying to see into the hood. "Are you hiding a bunch of warts under there? Or a long, pointed nose?"

Orla chuckled.

"Nothing so obvious but noticeable just the same. If you promise not to draw back in revulsion, I will take my hood off."

"Sure."

He watched in interest as Orla raised her hands and pushed the hood back, lifting her eyes to his. He blinked but otherwise didn't react.

"You see now why people would call me a witch?"

Russ shrugged. "It is unusual, for sure, but not revolting." He looked around. "I don't see a broomstick or a black cat."

"My walking stick is leaning up against a tree at the edge of the berry patch," Orla said, pointing. "And as for the black cat, no, but I do have a raven I raised."

As if on cue, a raven cawed loudly from the tree closest to them. Russ started, lifting his eyes to find the bird and went stone still. A shadowy figure stood next to a huge oak tree, the tails of his duster twitching in the breeze. Russ's breath went ragged as he took in the bloodstained shirt, pale face, and dark mustache. He blinked and rubbed a hand over his eyes, but when he looked back up, the figure was gone.

"Are you all right?" Orla asked, concern in her voice. Russ blinked several times and looked down at her.

"Yes, yes, I'm fine." He couldn't prevent a quaver from creeping into his voice. "I thought I saw something."

The woman looked over her shoulder and scanned the area. He noticed her brows furrowing as she turned back to look at him.

"Do you feel that?" she asked suddenly, bringing her hands up to rub her arms. Russ raised a brow.

"Feel what?" he asked a bit warily.

Orla shivered and her eyes went distant. "The touch of one who was betrayed by one of his own. Whose spirit lingers until it finds peace," came the soft reply.

Russ's eyes widened, and he stepped back several feet. After a few seconds, the woman shook herself and gave him a sheepish grin.

"I'm sorry," she said, lowering her eyes. "I should probably go. I see that what my mama called a 'gift' has upset you. It was nice to meet you, Russ."

She bent and gathered her basket, turning to leave. She moved a couple of steps before Russ could catch her shoulder with one hand.

"Wait, what gift?"

She glanced back at him. "You already think I'm odd, Russ. It's best I don't change that opinion to completely insane."

"But you can't just say something like that and then walk away. Tell me."

He tried to keep the note of hysteria from creeping into his voice but failed. Orla sighed.

"Since I was little I've been able to sense . . . something. Call it restless spirits; I don't know. It gets really bad around cemeteries. Especially the one in town. Usually I can ignore it, but occasionally I'll have an episode like the one just now. I didn't mean to upset you."

She pulled away from him and hurried across the meadow, stopping only to gather her walking stick. Russ stared after her for several minutes, emotions waging war on his insides.

"So, who was it?"

Russ nearly jumped out of his skin. Spinning, all he saw was Joe.

"Damn, Joe!" he bellowed. "Don't you know not to sneak up on a man like that!"

Joe laughed at his brother's discomfort.

"You always were jumpy. So tell me, who was it?"

"Our neighbor. Says she's a healer and was gathering flowers for a tincture. Nice gal."

"The witch, huh? What will people think of next? Giant ape men living in the woods?" Joe chuckled. Then he sobered. "Was she pretty?"

Russ raised a brow at the tone Joe's voice had taken but nodded.

"Yeah, very. And young."

Joe grinned. "Then we should go over soon for a visit. Just to be neighborly."

Russ eyed his brother. "What did you do to get the Rangers on your trail?" he asked. Joe folded his arms across his chest.

"Nothing to worry yourself over, kid. You did your part, now let's just leave it lay."

Before Russ could ask anything else, Joe walked away.

Orla heard Vince before she saw him.

"This won't take as long as we figured," she said as he came into stride next to her. "The guilt that man carries is immense."

Vince frowned.

"I would hope so since he got six of his fellow rangers killed," he growled. It was Orla's turn to frown.

"There is that, of course, but it's not all. Vince, please don't be angry, but I don't think it was intentional."

Vince stopped in his tracks. Orla stopped as well but didn't turn to face him.

"What are you talking about?" he demanded. Orla folded her arms across her chest and let her eyes drift up to the trees.

"There's the problem," she admitted. "I haven't figured that part out just yet. He's McNeally's half-brother, but he hasn't known him long. In my honest opinion, I think he was used by McNeally."

"You can't be serious," Vince scoffed, looking at her incredulously. "You sound like you're defending him."

The heat in Vince's tone made her turn around to face him, and the rage and betrayal on his face sent a hot pain through her chest. Pushing the pain aside, she faced him squarely, her chin held high.

"Perhaps in a way I am. I know better than anyone what it's like to be judged by people who don't know all the facts. All I'm asking is that you get all the facts before you condemn him."

Vince stared at her incredulously. She knew it was a lot to ask of him when she knew what they had done to his men and to him. Her heart dropped as his expression darkened.

"I can't do that, Orla," he said simply. Orla's arms fell, and she sighed heavily.

"Then I suppose this is where we part ways. Good luck, Ranger. I wish you peace in your decision." She turned away from him, pulling her hood up over her head. "One last piece of advice, Ranger, if you choose to take it. I would confront him tonight while the shock is still fresh."

With that, she walked into the forest, disappearing among the trees. She never made a sound as tears streamed down her cheeks.

SEVEN

"You have been jumpy all damn day, Russ. What the hell is the matter with you?"

Russ started, throwing off the swing of the axe and missing the log he was aiming at.

"Damn it, Joe! I told you not to sneak up on me!"

"It hasn't been hard. Seems like every time something moves, you jump like a scared rabbit." Joe rubbed his chin in thought. "You weren't like this 'til after the little witch paid us a visit. What did the two of you talk about?"

Russ leaned the axe against the chopping block and wiped his brow with his bandana.

"Just about who she was and why she was picking elder flowers."

"And you say she lives just west of us?" Joe asked next. Russ nodded.

"Yeah, about a mile. Why?" Russ's brows rose. "Now wait just a minute. Get that thought out of your head. If she saw anything that day, she wouldn't have come near here. Besides, she would have gone straight to the sheriff."

"Maybe you're right," Joe conceded, then smiled. "Come on in for supper, and then we'll play some cards. To settle your nerves."

Russ nodded and followed his brother into the cabin.

He couldn't sleep. Flashes of gunfire exploded behind his eyelids every time he closed them, and the screams of men dying echoed in his ears. He started at every creak of the floorboards or call of a night bird.

"Murderer."

Russ froze, the whisper hitting him like an icy wave. His breath came out in a rasp.

"Betrayal."

He sat up and looked frantically around the room. An owl called from a nearby tree, and he cried out in fright, turning toward the window. The door creaking open behind him caused him to freeze again. His breath coming in ragged gasps, he very slowly turned his head back toward the door.

Terror coursed through him at the sight of what stood in his doorway. The skin was pasty white, and old blood covered the torso. It stepped into the room, making no sound as it moved to the foot of his bed and turned slowly to face him. The first light of dawn peeking through the window illuminated the face, and Russ screamed, crawling backward and up until he was standing on his bed and pressed against the wall.

"This can't be happening!" Russ croaked. "You're dead! This is nothing but a nightmare!"

"Murderer," the specter whispered again. Russ crumpled, curling into the fetal position, and started to cry.

"No!" he sobbed. "I didn't know! It wasn't supposed to be that way, Vince! He told me he wanted to turn himself in!"

"Liar!" Vince snarled. Russ flinched.

"I swear! I didn't know about the ambush! I only met my brother last year after we inherited this place. I'm so sorry, Vince! I never meant for you and the others to die! Please, I'm so sorry!"

Vince stared at the prostrate form, deflated. His rage drained, turning to pity and then to guilt. He owed Orla a huge apology, if she would ever talk to him again.

Vince sighed. "Oh, for Christ's sake, get up, Russ." Russ's sobs turned to choking coughs. He unfolded his body slowly, rolling to look up at Vince.

"Vince?" he asked hoarsely after his coughs had settled. "You're alive? How is this possible?"

"Orla," Vince said simply. "She found me after the ambush, barely breathing, and she nursed me back to health. She did mention she was a healer this morning, right?"

Russ sat up, his eyes wide.

"That was you in the trees that I saw this morning. You set me up?"

Vince leaned against the bedpost.

"I needed to know, Russ," he explained gruffly. "After Orla told me that there was one ranger missing, I went to the undertaker and found out that you had survived. What else was I to think?"

Russ sighed. "I see your point. I would probably think the same way." He looked past Vince to the door. "I'm surprised Joe hasn't come running in to check out the noise. I made enough of it."

"I saw him ride out before I came in," Vince said. Russ stilled.

"Which direction was he riding?" he demanded. Vince raised an eyebrow.

"West. Why do you ask?"

Russ jumped to his feet, reaching for his pants. "We have to go," he said urgently, yanking his pants on and then reaching for his shirt. Vince's brow furrowed.

"What are you so worried . . ." Vince's voice trailed off as his eyes widened. "Orla."

"He showed way too much interest in her this morning," Russ explained, pulling on his boots. "And I have a feeling that has something to do with why the Rangers were after him in the first place."

Vince's eyes darkened. "It has everything to do with it," he growled. "Let's go."

Orla stepped out onto her porch, a steaming cup of tea in her hand. The morning was cool but had the promise of turning into a sweltering afternoon. She was tired. Bad dreams and thoughts of Vince had kept her up most of the night. She found herself thinking that if she had just minded her own business that day, this wouldn't be a problem. But afterward, a pain would shoot through her chest at the thought of not meeting Vince and she would start crying again.

Euan jolted her out of her doldrums when he cawed loudly, swooping down in front of her before shooting skyward and circling the garden. Perching on his favorite branch of an old oak, he cawed again, staring off to the north of the house.

A warning. Someone was watching her. Her awareness turned from sorrow to alert. She kept her posture the same, not wanting to make her watcher aware that she knew they were there. Staying relaxed, she turned and went back into the house to dress and prepare.

Joe was more than satisfied as he watched the witch walk out onto her porch. He remembered Russ mentioning her name but hadn't paid enough attention to commit it to memory. His brother had not exaggerated about her being pretty, though. She was beyond pretty; she was gorgeous. Her dark hair fell down her back in soft waves, and the thin cotton nightgown did not leave much to the imagination. It had been too long since he had had time with a woman. Being on the run from the Rangers had made it impossible, and after the shooting, he had thought it would be best to lay low for a while.

He had heard the talk of a witch living in the woods. He had thought it all a bunch of hogwash. There were no such things as witches. But in this case, he was glad of the rumors. He doubted anyone would wonder why she hadn't been to town in so long. A dark grin spread across his face. He could play with this one as long as he wanted. The prospect sent a warm tremor through him, gathering at his crotch. Oh, yes. He could take his time with this one.

He eased out of his hiding place, making his way closer to the house. Maybe if he waited long enough, she would have breakfast ready for him. Anything would be better than his brother's cooking, or his own for that matter. His mouth actually started to water as the smell of baking biscuits and fresh coffee hit his nose.

Before he knew it, he was at the porch. When he looked up, he started. The witch stood in the doorway, fully dressed, looking at him as if she had been expecting him.

Up close, she was a vision. His eyes paused at the white streak of hair over her left ear, but as he met her gaze, he went still. Her green eye gazed at him calmly, while the pale blue bored into him as if trying to reach the deepest part of his soul.

"Good morning, Mr. McNeally. The coffee is done, if you would like a cup. Breakfast will be just a few more minutes."

Joe stared, wide-eyed, as she turned and disappeared back into the house, a feeling of unease sparking in his chest. He was starting to rethink his view on witches being real. Stepping up onto the porch, he followed her into the house. His eyes scanned the interior, taking in the shelves full of crocks and bowls and the bundles of herbs hanging from the exposed beams. Her chuckle from the table had him starting again.

"The only animal sacrifices I make are for my supper, Mr. McNeally. Completely harmless." She held out a cup. "Coffee?"

He stepped slowly to the table and accepted the cup.

"How do you know me?" he asked warily. The woman smiled softly and poured hot water over her tea leaves.

"I have my ways," she replied simply. "You must be hungry. You've been out there quite a while. I've made some biscuits and sausage gravy."

"Thanks," Joe said, eyeing her. He stamped down his unease and admired her backside as she filled a plate. "I understand you visited my place yesterday. I'm sorry I missed you."

She smiled again as she set the plate on the table and motioned for him to sit.

"Your brother was very kind to let me harvest the elder flowers. I appreciated it very much."

Joe took a bite of biscuits and gravy, and his eyes drifted shut. It was divine. The biscuits were fluffy and the gravy thick and flavorful. Before he realized it, he had cleaned his plate.

"That really hit the spot, thanks." He sat back in his chair with his cup of coffee. He was quiet for several minutes, relaxing and drinking the dark brew. "This will make my stay here much more pleasant, knowing you can cook."

She raised a brow.

"Planning on an extended visit?" she asked carefully. Joe stretched.

"Oh, yeah. You and I are gonna have a lot of fun. Just like that other little gal. Damn, she was pretty. Though not nearly as pretty as you, darlin'. I guess it was just dumb luck she turned out to be O'Connor's little sister."

Orla's heart nearly stopped at McNeally's confession. She now knew where the rest of Vince's rage and guilt had come from. This man had killed not only Vince's men but also his sister. And Orla didn't want to think about what else he had done to her.

McNeally went on, his hands behind his head.

"When I found out my little brother was riding with O'Connor, I sent him a message telling him I wanted to turn myself in. And the dumb bastard led them right to me." He laughed. "It was like shooting fish in a barrel. I did feel bad about having to kill the rest of my men, but I couldn't have them talking, now could I?"

The laugh seemed to have jolted him back to reality a bit and he shook his head. Orla stared at him with wide eyes as he stood up, wobbling slightly.

"What did you do to me?" he demanded. Orla swallowed hard, trying to ease her racing heart.

"Just a little something to calm your nerves," she said, managing to keep her voice steady.

"You really are a witch, aren't you?" He walked unsteadily toward her. "You poisoned me!"

She reached for her knife, but even drugged, he was just a bit quicker. He pinned her up against the wall, one hand on her throat, the other pressing her weapon arm above her head.

EIGHT

That was what Vince saw as he threw open the door. White-hot rage flowed through him, nearly blurring his vision. Orla's gaze shifted toward him, and in turn, McNeally's. The smaller man's face lost all color at the sight of Vince standing in the doorway.

"O'Connor?" McNeally asked, his voice nearly a squeak. "This can't be happening! You're dead!"

"Not hardly," Vince growled. "It's over, McNeally. Let her go."

McNeally laughed, a high, hysterical cackle. He shifted, pulling Orla around in front of him, his hand still around her throat.

"Oh, no. The little witch here is going to assist in my escape. Now be a good ranger and move aside so I can take my leave." McNeally's hand tightened on Orla's throat when Vince hesitated. "Now, Ranger!"

"It's okay, Vince," Orla said softly. "Let him go."

Vince met her eyes and the rage eased, confusion taking over. She was calm, her arms loose at her sides. He stepped away from the door. McNeally moved past him, turning so Orla was always between himself and Vince.

"This isn't over, McNeally!" Vince snarled. "I will find you."

"I wish you luck, then, Ranger. You're going to need it."

McNeally backed out the door and instantly dropped, taking Orla with him. Vince hesitated before rushing out. Russ was helping Orla to her feet, and an unconscious McNeally lay stretched out across her porch. Russ holstered his pistol.

"Are you all right?" Vince asked, pulling Orla into his arms.

She wrapped hers around him in relief. "I'm fine, thanks to the two of you."

Russ grinned. "I thought you had seen me, but I wasn't sure."

Orla smiled back at him. "It was just a glimpse, but enough to make it work."

Russ looked between the two of them and stepped off the porch. "I'll take care of Joe. You two take a minute."

Vince nodded gratefully and led Orla to the garden.

"Are you sure you're okay?"

Orla nodded. "A bit shaken, but yes, I'm fine."

Vince gathered her against him again. "I am so sorry, Orla," he began, his voice low. "I should have listened to you. I let my anger get the best of me, and I used it to hurt you."

Orla rested her cheek against his chest, soaking in his warmth.

"And I'm sorry too, Vince, about your sister."

Vince stilled, and he leaned away from her. "How did you . . . ?"

She nodded at McNeally.

"One of the side effects of the concoction I fed him. He told me everything. I'm just glad Euan let me know that McNeally was watching me so I had time to put everything together." She chuckled. "You should have seen his face when I greeted him at the door by name. I truly lived up to the rumors today."

"You sure have. But I think there's also a bit of truth to them."

Orla looked up at him, her brow furrowed. "What do you mean?"

Vince raised his hands to cup her face. "You have bewitched me, Orla Milne. The thought of you being hurt was worse than anything I have ever felt. I was furious but also terrified. I never want to feel that way again."

"What are you saying, Vince?"

"I want to be with you, Orla, in any way you'll allow it, whether it be marriage or whatever tradition you favor. I want to have a family with you, with as many children as you can handle. I want to grow old with you." He paused. "I love you, Orla."

Orla gazed at him, her eyes glistening.

"Would you be willing to leave the Rangers for me?" she asked. He smiled softly, his thumb caressing her cheek.

"I would, if that is what you wanted. You mean more to me than anything in this world."

Orla raised her hand to his cheek.

"I love you too, Vince. And I wouldn't want you to leave the Rangers. It's a part of you. One of the best parts. To take that away would be like cutting off your arm." She grinned. "Besides, at least you know I'd be able to take care of myself when you're gone."

Vince laughed. "That is very true."

A startled yell broke them apart. Turning toward the sound, they witnessed Russ pressed up against a tree, Aksel sitting in front of him, his short tail twitching.

"About time you showed yourself, you mangy cat." Orla chuckled. "Leave Russ alone."

Aksel turned his head and gazed at his mistress, yawning wide to show his fangs. Russ looked between her and the cat.

"He's yours?" he asked incredulously. Orla smiled, turning in Vince's arms until her back was against his chest.

"I'm a witch, Russ. Don't you know witches can control animals?" she teased.

"Feel lucky he likes you, Russ," Vince chimed in, his arms around Orla's shoulders. "Her raven doesn't like anyone."

Russ relaxed a bit, but his eyes returned to the cat.

"So, he won't pounce if I walk away?"

Orla leaned her head to the side. "Well . . . that I can't guarantee. He may think you're playing with him. I guess you'll just have to take your chances."

Aksel chose that moment to crouch and spring into the trees.

"I guess he found better prey than you, Russ," Vince said, grinning. "Is McNeally secure?"

"Yes, sir. I'll just need help getting him up on a horse when we leave." He looked at Orla. "What did you give him?"

Orla shrugged.

"A bit of this, a dash of that. It won't kill him. But he will have a major headache when it wears off. Serves him right."

"Remind me to never get on your bad side," Russ muttered. "I'm going to go get Joe's horse. We should get him into town and safely in jail as soon as we can."

"Sounds good," Vince said, watching him go. His hands slid down Orla's arms and circled her waist, his chin coming down to rest on her shoulder.

"What will happen to Russ?" Orla asked. Vince sighed.

"I'll have a word with the sheriff. Tell him that he was held hostage or something. He's a good kid. I'll make sure he stays working with me in the Rangers."

She smiled and turned her head to kiss his cheek.

"I can't imagine a better man for him to look up to." She twisted her body until her lips reached his ear. "Weren't we interrupted earlier?"

She giggled as he growled and turned, capturing her lips with his.

Orla pulled her horse to a stop at the edge of town, taking a deep breath.

"Are you okay?" Vince asked, stopping next to her.

"I've come to town twice within a week. I'm not sure the citizens can handle it."

He chuckled.

"I'm sure most of them will get over it. There are some who will never accept you, but they don't matter. Who matter are the ones who love you."

She smiled at him. Russ came up on her other side, folding his arms and resting them on his saddle horn.

"I happen to think you're pretty great too, Orla." He winked. "Are you sure you wouldn't prefer a younger man?"

Orla laughed at Vince's dark look.

"Watch it there, boy," Vince growled, but there wasn't much heat to it.

"As tempting as that is, Russ, I'll have to pass." Orla patted his hand. "But don't worry. The right girl will come along before you know it."

"Let's get McNeally to the jail," Vince said. "There happens to be a pretty nice reward out on him. Plenty to take you both out to a nice dinner."

Orla started to frown, then sighed and straightened in her saddle.

"That sounds wonderful. It will be nice to not have to cook for myself for a change."

Vince winked at her. "That's my girl."

Bill stepped out of the jail as the horses walked up. Vince grinned as the sheriff's brow rose at the sight of McNeally sitting on the horse behind Vince, bound and barely lucid.

Vince swung to the ground. "I have a new resident for your jail, Bill. I hope you have a vacancy."

"Sure do. Best room in the house; saved it just for you," he responded with a grin. He tipped his hat to Orla. "Miss Orla, nice to see you again."

"You as well, Sheriff," she said with a smile.

"Let's get him down and into a cell," Bill continued. "I'll get everything taken care of and get you the reward money."

"Thanks, Bill." Vince turned. "Come on, Russ. Let's get him down. It'll take both of us to get him into the jail in his current condition."

Despite the trouble getting him into the cell, they were in and out of the jail in less than fifteen minutes. Vince counted out part of the reward money and handed it over to Russ as they walked across the street toward the general store.

"What's this for?" Russ asked.

"You helped bring in the prisoner, so you are entitled to a share of the reward. Besides, you'll need something to live on until your pay comes through from the Rangers."

"Miss Orla! Miss Orla!"

All three of them looked up, Orla turning just in time to catch a little blonde-haired girl who had thrown herself at Orla.

"My goodness!" Orla gasped, scooping the girl up. It took only a second for her to recognize the girl, and she smiled. "Carla! How have you been doing? Have you had any trouble breathing?"

"Nope," the girl chirped. "I'm breathing real good. I saw you from the store and had to come say hello."

"I'm glad you did. But where's your mama?"

"Here, Miss Orla. Hello, Ranger. I asked her to wait, but she was just too excited. My husband rushed us off before I could properly introduce myself. I'm Susan."

Orla adjusted Carla onto her hip so she could shake Susan's hand.

"It's nice to meet you properly, Susan." She looked around a bit nervously. Susan smiled.

"Don't you worry about Carl. He's finishing up loading the wagon and will be along shortly."

She was true to her word. The tall man joined them just a few minutes later. Orla shifted nervously. Susan caught her husband's eye and nodded toward Orla.

"Miss Milne, I would like to apologize for my behavior the other day. I wish I could blame my actions on the situation, but I can't. It was nothing but my ignorant prejudice. I want to thank you for helping my little girl, and if you are still willing, I would like to ask you about the tea you mentioned that would help with her condition." His posture was contrite. Orla's smile returned.

"Of course. I would be happy to supply you with tea as often as you need it." She paused. "And to accept your apology. I'm glad to see she is doing so well."

"We still try to keep her from exerting herself too much, but yes, she is doing great."

"Give me a day to get the tea mixed for you, and either I can bring it by or you can pick it up at my place. I didn't bring my kit with me today."

"That would be just fine," Susan said with a smile. "We can stop by and pick it up in a couple days. Carla, we need to get going, hun. Daddy has work to do at home. Have a wonderful day, Miss Orla, Ranger."

Carla hugged Orla's neck tightly before allowing her mother to remove her form Orla's arms.

"Bye, Miss Orla! See you soon!"

Orla waved as Carla skipped away with her parents. Vince slid an arm across her shoulders.

"That was unexpected," he rumbled. Orla looked around them. She was still getting a few dark looks, but most had changed from wariness to curiosity. A weight lifted from her shoulders, and she turned her smile to him.

"But like you said, it's a start. And we have to start somewhere."

THE BITE OF THE WOLF

DOROTHY TINKER

Beda was just laying her niece down for the night when her brother, Demason, burst into the house, shouting her name. Despite his urgent barks, Beda only rolled her eyes before crossing them and sticking out her tongue. Grayson, as pink and chubby as any human babe, squealed with glee and reached with her small hands for the white strands hanging down around Beda's face.

"Now, go to sleep, cub." Beda laid her hand over the babe's forehead and eyes. Grayson gave a wide yawn and then cooed softly as she drifted off into the land of Lodyma.

As soon as the babe was asleep, Beda silently slipped from the room and followed the sounds of scrambling downstairs to the first-floor bedroom. There, she found her wiry older brother, his pinched lean features partially obscured by his hanging gray hair and beard. Half his dresser drawers were open, and he was shoving clothes from within them into a travel pack.

"What's got your loincloth in a bunch?"

The shirt in Demason's hands tore, and he growled as he spun toward Beda. When his eyes landed on her, he snapped his teeth together and returned to packing.

"Go pack! We need to leave town."

Beda frowned but didn't move. "And we're going where exactly?"

Demason snarled wordlessly and slammed the dresser drawers shut. Grabbing his pack, he shoved past Beda and out into the main living area. "Go pack!" he repeated. "I'll get Grayson."

It was Beda's turn to snarl as she grabbed her brother's shoulder and spun him around. Before he could do more than open his mouth, she had her hand wrapped threateningly around his throat. As he hesitated, she leaned closer and pitched her voice low.

"I just got the cub to sleep, Demason. Like Gijs am I going to let you burst in there and wake her."

For a moment, he simply glared. Then his eyes softened, and his expression turned sulky.

"She's *my* daughter," he muttered, the words nearly lost in the gravel of his voice.

Beda rolled her eyes and dropped her hand from his throat. "Biologically, maybe." She eyed him sideways. "Now are you going to tell me why we're leaving Monalof?"

Demason's eyes darkened. "Drefan has betrayed us. He killed the Lioness!"

Beda's lungs stilled and her heart stuttered. Queen Leoma was dead? But she was supposed to be giving birth to Drefan's—

Her eyes widened. "Her cub! Did he…?"

Demason growled lowly. "The babe was alive when I last saw him, but there's no telling if Drefan will keep his word."

"Word?"

Her brother shook his head. "Pack and get Grayson."

Beda grabbed his shoulders as he tried to step past her and snapped at his throat. "You're going to tell me why you, captain of the queen's guard, left the cub with Drefan if he killed his own mate."

Demason snarled down at her, but now that Beda was looking for it, she could see the strain in his eyes. "I had no choice, Beda! It was leave with the promise that Drefan would spare the cub or watch him kill the only hope of our people. Or do you forget what the death of the last Royal would cost us?"

Beda's hands slipped from Demason's shoulders, her eyes staring past him into nothingness. Her chest felt like ice. "He…he would have killed him?"

Demason rumbled lowly but cupped Beda's shoulder comfortingly. "He held a knife to the cub's throat, Beda. Demanded we leave. The only way the babe survives is if we flee Monalof and don't return."

Beda shook her head. The urge to rush upstairs and clutch Grayson to her chest, never to let her go, swelled within her.

"We who, Demason? All the shifters? Just the queen's guard?" Neither made sense, though, even as Beda spoke the words. The first seemed too many when more than half of Monalof was inhabited by shifters. And if it was just the queen's guard, then Beda wouldn't have been included.

Demason shifted, drawing a frowned from Beda. He sighed, his shoulders drooping. "Just Howlers. *All* the Howlers."

Beda's mind raced. "But if the only Royal alive can't shift yet…" She cursed. "He's going to lay the blame on us Howlers, isn't he? The rest of our people will wake to the knowledge that Lodyma's touch is gone, and he'll point them after the ones who fled, the only ones who can still shift."

Demason shuddered but nodded. "And if we try to fight it, he'll simply kill his own cub, ensuring Lodyma's power never touches our people again." His head snapped up, and his eyes burned. "But if we leave, we at least still have hope for our people's future. Now go pack and get Grayson."

Beda nodded and loped up the stairs, packed quickly, and collected her slumbering niece. Any human child would have been awake and squalling with the ruckus her sire had made earlier, but the bond between the shiftling and Beda was strong enough to keep the cub asleep.

With the sleeping Grayson curled against her chest and her travel pack slung across her back, Beda followed Demason away from their home. A heavy silence settled between them as they moved quickly through the dark city. When Beda realized where Demason was leading them, though, her steps faltered.

"Are you sure we should be going this way?"

Demason cast an irritated glance over his shoulder. "The eastern gate is the closest to the forest. And the smallest. We're less likely to be noticed slipping out there and into the forest."

Beda slowed to a walk and glanced around. The streets they passed through had been mostly empty, which would have been unusual on any other night. It was only the New Moon—the lowest point of Lodyma's power—that kept the city so still.

"I think we might have better luck with a different gate," she muttered.

"Don't be ridiculous. It's the only gate guarded by a single man. Besides, I already told the others to meet us there."

Demason broke into a trot once more, and Beda had little choice but to keep pace. She only hoped her brother didn't get too angry when they reached the gate.

The gate itself was only as wide as three men standing shoulder to shoulder. It usually stood open twice as tall as a man, but on nights like this, the portcullis barely hung high enough for a man to pass through without ducking.

As they approached, Beda spotted other Howlers gathered just inside the gate, standing in the shadow of the city walls. Each bore a pack upon his or her back. Some, like Beda, carried babes or held the hands of older shiftlings who weren't yet old enough for the shifter bite and their first shift. Others cradled their mates, most of whom were also Howlers since few other moon shifters could handle the power and temper of a wolf.

There were those who tried, though.

"Rover, I told you, no humans," Demason growled as they got closer to the group.

Rover, a tall man with black hair and golden eyes, curled his arms more tightly around the woman within them. She, in turn, pressed back against his chest, despite the defiance blazing within her eyes.

"And I refuse to leave behind my mate, Demason. Besides," Rover added with a narrowing gaze, "she's with pup."

Demason snarled. "We have no idea what lies Drefan will spread among the humans and the rest of our people once we're gone. If they accuse us of kidnapping as well as—"

"I'd prefer that," snapped Rover, "to them killing my mate and unborn child!"

"Brother," Beda hissed, gripping Demason's arm. She had finally spotted the guard who stood on duty for the night, and the man was watching them with curious eyes. She doubted he could yet make out their features—he was only human, after all—but she could see him clearly. He was exactly who she had feared he would be.

Or had hoped. She wasn't sure which was worse.

"What?" Demason ground out. He seemed to catch the direction of her gaze and turned to eye the single guard. "Right. There goes knocking him out before he sees us."

Beda rolled her eyes. Despite being captain of the Lioness's personal guard, her brother could sometimes be quite the brute and simply unimaginative.

"The last thing any of us needs is to leave behind someone unconscious." Glancing quickly at the guard, she added, "Let me talk to him."

Demason didn't look happy with the idea, but he admitted to not having any better ones. Not bothering to leave Grayson with her sire, Beda strode confidently toward the gate.

She knew the second the guard could make out her white hair and lean features. His icy blue eyes brightened, his smooth chin tilted up, and his thin lips curled into a warm smile. Leaning back against the wall, he tugged at the edge of his crimson uniform jacket, slipped his hands into the pockets of his black pants, and cocked his head to one side.

"I was wondering where you were, Beda."

Heat filled Beda's cheeks, and she ducked her head. It wasn't how she had meant the conversation to begin, but Holt's forwardness always surprised her. "Surely you didn't expect me to hunt tonight?"

Except he had, she knew. Every New Moon for the last two years she had left through this gate, taking to the forest to hunt in human form. It had only been the queen's labor that had kept her brother from returning home earlier to care for Grayson. The sudden reminder of their lost queen and her threatened cub made Beda's chest tighten.

Holt stepped forward, his sudden proximity enough to draw Beda's gaze back to his. His icy eyes were intense, and he lifted one hand, palm up, between them. "What do you think?"

Beda stared into his eyes, unblinking and unbreathing. The words might have been innocent but for the gesture and his proximity. Both invited her to join him in more than just teasing conversation—an invitation that was older than she liked to admit. Because for every New Moon that she had left through this gate, Holt had stood here on duty, watching and teasing.

"Beda." The word was a sharp grunt from behind her, and Holt's icy eyes left hers, his hand dropping to his side.

"Sir Demason," Holt greeted with a short bow. "Is there something I can do for you, sir?"

Beda glanced back at her brother. Demason glared at her, ignoring the guard. "I thought you were going to take care of him."

A prickling sensation broke out across Beda's neck and back. "I was *talking* to him, Demason. I never said anything about *taking care of* him."

Demason scowled. "Now he's recognized us—"

"We wouldn't have been able to pass without him recognizing us." Beda's cheeks burned as she thought about why.

Her brother's gaze flicked between her and Holt. "No."

Beda frowned. "What do you mean, no?"

"I mean," he rumbled, so lowly Beda as much felt it as heard it, "you cannot be with him. He's human, Beda, and one of Drefan's guards, no less. He'll turn on us as suddenly as Drefan did."

Beda tried to protest, but Holt beat her to it. "With all due respect, Sir Demason, I'd never—"

Demason snarled and lunged for Holt. Despite the sudden panic in Beda's thoughts—the babe in her arms prevented her from bodily stopping her brother—she sidestepped in front of Demason and put out a hand to catch the middle of his chest. Immediately, he froze, his eyes widening. His right arm hung a finger's width from Grayson's head.

"What are you doing?"

Beda huffed. "He's done nothing wrong, brother. You have no right to attack him."

"And you have no right to threaten our people's livelihood by courting a human! Not after tonight!"

Beda's breath caught in her chest, but she snapped her teeth together. "That is not your decision to make, brother. I am my own wolf. Just because you couldn't protect—"

"Demason."

He jerked around. Witter, Demason's second, stood behind him. The older Howler stared into the city before turning his sharp gaze to Demason.

"We need to leave. If Drefan sends soldiers to hunt us down…"

"Go," Holt insisted, stepping to the side of the gate. "If anyone comes seeking Howlers, I'll insist you didn't come this way."

"Or run off to Hehmona Hall to give them a head start?" Demason sneered. "I don't trust you enough to turn my back on you."

Holt lifted his chin, though Beda noticed the way his eyes flashed toward her. "Then take me with you. I won't cause you any trouble either way, but if you'd rather keep an eye on me…"

Demason growled, spun toward Beda, and snatched Grayson from her arms. The cub grumbled before settling against her sire's chest.

"Tie his wrists." He turned away, though not without a final snarl at Holt, and led the Howlers through the gate, away from their city and into the forest.

Holt couldn't believe his luck. Being out from under Drefan's command and running away with the woman he loved was almost more than he'd ever dared dream. Of course, they were technically fleeing to escape persecution by Drefan, but Holt wasn't choosy.

He also wasn't usually this clumsy, even in the dark. He kept tripping over logs and stepping on sticks, advertising their location better than the Howlers would have if they'd actually been howling. Beda kept shushing him, but there was little he could do with his hands tied behind his back.

After the seventh time, Beda shot him an irritated glance that was clearly visible even in the darkness. Holt shrugged as she tugged him back to his feet. "Look, I can only be so quiet when I can't steady myself. If you unbound my hands—"

"My brother would kill you."

Holt grimaced. That was probably true. "Then tie my hands in front of me. I'll at least be able to keep my balance."

Beda didn't answer. When Holt nearly tripped again, she sighed. "Fine," she muttered, stopping. "But don't blame me if my brother decides even that's too much freedom for you."

As soon as his hands were out from behind his back, he rubbed at his wrists. "Thank the gods."

Beda paused in coming back around him. "The gods?" she asked. "I thought you humans praised Gijs alone?"

Holt shrugged. "When Lodyma shows the power she holds, it's kind of hard to ignore her."

Beda frowned but didn't say anything else. She tied his hands in front of his body, and they continued on, running to catch up with the rest of the pack. With his hands in front of him, Holt had little trouble running—or staying quiet. In fact, he felt a sense of peace as the scents and sounds of the forest reminded him of his younger days.

By the time they'd caught up with the pack and could slow,

Holt's breathing was heavy. Beda's was steady, and he shook his head as he kept pace with her.

"Sometimes, I wish the shifter bite worked on us humans. What I wouldn't give to run with a pack on a Full Moon. Or any moon, for that matter."

Beda was silent a moment before asking, "Why?"

Holt shrugged. "Why not? Racing through the forest with boundless energy? Watching the moonlight dance upon rippling fur?" He flashed Beda a grin. "It sounds beautiful."

Beda didn't answer. She remained silent for the rest of the night.

"We'll make camp here."

Beda lifted her head to blink wearily past the hanging heads before her. Gijs had risen several hours ago. His light shone down heavily toward the head of the pack, where Demason stood, calling them to a halt.

"Finally." She rolled her shoulders. It was true that moon shifters spent most nights awake, never sleeping before Gijs had risen. But that wakefulness was driven by the power of Lodyma, who gave all moon shifters the energy to shift and forge through the night. Most fell asleep as soon as they had shifted back to human form.

That the night before had been a New Moon, the one night each month when Lodyma's power was at its lowest, only made everyone's exhaustion worse. Most moon shifters slept nearly as much as humans did on the nights of New Moons.

Even Howlers.

"I don' s'pose we could jus' lie down here an' sleep," Holt muttered. He leaned against a nearby tree, his eyes already closed.

Beda snorted. Despite her own desire for sleep, she gripped his arm and tugged him upright. He groaned but met her gaze with a flashing smile. "Didn' think so."

Beda shook her head and tugged Holt forward, following the other Howlers as they spread out through the small heather meadow

Demason had found them. Where meadow met the surrounding tree line, heavy patches of lavender and lemongrass grew, thick enough to help mask the musk of unwashed bodies. By the sound of it, there was even a small creek nearby. Beda made a note to stop by it before she crashed out on her bedroll.

A piercing wail jerked Beda's thoughts back to the present. She steered Holt toward the center of the clearing, where Demason still stood.

"Give her to me," she insisted as soon as she was close enough to her brother not to shout.

He scowled. "I can take care of my own cub."

Beda rolled her eyes. "Not when you're trying to direct Howlers to set up camp, you can't." Demason's lips parted, baring sharp teeth, but Beda only motioned toward the wailing babe with both hands. "Hand her over, and maybe we can all get some rest soon."

He grumbled but handed the shiftling over. As he turned away to direct the pitching of tents, Beda bent her head over Grayson's scrunched-up face and blew lightly across her nose and mouth. The screams paused as Grayson opened dark eyes to peer up at Beda curiously. Beda smiled, crossed her eyes, and offered the shiftling a finger to suckle.

Grayson cooed and laughed before she accepted the finger and began gnawing on it with toothless gums.

"Wow. Wish my sisters had been that easy to appease."

Beda blinked and raised her eyes to Holt, who still stood beside her. He looked more awake than he had earlier.

"You have sisters?"

Holt's smile turned to a grimace. "Had, actually. Three of them, all younger. They, uh…disappeared when…"

"When your people were driven from their homes?" Beda offered. She had never really understood the humans' circumstances when they arrived in the moon shifter kingdom asking for acceptance, but she wasn't going to press if Holt didn't feel up to talking about it.

Besides, Beda suspected any conversation concerning the origin of Drefan's people was more likely to lead to Demason killing Holt than to any kind of understanding right now.

Holt nodded slowly and ducked his head to peer down at Grayson. "Looks like the little thing's hungry, even if she is being nice and quiet."

Beda nodded. "Quieting her is the easy part, what with the shiftling bond between us. The tricky part will be finding her something to eat out here. I'm accustomed to giving her goat's milk or mashed fruit from the market."

Holt's smile returned to its full, flashing breadth. "Oh, that's easy enough. You just need to know what to look—"

A sudden hand on his shoulder jerked him around, interrupting him. Demason stood behind him, his teeth bared.

"You," Demason growled, "are going in there!"

He shoved Holt toward a small tent that seemed barely large enough for him to crawl inside. Beda stepped forward, protests on her lips, but Demason turned and stopped her with a hand on her shoulder and a snarl in her face.

"I told you, Beda. You can't risk our people's livelihood by courting a human!"

A rumble rose up Beda's throat. "And I told you—"

A soft cry cut through her protest, and Demason's dark gaze cut to the babe in Beda's arms. "And I thought you were supposed to be caring for her. Or is a human worth more to you than Grayson's welfare?"

Beda bared her teeth as she began to rock the shiftling to ease her fussiness. "I was trying to, Brother, but it's kind of difficult when—"

"Demason!"

Beda snapped her mouth shut as Witter waved from the other side of the meadow, where an argument had broken out. With a loud rumbling in his chest, Demason shoved Holt into the tent, ordered a young Howler to guard him, and trotted off toward the fight that was already turning physical.

Beda huffed as she watched her brother wade into the fight. She was tempted to stick around so she could force him to let Holt out of the small tent, but Grayson's strengthening cries urged her to move before he was finished.

"All right, all right." Eyeing Holt's tent one last time, she left to seek out one of the other mothers. Surely someone other than Holt would know what she could scrounge to feed the shiftling.

The following days passed slowly for Holt. He was little more than a prisoner to the Howlers. Since he was thrown into the small tent, he was almost never allowed to leave it. Only the kindness of Meghan, the pregnant human, kept him from starving, and the early-morning patience of her mate, Rover, kept his muscles from shriveling. The rest of him was neglected: his face went unshaven and his crimson uniform, already stained from the long trek through the forest, only grew darker.

Whenever Meghan visited, Holt spent just as much time offering her tidbits about the forest as he did gleaning news of what was happening. Several times she offered him thanks from not only her but the other mothers, as apparently none of them were versed in what plants were edible outside of the market and farmland. In exchange, she shared the true depth of Drefan's betrayal.

Other than those small interactions, only the nights held interest for Holt. Laid out on his bedroll, he closed his eyes and listened to the yips and growls that filled the clearing each night. He didn't dare peer past his tent flaps, but he could picture in his mind's eye the large lupine forms that chased each other around the clearing and tumbled through the dirt. The voices of the wolves soothed him into slumber, and he dreamed of running through the forest alongside a pearly white wolf with ebon eyes.

It had been a week since they'd settled into the clearing when Holt's attention was caught by an argument between Demason and Beda. Arguments weren't uncommon among Howlers, but this one featured his name.

"Holt's not an animal, Demason! You can't just keep him locked up."

"Enough, Beda!"

Holt pulled aside one flap of his tent and peered out. Beda stood before her gray-haired brother, her head barely reaching his nose. In the bright morning sunlight, her hair shone a pearly white, piled atop her head in a messy knot. Her face, pale and lean like her brother's, was twisted in a snarl, and her ebon eyes, her only darkness, flashed.

Beautiful.

"But he'll rot!" Beda protested.

"Let him!" Demason answered. He tried to walk around her, but she caught his shoulder with the heel of her hand.

"Don't!" she snapped. "You can't just walk away from me! I'm your sister and the caretaker of your cub. You owe me some consideration!"

Demason growled. "I have a camp to run, Beda. I don't have time to entertain your fancies for one of our people's enemies."

"I'm not—he's not—" Beda gave a sharp wordless scream. Her hands clenched into fists, and her teeth flashed. "Why do you *refuse* to listen to reason?"

The entire camp stilled. Though Holt couldn't see the other Howlers, the color that flushed up Beda's neck and cheeks in the next moment was enough for him to imagine the looks she was receiving.

Demason sneered and brushed past her. "I'll listen to *reason* when you can speak something untainted by your emotions."

Holt snorted and dropped the tent flap before anyone noticed him watching. He knew as well as any shifter that Howlers lived and died by their emotions. That Demason would say such a thing was only piling insult on top of injury.

At least I can be certain that Beda's too stubborn to give up, especially after that. Remembering her expressive features and the tight coil of her lean form, he grinned. *And the boredom will be worth it if I can get more moments like those.*

That day's midday and evening meals came and went without a single visit from Meghan, and Holt sighed, laid out across his bedroll. They weren't the first meals she hadn't been able to sneak him food, but he had come to enjoy the small conversations they shared. If nothing else, they were a reprieve from the constant monotony.

At least I have that glimpse of Beda to distract me.

He was replaying the argument in his mind—*she was even defending me to her brother*—when the flap of his tent was thrust aside and a hand grabbed his ankle. Yelping, he jerked his knee toward his chest. His attacker didn't let go, instead gasping and falling forward across his upraised leg. Blinking, Holt found himself staring into ebon eyes framed by pearly tendrils.

"Beda?"

Even in the dim light of the tent, Holt could make out the color filling her cheeks. She squirmed around, apparently trying to get up, but when she lifted up and placed her hand on his knee for support, he wasn't expecting it. He winced as she collapsed on top of him.

"You know," he gritted out, catching her hips to still her continued squirming, "I've dreamed of you getting me in a position like this for months, but I suspect your brother would kill me if he saw us."

Beda inhaled sharply and froze. After a long uncertain moment, she planted her hands on either side of Holt's head and thrust herself back up onto her knees. She stared down at him with wide eyes and dark cheeks.

Hoping to ease her embarrassment—and to hide the results of her lovely movements upon his body—Holt sat up and scooted backward, crossing his legs together in front of him. Leaning his elbows on his knees, he offered her his usual smile. "So…any chance I can get out of here?"

Beda ducked her head. "I, uh…asked Demason if I could take you out into the forest…"

Holt refrained from mentioning that he'd overheard the argument. Instead, he nodded encouragingly, though he doubted she noticed. Her eyes appeared to be locked on her knees.

"He said no," she muttered.

Holt frowned. "Then why are you here?"

Beda's head snapped up, and her eyes flashed. Holt hoped she didn't notice the way his breath caught.

"It isn't right, the way he's treating you! You need food and exercise and—What?"

Holt was grinning. "Have I ever told you how beautiful you are?"

Beda wrinkled her nose. "I'm a wolf, Holt. We don't do beautiful."

Holt snorted. "Right. Except I've thought you were beautiful since I first met you. And your shifted form…" He offered her a softer smile. "There's a reason I wish I could run with a pack."

Beda's eyes widened again, but this time Holt didn't think it was embarrassment. Her breathing had sped up, and her eyes darted back toward the tent's entrance, her nostrils flaring. Abruptly, she grabbed Holt's hand and tugged him toward the tent's flaps.

She didn't even bother to check if the coast was clear before bursting out of his tent and dragging him with her. She tugged him along, and they ran through the surprisingly deserted camp.

As they passed into the forest, Holt glanced back into the camp. "Where is ever—oof!"

His back hit a trunk, and he snapped his head back around. Beda's eyes, despite their dark color, seemed to glow in the late evening light that filtered through the forest canopy, and she leaned her body along his. The press of lean muscles against his own stirred Holt in ways he had only dreamed of.

"Did you mean it?" Beda whispered. Her breath caressed Holt's neck, sending a shudder down his spine. "About my wolf?"

"I mean everything I say to you, Beda," he murmured. "You're beautiful. It doesn't matter the form."

"Good."

It was the only warning Holt had before Beda's lips pressed hard against his. His teeth cut into his lips, and the taste of iron filled his mouth, but he could only groan and catch her hips with desperate hands, pulling her even closer. Her nails dug into his shoulders, and for one wild moment he wondered if she would rip his sweat-crusted jacket and shirt from his body.

The reality turned out wilder than he'd hoped. She reared back, pulling his body with her away from the trunk. Next thing he knew, he was sprawled across the forest floor, only leaves and moss cushioning his fall. Beda stood over him, her white hair a halo in the evening light.

"You speak prettily," she growled, dropping into a crouch, "but can you handle the power of a wolf?"

Before he could even groan, she leaped upon him, her lips mashing into his and her fingers worming in between the buttons of his stained jacket, ripping it open. Holt grabbed her hips again and slammed her groin down against his. She broke the kiss with a whine, but he reached for her hair and pulled her head back down, catching her bottom lip between his teeth.

Her voice rumbled deep in her throat as he bit down on the plump flesh. Nails dug into his stomach, and he hissed but held on. Rolling her hips against his, she eased up on his stomach and reached for his waistband. She slipped her fingers underneath, and he thrust up against her as they grazed his manhood.

He released her bottom lip and shoved her off to the side. She flashed her teeth and grumbled, but he was already leaning over her and hooking curled fingers into clothes and flesh, all too aware of the approaching night.

It seemed only a moment before she realized what he wanted. Her growls turned to whines as she rolled onto her stomach and lifted herself onto her hands and knees. With one hand, he dragged her trousers down over her hips, while his other shoved his own down to his thighs.

As Holt carefully palmed his erection, he paused just long enough to admire the shadows of filtered evening light playing across her pale cheeks. Then a soft snarl urged him forward, and he plunged home.

White blanked his vision, and a howl filled his ears, so loudly Holt wondered if the king could hear it in Monalof. He couldn't find the will to care. All that mattered was heat, moisture, and the passion and power of the woman below him.

"Move!" Beda snarled. She leaned forward and thrust herself backward. Holt nearly laughed with the joy filling him, but the sound came out choked and he could do nothing more than follow his love's lead.

Holt lost the individual movements among the pleasure that curled within his gut and reached for his chest and limbs. It grew stronger and reached farther, and he was gasping and shuddering as he clutched Beda's hips and hammered into her with a passion he could only hope equaled hers.

When Beda howled again, her channel tightened around him. He gasped and stilled as the pleasure that had been building within him exploded through his chest and limbs and emptied into her.

Somehow, he and Beda wound up curled together on the forest floor, her juices and his seed spilling across their half-naked legs. She nuzzled his neck lazily, despite the encroaching sunset, and nipped lightly at his skin.

"You know," she murmured, her voice gruff. "You don't need to shift to run with a pack. You seem to keep up with me just fine as it is."

Holt felt his cheeks flush. "What about your brother?" A thrill of dread raced up his spine, but Beda's hot form pressing tightly against his eased that fear almost immediately.

Beda shook her head, her hair trailing softly against his shoulder and chest. "I'll make sure he accepts you. I'm not giving you up now that I've claimed you as mine."

Holt's whole body flushed then. Beda stirred beside him, and he opened his eyes as her warmth disappeared from his side. He wondered where she found the energy to move, but that became apparent in the next moment.

Beda's ebon eyes met his, and suddenly her body was bending

forward, growing larger, and sprouting fur as pearly white as the hair atop her head. Her face elongated and became even sharper. Soon, a giant wolf stood where she had.

Holt climbed to his feet slowly—not from fear but from an awe he couldn't hope to contain. Standing in front of Beda, he cupped her chin and smoothed his hands back over her neck, burying them in the thick fur he found there. "Beautiful," he whispered, pressing his stubbled cheek to her furred one. "Absolutely beautiful."

They spent the night together, running through the forest and tumbling around in the underbrush. As midnight passed and yawns plagued Holt, they settled down under a thickly branched willow. Holt ran his hands through Beda's pearly fur, dislodging dirt and twigs, before settling down to sleep. Beda curled around him, her warmth a lovely substitute for a blanket.

As Holt drifted off into slumber, he felt safe and warm. Beda, he knew, wouldn't sleep until sunrise. Moon shifters never did.

Holt woke to gentle shadows and the cool mist of early morning. Rubbing at bleary eyes with one hand, he wondered what had wakened him. Gijs had risen, but not yet high enough for his light to penetrate the forest canopy.

Lifting himself onto an elbow to peer through the willow branches, he paused as something tightened across his chest. Laid out against his side, Beda was fully clothed and snoring lightly, her arm tight around his torso. Holt smiled and smoothed pearly strands of hair out of her face.

The crack of a breaking branch startled Holt from his reverie. The sound was followed by a curse and shushing, and he narrowed his eyes. Those weren't the voices of Howlers.

Carefully disentangling himself from Beda's grasp, Holt stood and pulled aside the willow's branches to peer out into the larger forest. Not a body's length away stood three men. Two of them glared at the third.

"Sorry," the third hissed, raising his hands. "You know woods aren't exactly my expertise."

Holt raised an eyebrow, recognizing the human. Bar had once been a brawler. The quiet and stealth required by the forest were definitely not part of his capabilities. As he observed the other two, he realized none of these humans were accustomed to the forest.

"That's not the point," hissed one of the other two. "If you wake the Howlers before we find them, it'll be our heads rolling, not theirs." He grabbed Bar by the elbow and jerked him forward.

Holt nodded grimly. As he'd expected, they were here to hurt the Howlers, and that was not something he could let happen. The Howlers were Beda's people—and his, if they would accept him.

These men fear the Howlers they hunt, but they've entered my terrain now. Let us see how quickly they regret that.

Beda startled awake to the scent of blood. It wasn't unusual for her to wake next to a kill, but this blood smelled distinctly human. Her nostrils flaring, it took her a moment to notice Holt leaning over her, one hand on her cheek. He, she realized, was the source of the scent.

"Holt?"

He dipped his head and brushed his lips across hers. "Just a few humans," he murmured. "By the sound of it, they followed your brother and the others from wherever they disappeared to yesterday evening."

Beda gasped, her cheeks growing warm. *The camp! The children!* She tried to scramble to her feet, but Holt pinned her to the ground, his hands gentle but firm.

"Don't worry," he murmured, dropping kisses to her cheeks and forehead. "There were only three of them. They didn't even find the camp."

Beda stared at him, wide-eyed. "You…killed them?"

Holt nodded, his icy eyes as intense as they'd been the night they'd fled Monalof. "They planned to hurt our people. I couldn't let that happen."

Warmth filled Beda. *Our people.* She lifted a trembling hand and traced his lips with her fingers. "I thought last night had taught me how well you matched me, but this…you're already a Howler at heart, aren't you?"

The smile Holt gave was as fierce as any wolf's. He leaned down and captured her lips in a hard kiss. Beda eagerly returned it.

Demason was waiting for them when they returned to camp, both of them disheveled and Holt's uniform jacket gaping open. They'd barely entered the slowly waking camp when Demason grabbed Holt by the throat and shoved him up against a tree.

"What," Demason bit out, his voice more gravel than words, "do you think you are doing?"

"Demason, stop!"

Beda grabbed her brother's shoulder. He tried to throw her off with one hand, but she slid her hand along his arm, using his own momentum to get a grip on his wrist and twist his arm up behind his back. He turned his head and snarled, but he couldn't move far in that position.

"Let him go!" she insisted. Behind her, a soft murmur rose from the gathering Howlers, but she knew none of them would interfere. Only more powerful Howlers ever dared to interfere in a fight, and despite the death of the Lioness, Demason was still considered the most powerful.

"Why should I?" Demason demanded. "He's one of Drefan's men, Beda. If we let him roam free, he'll just run back to Monalof and lead Drefan right back here."

"I won't—"

Demason snapped his teeth and tightened his hold on Holt's throat. In turn, Beda wrapped her free hand around her brother's throat.

"Let him go, Demason. He's not the enemy. He's family!"

Demason's whole body spasmed, and Holt twisted free of his

grip in the moment it loosened. As Beda slammed her brother up against the tree in Holt's place, Demason screamed, "You didn't!" Whether it was aimed at Beda or Holt, she couldn't be sure, but the distinction didn't matter.

"He's my mate, Demason. I won't let you harm him or keep him locked up any longer. Especially," she added before her brother could shape his snarls into words, "when he could be our only defense when we need it most."

Demason jerked within her hold. "What is that supposed to mean?"

Beda tightened her grip and growled. "It means that wherever you and the others disappeared to last night, *you* led humans straight back to our camp." Demason stilled. "The only reason most of us aren't already dead is because Holt killed all three of them. To protect *our* people."

As Beda had hoped, that seemed to break through Demason's resistance. He suddenly went limp, his shoulders drooping and his face pressing into the bark of the tree.

"By Lodyma," he whispered. "That wasn't—we weren't—"

He flinched and fell silent. Beda turned her head to follow his gaze and was surprised to find Holt standing in Demason's line of sight. Holt's expression was stern, his arms crossed over his bared chest.

"Is that enough?" he demanded. "Or must I take on Drefan himself to prove to you that I'm not the traitor he is?"

"You wouldn't stand a chance against him," Demason retorted shakily.

Holt snorted. "Perhaps not, but if there's no other way to prove that I love your sister and care for your pack, then I'll gladly try."

Beda blinked, shock numbing her entire body. "What?" she gasped out.

Holt didn't answer as he turned away. Demason, slipping out of Beda's loosened hold, leaped forward and grabbed his shoulder with a panicked "No!" Holt turned back to meet his gaze narrowly.

"You're afraid of him."

"Of course I'm afraid of him," Demason grated out. To Beda's surprise, there was a tremor in his voice and in his hands. "He killed the Lioness, and we still don't know what has become of her cub."

Holt observed Demason with a quiet, sharp gaze. "Is that what you were trying to learn last night?"

Demason shivered and dropped his head. Beda stepped up behind him and smoothed a hand along the curve of his back. "Demason?"

Her brother took in a shaky breath and shook his head. "I wanted to verify…I had hoped…"

"We needed to confirm that all the other shifter breeds had lost the shift," Witter spoke up. Beda snapped her gaze around to Demason's second. The older wolf bowed his head once in acknowledgment of the warning and stepped back.

Hoping none of the others would risk interfering, Beda huffed and laid her head upon Demason's back. "Brother, you knew the truth." His back tightened beneath her cheek, and she sighed. "You've seen it every night when Heather and Fleta couldn't shift."

"That was only two breeds," Demason muttered.

"I don't understand."

Lifting her head, Beda met Holt's confused gaze over her brother's shoulder. She offered a sad smile.

"The Royals channel Lodyma's power," she explained. "If no Royal can shift, then neither can the other shifter breeds."

Holt's confusion only seemed to deepen. "But you—"

Demason grunted. "We Howlers are the only moon shifters wild enough to hear Lodyma's call without a Royal channeling her power. It's why we have always acted as the Royal's personal guard. We…we can protect a shiftling."

Holt grimaced. "And Drefan has hidden his son away beyond anyone's knowledge."

Demason snapped his head up. "What?"

Beda stepped around her brother to stare at Holt. "How do you know that?"

Holt's smile sharpened. "The three humans I killed were…talkative. They knew that Drefan's son was alive but also that his whereabouts were unknown."

Demason straightened. "Then there's still hope." He eyed Holt for a moment, and Beda found herself holding her breath as he made his judgment. When he nodded, Beda sighed.

"I may not like that my sister has chosen to mate herself to a human, but you saved us when we weren't even aware we were in danger and brought us hope when I feared it might be lost. For that, I thank you and…" He grimaced and sighed. "And I welcome you as part of our pack." In a softer tone, he added, "As much as you can be."

Beda whooped and threw her arms around Holt's neck. His arms curled around her waist as he met her seeking lips with his own. Beda reveled in the embrace, even as her mind whirled with joy.

Holt may not have been born a Howler, but he is as much a wolf as the rest of us, in his own way. Demason will come to see that.

And so will Drefan. One way or another, we will find and reclaim his cub, and Drefan will know the bite of a wolf.

CAPTURED

CHARLEIGH BRENNAN

ISPIE CASE FILE #SF27

Tegan Quinn hated these meetings.

It wasn't just the high heels she had to wear. Hunting down the idiot who thought those were a good idea was a fantasy of hers. It also wasn't that she had to wear a stuffy suit that made her look like one of the Men in Black. Hunting down aliens seemed right up her alley, though. It wasn't even that she had to bring Noel along with her . . .

No, wait . . .

Yup, it was because she had to bring Noel.

Not that Noel wasn't a great guy. She enjoyed the company of the big lug. He was extremely well read and had more than one PhD. His education and background certainly gave her business a touch of legitimacy.

No, the problem was that Noel was the one who looked like he could kick ass and take names. At six foot five, he had the kind of muscles that a pro wrestler would be proud of. He also had a serious case of resting bitch face, which had consistently gotten in the way of him being hired as a professor. People either were afraid of him or wanted to pick a fight with him.

In reality, he was a marshmallow who had realized that if he didn't work out, he'd easily get out of shape because he'd rather sit around studying one thing or another. He had been her dearest friend for years. He was always there to look out for her, holding her back when she got too ahead of herself, scaring off unwanted male attention, and making his incredible key lime pie to cheer her up when a mission went wrong. A person couldn't buy friendship like that.

His job was to make sure their business had all its *i*'s dotted and its *t*'s crossed. He made sure things ran seamlessly so they could continue to run within enough of a legal gray area that Tegan didn't end up dealing with lawsuits and possible jail time. It was Tegan who did the majority of the grunt work, and she was good at it. She was the one who tracked and hunted down the strange and the paranormal.

Nobody believed it, though. Noel looked the part. On the other hand, she was born with the curse of looking like a cartoon princess. Big brown eyes, small mouth, rosy cheeks . . . it was no wonder she still got carded. No amount of makeup could make her look at least a little more . . . in charge.

This was why she and Noel had to play their little business meeting game. Noel came with her looking all badass; his shaved head made him look like a multiethnic version of Mr. Clean, and he usually wore at least one article of clothing with a camo print. Meanwhile, she dressed as though she were the secretary.

She hated it, but damn it, it worked. It got her jobs. It kept Noel in cash so he could pay off his student loans and afford his fancy foreign teas, and it helped her maintain her abundant and coveted weaponry collection. That was why she put up with the heels and the suit that made her neck itch but hid her "war wounds." She managed to appear innocent and sweet while still getting contracts for more prey.

They walked down the hall to the meeting room in their purposefully nondescript office suite, Tegan ahead of Noel by a yard.

"Are you ready for this?" Noel's velvety voice came from over her shoulder.

Tegan sighed. "Yeah. I just want to get it over with so I can get my gear on and do my thing." She scratched at her arm where a recently healed scar still itched beneath her sleeve.

"Stop," Noel stated. Tegan turned and looked up at him. "I know you hate this part of the job. Just remember that I believe in you. Other people may look at what's on the outside, but you take the time to look further. I respect you for that. You don't just go in guns blazing; you go in smart . . ." He gave her a little grin. "And with guns blazing."

"Well, we're a team. Without your research skills combined with my . . . talents, I wouldn't be able get the job done as well. I wouldn't keep you around if I didn't respect you too." Tegan smiled and gave Noel a friendly pat on the shoulder.

"If those people in that meeting room assume I'm the brawn, just remember that at least one other person in that room knows the real story. Two, with Haruka there." Noel returned her shoulder pat with one of his own. "Don't let their ignorance get you down."

"Haruka's here?" Tegan asked.

Haruka Sato was a fellow member of the International Society for Paranormal Investigation and Exploration, or ISPIE. Their organization was small but close-knit, as they frequently worked across international lines in order to cover all the cases that came to them. Haruka frequently sent client referrals to Tegan when her boss, Ryutaro Kimura, was unable to take a job. The presence of Haruka herself in Tegan's San Francisco office was quite unusual, which made her wonder if this job was particularly serious.

"I wanted to surprise you." Noel smiled. "I know how much you like working with her."

Tegan gave him a grin. "What would I do without you to perk me up?"

"I don't know, but if you want to repay me, there's this new tea blend I've been dying to try . . . ."

Noel was the only one who could get her to giggle, and giggle she did. Once she stopped, she took a deep breath, squared her shoulders, and gave him a businesslike nod, though her eyes still sparkled with mirth. Then she continued down the hall to the room she usually referred to as "the mouth of doom" instead of the meeting room.

Entering the meeting room, Tegan and Noel found a middle-aged Asian couple, both of whom had concerned expressions on their faces. A young woman sat next to them, speaking to them reassuringly in Japanese.

"Haruka-chan! It's so good to see you again!" Tegan exclaimed as she approached the young woman. Haruka was one of the few people she could drop her guard with. Her irrepressible sunny nature tended to be contagious.

"It's good to see you too, Tegan!" They bowed respectfully to each other and then turned to the couple.

"This is Mr. and Mrs. Maruyama," Haruka said, introducing them. She turned to the Maruyamas. "Kochira wa Quinn-san desu."

"Hajimemashite," Tegan replied and bowed.

Haruka gestured to Noel. "Kochira wa Gray-san desu."

Everyone bowed in greeting.

"Kanojo wa kawaii ne!" said the woman, looking at Tegan.

"I'm sorry, what was that?" Tegan asked, looking at Haruka.

Haruka smiled. "Oh, she just said you were cute."

Tegan cringed inside a bit, hoping it didn't show on her face, but replied in thanks. "Arigato gozaimasu."

Once everyone had settled in their seats, Tegan picked up the pad of paper and pen she had left on the meeting table ahead of time. Noel probably would have taken better notes, but having her do it fit the image they were trying to convey.

Through a series of translations, Tegan was able to get the full story. The Maruyamas' teenaged daughter, Asuka, had gone missing, along with several other young women in their prefecture. The police had been unable to do anything as there was no evidence that could be used to find the missing women. The Maruyamas, as well as families of some of the other women, suspected the abductions were connected. The area they lived in had some unusual folklore regarding abductions, and they were so desperate for help of any sort that they had decided to give ISPIE a try.

It was exactly the type of job Tegan liked to take. ISPIE was often a last resort in cases like these, so she never felt insulted when she was hired as a last-ditch solution after all other avenues had been explored. She merely wanted to use her skills to help others, and she was a sucker for trying to help families in need.

She looked at Noel and gave him a nod to confirm she'd take the job.

"We'll do what we can to help you," Noel said and waited for Haruka to translate.

The relief on the Maruyamas' faces was all it took to reconfirm to Tegan that this job (and having to wear the heels and stuffy suit) would be worth it.

After negotiating salary and travel expenses and several "Arigato gozaimasus" from the Maruyamas, Tegan and Noel said their goodbyes and immediately began preparing for their trip. They had to move fast with an abduction case, so Noel immediately booked a flight for the next day. There were also phone calls to make to arrange for weapons in Japan and some quick research by Noel on supernatural occurrences in that particular prefecture, among other tasks.

"So, brush me up on all the info we have so far," Tegan said as Haruka drove them through the Japanese countryside.

"Local news has little to offer," Noel began. "Six women have been abducted so far. There's little to no useful evidence to help determine who the culprit, or culprits, might be. Some sources even theorize that the women weren't abducted at all but rather ran away on purpose. There's little to link the cases other than that they're all young and rather lovely, and each one is particularly talented in some way. One is a gifted student, another a skilled opera singer—

however, none of their talents seem to necessarily be related." Noel paused, sipping at a travel mug of tea.

"History of the area?" Tegan asked.

This time, it was Haruka who answered her. "Before I brought this mission to you, I did a little research with the Maruyamas. I didn't want them to travel all the way to San Francisco unless I thought we could actually help them. Apparently, there has been a history of strange abductions going back for centuries in that prefecture. Very few people are familiar with it because the area has been abandoned several times in the past. These times of exodus sometimes coincided with similar abductions; others were due to environmental disasters, like flooding or earthquakes."

"That's right," Noel added. "The current incarnation of this town is a relatively recent development. The houses are no older than twenty years, and it was built up to be a relatively nice upper-middle-class suburb."

Haruka nodded. "Previous to that, the town that was there had been abandoned for about a century. It was a small, rather impoverished village. Ten young women had been abducted, leading the inhabitants to believe the village to be cursed. They gathered their belongings and left everything behind rather than risk staying and losing more of their loved ones. The only thing left of that village is the rumor of a temple on the mountain overlooking the site of the former village."

"Hmm . . . the abandoned temple may be our best link, depending on what was worshipped there." Tegan glanced thoughtfully out the window at the bright greenery passing by in a blur.

Haruka continued. "I think so too. Also, it's always ten young women, no more, no less. The time between abductions varies throughout history. The longest period without an abduction was three hundred years. The shortest was about fifty. It's harder to tell the time frames from the older accounts, but it seemed to happen more frequently the further back in the past I looked."

"There have been six abductions so far. If we can't find the women, let's see if we can at least prevent more from happening," Tegan stated. "Any pertinent history of yōkai in the area?"

"Yes," Noel offered, having specifically researched Japanese demons and spirits for the case. "There are several photos of deteriorating statues found at the ruins of the old town before everything was knocked down for the new development. Kitsune and tanuki statues mostly, as well as a tengu or two."

"So we have a possibility of yōkai who are known to be tricksters, abductors, or both," Tegan noted, remembering her folklore about the fox, raccoon, and bird demons. She held out her hand to accept the photographs Noel offered her to sift through.

"That's why I decided the Maruyamas could use ISPIE's help," Haruka explained. "It's still a mystery, but given what we know of the area, it's worth it to see if we can help in some way, even if it's simply to eliminate the possibility of supernatural activity. Also . . ." She paused.

Tegan and Noel glanced at each other. They knew what that "also" meant. Haruka had a bit of extrasensory perception. It wasn't particularly powerful, but at times, she caught glimpses of things or got a general bad feeling about something.

"You noticed something?" Noel prompted her.

"Yes." Haruka took a deep breath and sighed. "Something felt wrong when I visited the Maruyamas. I even visited the homes of some of the other abducted women. Something felt . . . influenced, maybe? There may have been manipulation of some kind." She sighed again. "I'm sorry. I know my ESP is weak, but this feeling was strong enough that I felt uncomfortable."

"Don't worry, Haruka. I trust your instincts." Tegan gave her shoulder a squeeze. "Were you able to pull yourself back together again?"

"Yes. Usually Ryutaro is around to make sure I'm not overdoing it, but he left for a mission in Russia the day before the Maruyamas showed up. Apparently, Baba Yaga is up to something again."

"She still roaming the countryside in her chicken house?" Tegan asked, taking Haruka's change of subject as a sign that she didn't feel comfortable saying much more about what she felt at the Maruyamas' house.

"Strangely enough, no. She has a camper van now. I guess she decided to update her mode of transport. It still has chicken legs instead of wheels, though."

Noel gave a rumbling laugh. "Some things never change."

Tegan smiled. She could feel some of Haruka's tension dissipate—not all, but at least some. She guessed that Haruka was feeling reluctant to return to the scene of the crime. Tegan decided to move on to other business.

"What kind of team do we have in place?"

"There's us and one more. A freelance nature photographer who works as a wilderness guide on the side. Ryutaro and I have worked with him a few times before. His name is Michio Kageyama. He claims he found the location of the temple while out taking photographs. You won't need me to translate for him, either. He speaks fluent English."

"That should be helpful," Noel replied.

A hush fell over the car as Haruka continued to drive. A familiar feeling of anticipation and worry came over Tegan. She always felt eager to be in the field, but that feeling was usually tainted with a concern that there might be little she could do, if anything. Paranormal involvement was often questioned in the cases she took, and sometimes people saw her as a quack. Knowing that others doubted what she did, even though her track record was stellar, tended to cast a pall on her excitement. Once she got started, that worry usually dissipated, but she hated feeling it at all.

"Looks like we're nearly there," Noel observed eagerly.

The countryside seemed to fade away as they came over a hill to find a pristine town nestled in the valley below. Straight ahead was a small mountain overrun by lush forest. It stood in contrast to the ordered, somewhat uniform homes dotting the streets. They drove past the outlying residential homes and soon parked in front of a quaint hotel.

"I'll go check us in if you both grab the rest of the luggage," Haruka offered as she slung a duffel bag over her shoulder.

"Sounds fine to me." Noel opened the trunk and began to pull out their supplies.

"Once we get settled, I'll go meet with this Michio guy. You think you both can get things organized without me?" Tegan asked.

"Yes," Haruka answered. "I'll give him a call to meet you at the fountain in the center of town. Does that sound okay?"

"To quote Noel, 'sounds fine to me,'" Tegan responded with a wink.

"You're the ISPIE," stated the man waiting by the fountain. His back was turned to Tegan as he aimed a camera at a plum tree.

"You haven't looked at me and you know I'm 'the ISPIE'?" Tegan replied.

Without turning, he handed her the camera. She looked at the viewer and saw a picture of herself from moments before, when she had first spotted the fountain. He'd captured her in a way no photographer ever had. Her firm determination showed on her face, making her look less cute and more strong, maybe even fierce. Her excellent posture, honed from years of martial arts training, made her look taller than she really was. It may have been the first photograph she'd ever seen of herself that showed a glimpse of who she was on the inside, rather than just a pretty picture of the outside, and she was stunned by how beautiful she looked.

"Hmm . . ." she muttered under her breath, refusing to show just how impressed she was. She looked up to hand the camera over, and her jaw dropped a little.

For some reason, Tegan had expected someone older and grizzled. She had envisioned someone who looked like he belonged behind a camera—not necessarily unattractive, but nothing like the man who stood before her. If anything, this man looked like he belonged in front of a camera. Slender but nicely muscled, almost a foot taller than she was, and with a trendy shaggy haircut with bangs that seemed inclined to flop over his left eye, he could easily have graced the cover of a fashion magazine.

It was his eyes that made her breath catch, though. They made her think of a bird of prey; they seemed to pierce through her soul, despite his friendly, carefree expression. While his looks drew her in, his gaze threatened to catch her in a trap from which she didn't want to escape. Judging by the giggles of a nearby group of uniformed high school girls sitting at a cafe, she wasn't the only one who saw it.

"Hello," Michio said with a wry smile as he pushed his bangs out of his face.

Tegan gathered herself quickly and put out a hand to shake his. "I'm Tegan Quinn. I take it you're Michio Kageyama?"

He looked at her hand, one eyebrow raised, then reached for it and gave her a firm shake. "I am. However, it's considered more respectful to bow here, just so you know."

His response sounded a bit smug, leaving her with a feeling of doubt. She had a thing about people being condescending. With her youthful appearance, it happened to her all too often.

Usually she got angry, but this time, she just felt disappointed. Maybe it was because she was a little jet-lagged. Maybe it was because she felt like this case was important and she really wanted to have a good team. It might even have been because she had felt a bit enthralled by him. Whatever it was, if this guy couldn't listen to her, they might have to find someone else.

Unfazed by her scrutiny, he added, "Has anyone ever told you how—"

She held up a hand to stop him. "Yes, many times. 'You're so adorable and cute, Tegan!' 'You're like a little doll!' 'Aww!'"

He laughed at her sarcasm, and his response sounded more genuine. "I was going to say you were strangely intimidating, despite your appearance, but you are quite cute too."

Reminded of the photo he had shown her, she narrowed her eyes, trying to get a bead on him. It was hard to read him. Was he going to underestimate and undermine her, or was he going to work with her? She stood for a moment, brows furrowed, trying to determine what his motivations could possibly be. She soon gave up and decided that if he was being honest about finding her a little intimidating, maybe she could work with him. Considering how he had captured her in the photo he had taken, he might be more likely to see past appearances.

"Did Haruka catch you up on the case?" Tegan asked.

He turned away, once again brushing his artfully styled hair out of his face, and aimed his camera back at the tree. "Yes. It sounds bad. I can get you to the temple easily enough. I'm not sure you'll find the answers you're looking for, but I'm in." Pushing a button on the camera, he pulled back and checked the screen. "I'll be able to take some photos along the way, so even if it doesn't pan out, I'll get something out of the situation."

"All I ask is that you're helpful. You're welcome to take photos; as long as you're focused on the work we're doing, I'll be happy. If we get to a point where you feel you can't be helpful, you'll still be paid for your time." Tegan considered him as he carefully aimed his camera again. She had to admit that even though he seemed a bit patronizing, when he had laughed earlier, it had been like a ray of sunlight peeked through stormy clouds to shine on his face alone.

Michio smirked. "At least you'll have something nice to look at along the way."

"Hmm?" Tegan asked, distracted. Then she realized she had been staring and immediately frowned in irritation. "I'm assuming you mean yourself?"

"You said it, not me," Michio replied nonchalantly, snapping another photo.

Tegan sighed and crossed her arms in annoyance. She did not need weird guy drama on this mission. "Look, the task ahead is serious. I don't need nonsense. I need people I can rely on. I don't care what they look like as long as they get the job done. People's lives are at stake here."

Michio turned to her and placed a hand on her shoulder. "Don't worry; I get it. It's serious. A little flirting won't harm anyone, though, will it?"

"Well, if a little flirting is why those women are missing, it might." Tegan lifted his hand from her shoulder and let it drop back to his side.

An expression of anger crossed his face so quickly that she barely noticed it before he pasted on a smile. "I'll do the job you asked me to do. Fair?"

"That's all I ask," Tegan stated.

Michio handed her the camera again so she could view the screen. On it was a perfect plum blossom, dappled with shadow and light. The guy might be a bit annoying, but he certainly had a talent for finding beauty.

"So, when do we start?"

"Do you have my crossbow?" Noel asked. "Where's my crossbow?"

"What is it with you and crossbows? We're in Japan; there are all kinds of cool, distinctly Japanese weapons that you can use, and you still want a crossbow," Tegan teased. "It's the Buffy thing, isn't it?"

Noel perked up as he found the crossbow in the pack he'd pulled out of the car. "I happen to think they're useful. Besides, I'm hardly the weapons expert. You're the one with the training."

"Yeah, the training to know that they're not as practical as you'd think." Tegan gave Noel a playful slap on the shoulder.

She then carefully checked the variety of knives she had tucked into convenient harnesses on various parts of her body, making sure they were all secure. She glanced at Haruka, who was also making certain her weaponry was in place. A particularly impressive katana was strapped to her back, and Tegan had to admit, she was a little jealous. It was a beauty of a sword. She didn't want to be so obvious about their task, though, so she stuck with knives that could easily be interpreted as being used for hiking or ones she could hide. Haruka tended to rely on that katana, however, so Tegan couldn't deny her friend her prized weapon.

They were standing at a meeting point at the base of the mountain, rummaging through the car to make certain they had everything they needed for the hike. Michio hadn't arrived yet, making Tegan feel unsure of him again. There was just something about that guy. His skills weren't in question, and his reasons for being there made sense—making a little money and getting to take more photos fit with his trade. She just couldn't put her finger on it; it was like there was something else driving him, and his nonchalance and veneer of confidence were covers for . . . well, who knew?

It didn't help that he was so striking to look at that she was still finding herself catching her breath when his image came to mind. She couldn't allow herself that kind of distraction, but she didn't have time to look for someone else. Every hour lost could mean the difference between life and death for those women, so she had to trust him. She just didn't have to trust him completely.

"You ready?" Michio shouted as he walked over from the road.

"Did you walk here?" Haruka asked.

"No, I flew," Michio joked. Haruka gave him a friendly punch to the shoulder, and he playfully responded by pretending that it hurt.

While the two laughed together, Tegan noted his somewhat windblown hair. It wasn't a particularly windy day. Maybe he had just styled it that way? It certainly made it look like he had actually flown there.

Noel stepped forward and gave Michio a polite bow. "I'm Noel."

"Good to meet you," Michio replied, returning the bow.

"Yes, Michio, Noel. Noel, Michio." Tegan watched as Michio seemed to analyze Noel's broad shoulders and bulging muscles. *As long as Michio is a little daunted by Noel, he might keep in line,* she thought. "Does everyone have everything? Let's get going."

With backpacks straightened and boots tied, they followed Michio in among the trees and began their trek.

They walked down what could loosely be called a narrow path. The trees quickly seemed to close in behind them, cutting them off from the sounds of the modern world. If it weren't for the task at hand, Tegan could have thought of this as a relaxing hike. Instead, her instincts were on high alert. While she could have been gazing admiringly at the greenery around her and the hypnotic way the light and shade changed the appearance of the trees around her, she instead kept her eyes and ears open for what could be hiding behind the surrounding foliage.

"If you look over here, you can see some of the crumbling remains of the stone steps that led up to the temple," Michio pointed out. "We won't be going that way."

The other three members of the group stopped to examine the area for any sign of recent activity.

"Why won't we be going that way?" Haruka asked. "Wouldn't it make sense to take that route?"

"It would, if not for the landslide that wiped out a large section of the stairs. We're going a longer way around, but it will be safer." Michio turned and winked at Tegan. "I hope you don't mind getting dirty; it won't be easy going."

A sudden outburst of laughter from Noel startled Michio. He looked at Noel, an unspoken question on his face.

Once Noel caught his breath, he explained himself. "Man, you're talking to the wrong person. If anyone here doesn't mind a bit of mud or dirt, it would be Tegan. I'm the one who doesn't like to get too messy."

Michio raised an eyebrow. "Really?"

Tegan smiled. She liked the idea that Michio might be a little flustered. She knew that self-assured veneer had to have some weak points. Instead of saying anything, she let Noel continue.

"I've known Tegan since . . ." Noel glanced at Tegan. "Were we both eight years old?"

"Sounds right to me." Tegan nodded as she gently shoved a branch out of her way to examine the crumbling steps.

"Right." He looked back at Michio and continued. "Even then, she was a force to be reckoned with. Her father is an Olympic-caliber martial artist, and early on, Tegan preferred to spend nearly all her free time trying to be even better than him, much to her mother's disappointment."

"She wanted me to take ballet and wear dresses," Tegan

interjected playfully. "Luckily, I have a younger sister, who dances for the San Francisco Ballet. She fulfilled my mom's fairy-tale dreams, so I didn't have to."

"Nobody messed with Tegan, even back when we first met. Most of the kids already knew her as the kid you didn't pick on. They also knew not to pick on her friends. If someone was dumb enough to bully anyone in her presence, well, things didn't turn out so well for them," Noel explained.

"I can see you being like that as a kid," Haruka mused, giving Tegan a playful nudge.

"I got into so much trouble. Mom hated it. Dad . . . well, Dad understood. He pretended to get mad at me, but then he'd secretly take me out for ice cream as a treat. He always told me how proud he was that I believed in defending those who couldn't defend themselves." Tegan looked around. "Should we continue our hike?"

"We can do that, but I'd like to hear more," Michio replied.

They began walking again along uneven ground, and Noel continued his story.

"I had just moved into the area, and some kids were bullying me. I was a skinny kid back then, with bottle-thick glasses and awkward limbs I hadn't grown into. I'm sure I looked like an easy target. One day, a kid a couple of years older than me tripped me as I was walking home. His group of friends all laughed at me. Then out of nowhere, this tiny girl darted out and grabbed him by the front of his shirt. I looked in awe as everyone froze. Nobody said a word. She stared the kid in the eyes with such fierceness, and you could see he was starting to panic. He gulped and put both hands up in surrender. She gave him a huge grin, let go of his shirt, and straightened his collar out a little. 'You know what to do now,' she said calmly, and the kid turned and ran."

"Did he now?" Michio asked, humor evident in his voice. He was clearly enjoying the story.

"Apparently, Tegan had beaten up his older brother the week before because he was harassing some neighborhood girls. He'd ended up with a black eye and several scrapes and bruises. Tegan merely had a small scrape on her elbow. Few kids ever told on Tegan because they didn't want to admit such a cute, tiny thing was such a terrifying fighter. Most kids wanted to be her friend because they knew she believed in doing the right thing." Noel laughed. "While she was fair with everyone, she seemed to take a greater interest in me, and we became close friends. She even got me into doing martial arts with her."

Tegan smiled and patted Noel on the back. "I haven't regretted it since."

Noel gave her a smile. "Neither have I."

Everyone continued on in silence for a while, making a slow climb through the brush with no clear path in sight.

"Help me understand something, Michio," Tegan began.

"What's that?" Michio replied while clearing some branches out of their way.

"You know the way to this temple, but it looks like nobody has traveled through this area before." With her tracking skills, Tegan could tell they weren't even following an animal trail.

"I came a slightly different way last time," Michio responded smoothly. "I also saw the remains of the temple from above. I've never made it all the way to the temple on foot. This seemed like the best way to go with a group of this size and made sense according to the photos I had taken and the map I had of the area."

"Hmm." Tegan nodded. "So you took pictures from a helicopter?"

"Something like that," Michio replied.

Tegan heard a branch break off to one side and instantly threw a knife. The sound of flapping wings followed. "Probably just a bird?"

"Impressive reflexes," Michio observed. Tegan glanced at him, and the approval on his face looked genuine. "It got away, though."

Tegan rolled her eyes. "I wasn't aiming to hit it, just to find out what it was." She walked over to the tree where her knife was embedded and pulled the blade out carefully. She had pinned a feather to the tree.

"When we reach a stopping point, let me show you something.

Not that you're bad at throwing, but there's a slightly different grip that I use that could be less tiring if you have to do repeated throws." Michio smiled.

"Okay," Tegan said cautiously, as she checked her blade and tucked it into its harness.

Michio raised an eyebrow. "Okay? I'm surprised. You seem to be a bit . . . I don't know . . . put off by me."

Tegan shrugged. "Doesn't hurt to learn something new, whether or not I like the teacher."

Michio mockingly put a hand over his heart. "Ouch, you've wounded me!"

Tegan gave a half-smile and continued to walk. Her mood quickly became pensive. Maybe she really hadn't been fair to Michio. So far on the hike, he had asked questions more often than he'd made assumptions. She respected that in a person. He may have said a few things that triggered her, but maybe she'd been focusing on that more than was reasonable. Also, even though she didn't like to admit it, there was something about him that . . .

No, did she want to pursue that thought? She'd been avoiding romance for a good long while. Most guys who wanted to date her thought that because she was so cute, she'd be a pushover. Those weak stabs at relationships hadn't lasted long enough to actually become relationships. Her work had become her life, and any thoughts of romance had been put on the back burner. With, Michio, though . . .

Maybe her suspicion of him wasn't about his seeming overconfidence. Maybe it was more that she was afraid of the immediate attraction she had felt toward him and the fact that he seemed to look a little deeper than her surface from time to time. It was unsettling. She sighed. That was as far as she was willing to take that rather unwelcome thought process, so she wiped it from her mind and focused a little harder on their surroundings.

"I feel like something has been monitoring us," Haruka said, her soft voice cutting through the silence.

Everyone stopped and listened carefully to their surroundings.

"What do you think it is?" Noel asked.

"Not sure. It doesn't feel dangerous—at least, not yet." Haruka squinted into the shadows, which had grown thicker the longer they continued their hike.

"It's about noon now. Why don't we stop to eat? Maybe if we stay still for a bit, you can figure out what you're sensing," Tegan offered. She thought of the bird she had almost hit with her knife. A tengu in its bird form, perhaps?

Haruka nodded. "Let's do that."

As Haruka and Noel began to pull out food, Tegan decided to practice her knife-throwing skills. Maybe it would help her take out some of her frustrations, instead of stewing in her conflicting thoughts. She found a dead, gnarled tree a little ways away from everyone else and cleared her mind. After she took a couple of deep breaths, she began to throw, each knife hitting the center of the knot she aimed for on the tree. A couple of minutes later, all her knives were sticking out from various parts of the tree.

"Would you like some help with those?" came Michio's voice from behind her.

No, I wouldn't, Tegan thought. "I can get them myself," she muttered out loud. She scrambled to grab her knives before he could touch them. He was the last person she wanted to talk to right now, and she didn't particularly like having anyone else touch her weapons.

When she returned to where she had been standing before, Michio was there, looking unexpectedly hurt.

"Did I do something wrong?" he asked.

Suddenly, a wave of guilt washed over Tegan. Was there really something wrong with him, or did she just not want to admit to any attraction on her part? Usually she trusted her instincts, but with men, those instincts tended to be easily overridden by her usual guarded state.

She put a hand to her forehead and sighed. "No. No, you really haven't. It's me. I don't trust easily, that's all. Men I encounter usually want to gain testosterone points over me by either beating me at fighting or dominating me in relationships. It makes it hard for me to trust right away."

She hoped that explanation was good enough because there was no way she was going to tell him all the other thoughts running through her mind that had cast him in the starring role.

Michio shrugged and pulled out his own small set of throwing knives. They were beautifully carved to look like bird feathers. He adjusted his stance and threw one at the gnarled tree. The knife effortlessly struck the center of a knot near the base of the tree. "That's not a bad thing. Maybe it was the inability of the abducted women to reserve their trust that made it easy for them to be taken."

Tegan took up a stance next to him and threw one of her own knives. She hit a bend on one of the tree's branches. "That's the first thing I've heard you say specifically about the case."

"Those women shouldn't have been taken," Michio stated bluntly, a hint of anger in his voice. He threw another of his knives. "They should be with their families."

Tegan threw another knife. "You're right about that." Her aim was a little off, and her knife hit too far off the center of an exposed knot for her taste. "Shit."

"Show me how you hold your knives for throwing," Michio said. When Tegan showed him her grip, he carefully adjusted her hand. Even though her usual grip was loose enough to throw and steady enough to keep the knife from leaving her hand until she was ready, she immediately noticed a decrease in tension with the new position.

"Throw it," Michio stated.

Tegan nodded and aimed for the knot she had hit before. The knife flew gracefully and hit the center of the exposed knot with ease. Forgetting that the reason she'd decided to step aside and throw knives in the first place was the man standing next to her, she grinned excitedly and turned back to him. "Show me that grip again?"

Michio laughed. "I see the way to your heart is through your weapons."

"Maybe not to my heart, but it might help . . . a little," Tegan replied slyly.

He showed her the grip again, and then they both continued to throw their knives until the tree looked like a porcupine. They stepped forward and began to gather their knives after the last knife had thunked against the trunk. Tegan noticed one of hers near Michio's hand, and when she grabbed the hilt, his hand was suddenly on hers.

She instantly drew her hand back. "Sorry," she said. He pulled her knife out and handed it to her.

"Nothing to be sorry about."

She was hyperaware of him as he smoothly pulled back. She didn't dare glance back, but she could tell he was looking at her, maybe puzzling out why she was so confident at one moment and reticent the next. She felt horrifyingly awkward . . . and when she felt awkward, it usually quickly dissolved into irritation.

He then reached for another knife that was a little farther away from her. "This was fun. If your throwing skills indicate anything about the rest of your fighting skills, consider me impressed."

Tegan hadn't expect that. The compliment was such an unexpected jolt that her irritation gave way to shock, and her shock gave way to bashfulness. She was thankful the trees were dense enough to provide a lot of shade, because it helped hide her blush. She mentally chided herself. Blushing? A guy could have complimented her hair or clothes, and it would have meant nothing to her. One man complimented her skills and she went weak at the knees? *Get it together, Tegan!*

"Are you guys going to eat?" Noel's voice came from a few paces away.

Thankful for Noel's distraction, Tegan quickly replaced her knives in their various holsters and began to walk back to where Haruka was sitting. "I'm starving!" she exclaimed with what she hoped didn't sound like false enthusiasm.

She heard Michio following behind her. Once they had settled down and begun to eat, she thought about what had just happened. She didn't feel frustrated anymore. However, she was still confused as hell.

They continued their hike in relative silence for a couple more hours after they finished eating.

"We're almost there," Michio declared, swiping away at undergrowth with his machete. "We should be able to make it to what's left of the path soon. It would have taken far less time to make the climb if it was still there. Sorry we had to take such a roundabout route."

"All that matters to me is that we get there as quickly as we can," replied Tegan, surprised by Michio's humility.

"Oh, believe me, nobody could have gotten you here faster than I could." Michio gave his trademark smirk.

Tegan rolled her eyes from behind his back. So much for humility.

"I heard that," Michio accused and continued to lead the way.

Tegan smirked at the accusation. He had to be pretty talented to hear an eye roll.

"Is something up?" Haruka whispered to Tegan when they had fallen a little behind.

Tegan observed Noel approaching Michio and striking up a conversation. *Leave it to Noel to know when to be a distraction.*

"Does something seem a little odd about him?" Tegan whispered back. She just couldn't give up on her feeling about him, despite the moment they had had earlier.

Haruka glanced at Michio, then looked back at Tegan. "He helped Ryutaro and me on a mission a couple months ago, and he was pretty reliable. Nothing about him ticks off my ESP. Why? What are you thinking?"

"I don't know. I want to trust him, but I keep wondering if he's just shining us on. It's like he's going through all the proper motions but something else is going on." The anger she had observed in him each time the subject of the missing women came up was something she couldn't let go. His anger was genuine. Maybe one of those women was someone he cared about? How would she feel if that was the case? She didn't want to acknowledge the uncomfortable feeling she had in the pit of her stomach at that thought.

"Hmm . . . I don't know. If he doesn't tick my ESP, it could mean two things. He's either completely normal or so powerful that he can hide himself from me." Haruka sighed. "I'm sorry. I wish my skills were more useful."

"Nonsense. Your skills are valuable enough." Tegan suddenly felt a little guilty for questioning Haruka's choice of guide. "If you say he's reliable, then he's reliable."

"Ah, here it is," Michio's voice came from ahead.

Tegan and Haruka caught up to the two men. They were standing at the edge of a clearing that was a jumble of bricks and weeds. In fact, the weeds had grown so abundantly between the bricks that the clearing almost appeared to be a meadow. A rotting entry gate seemed to barely stand on its own, and several yards away stood a grim-looking temple. It might have been quite majestic in its prime, but now it looked like it would be dangerous to step foot inside it unless one was really careful.

"Why don't we take a break to discuss our next steps," Tegan proposed as she began to remove her backpack.

Noel and Haruka both nodded and pulled off their packs.

"I think I spotted something I want to photograph," Michio announced. "I'll be back in a bit."

He set off to one side of the temple. Tegan watched as he rounded the corner of the temple, and once more her suspicion kicked in. How could he have spotted something around the back of the temple?

"Noel, stay here," she whispered. "Haruka, come with me."

"What is it?" Noel asked.

"A hunch," Tegan replied.

Haruka and Tegan quietly walked to the temple, then hugged the wall as they crept in the direction Michio had gone. They soon heard two voices speaking in Japanese. Tegan was grateful she had had the foresight to bring Haruka along with her.

"That guy is saying that he's glad Michio is finally on board with bringing tributes," Haruka whispered.

"Tributes?" Tegan mouthed.

Haruka nodded and listened closely. She covered her mouth to stifle a gasp. "They mean us!"

"Us? They mean to take us as well?" Tegan whispered.

"Michio is arguing, though. He didn't bring us for them, whoever they are . . . wait, what?" Haruka stood silently, listening carefully.

Tegan stared, trying to gauge the emotions crossing Haruka's face. As they listened, Haruka's complexion became ashen, and she finally mouthed to Tegan, "We have to leave . . . now."

Tegan nodded. Her curiosity almost got the better of her, but she knew to trust Haruka, so she followed carefully. She turned to glance back once she realized the talking had stopped.

"Going somewhere?" came a silky voice from ahead.

Tegan's head turned so quickly she almost got whiplash, and she pulled her two most convenient knives from their sheaths. Haruka pulled out her katana, and they both took fighting stances.

Before her and Haruka stood a man with silvery-white hair, fox ears, and five graceful, fluffy tails.

"They're not for you, Takumi," Michio stated. At least, it sounded like Michio—except he had large black raven wings sprouting from his shoulder blades. Tegan's heart dropped. She remembered his joke about flying and his cagey response to her question about helicopters. Had he been using them this whole time?

"Why not? They're both lovely and have those interesting talents you mentioned . . . languages and ESP for one, fighting skills for the other. They'd make excellent offerings," the kitsune, Takumi, stated, grinning from ear to ear. "Then we'd only need two more. You needn't worry so much, tengu."

"So we were just convenient for you?" Tegan asked as she glared at Michio, anger dripping from every word. "I knew there was something wrong with you."

He gave her a loaded glance, like he was trying to tell her

something, but she couldn't read it. "These women are mine." He positioned himself between them and the kitsune.

Takumi smirked. "How greedy of you, little tengu."

"I haven't accepted a tribute in centuries. Aren't I overdue?" Michio stated smugly, arms crossed over his chest.

"Perhaps," Takumi replied vaguely. "It will have to be discussed in council."

Suddenly, an arrow flew toward the kitsune from behind. He deftly caught it in his hand before it had a chance to hit anything. Tegan spotted Noel, standing a few yards behind the kitsune, preparing his crossbow for another shot.

"That was not smart, human," Takumi growled, turning to glare at Noel.

Michio grabbed Takumi's shoulder. "No, this isn't the time. Just bring us to the council."

"Yes, let's explain your sudden greed. The foreign woman may be argued over. Perhaps some of the council will be appeased by an additional male tribute, though." Takumi began to walk toward the entrance of the broken-down temple. With a graceful gesture from the pale creature, Tegan, Haruka, and Noel found themselves completely bereft of all their weapons, which appeared in his arms the next moment.

Michio turned to the women and moved to take hold of them. As he grabbed Tegan's arm, he whispered in her ear, "I need you to trust me on this, okay?"

Tegan noted that while his grip on her arm appeared firm, it was fairly loose. She nodded at Haruka and gave Noel a loaded glance. Whether she gave Michio her trust or not, the element of surprise had already been lost and the easiest way to find the other women was to follow the kitsune. The three humans began to walk toward the entry, with Michio behind them.

Crumbling beams and warped floorboards were all Tegan could see through the door, and she was a bit mystified as to why they'd even enter the place. Then, before her eyes, the kitsune strode straight through the opening and disappeared suddenly.

"Go through," Michio stated. "It's a portal."

Undaunted, Tegan stepped through. Instead of a room full of rot with holes in its roof, she found herself standing in a magnificent hall with a dais at the far end. There were several beings lounging about the room. A raccoon-like tanuki drank sake straight from a bottle while laughing with a kappa. The kappa had his arm around a serving girl while water dripped from the traditional bowl of water sitting on his head onto one of his scaled shoulders. A rokurokubi observed a young woman playing a koto, his snaking neck stretched out several feet toward the girl as she blushed shyly. Several other creatures who looked part human and part—well, animal or object—lounged around the room, interacting with or being served by several young women who looked perfectly human.

They must be the abducted women, Tegan thought.

"Takumi!" shouted an ōkami, his wolf tail swishing behind him. "We have eight now!" He glanced at Tegan, Haruka, and Noel. "Wait, two more? Now we have ten and even an extra human to play with. Perfect!"

Tegan looked at Michio, who was scowling at the indulgent scene. She tugged on his sleeve to get his attention. He looked her in the eyes, and she could read anger, sadness, and even a hint of ages-old fatigue in his gaze.

"Go ahead; tell them what you're here for," he said. He guided her to the center of the room, amid the various beings who seemed completely unconcerned.

"We're not here as offerings." Tegan's voice rang clearly throughout the room. The koto player stopped and everyone looked at her, confused.

The tanuki shape-shifted to appear more human as he drunkenly replied, "Well then, human, what are you here for?"

"We're here to take the women back to their families."

The room erupted in laughter.

A hebi stood from his spot, his snakelike tongue flickering and his slit pupils glaring as he spoke. "You're quite short-sighted, young lady. Look around the room. Do these women look like they want to leave?"

As if on cue, the abducted women giggled in chorus, then stopped abruptly and continued with whatever task they had been doing before.

"Their families are scared that they may be hurt. They deserve to know that their daughters are at least safe," Haruka said, backing Tegan up.

"If they were so concerned about their daughters' safety, they should have made offerings to us at the temple so we wouldn't have had to take them," Takumi retorted condescendingly as he stepped forward and took Tegan's chin in his hand.

Immediately, Tegan grabbed him and flipped him onto his back. The room erupted in more laughter.

"Oh, this one is quite entertaining," the wolf-like ōkami pronounced. "I wouldn't mind taking her for myself."

Takumi stood and grabbed Tegan's chin again, this time much more forcefully. "That will not happen again," he said with venom in his voice.

Tegan stared back at him, undaunted.

Michio stepped forward and pulled Tegan out of Takumi's grip. "The humans don't even know the temple exists."

"How is that our problem?" the hebi asked as he approached Haruka, sizing her up. As he made his way toward her, he shifted from his human form into a large snake, still retaining his human head. "This one is quite pretty. I haven't chosen one yet. Can she be mine?"

"These women aren't yours," Michio stated, pulling Haruka behind him.

"Oh, but this man will do well for me. We really should be taking male tributes as well." A beautiful but strangely skeletal woman grabbed one of Noel's arms and cuddled up to him. "He'll last me a good, long while, as strong as he is."

The kappa laughed and held up a scaled, webbed hand. "Absolutely not! You'll suck the life out of every man you take with your wanton ways. There would be no more men to father daughters who could be offerings to the rest of us."

Michio glared at the hone-onna, and she quickly let go of Noel's arm.

"So greedy, Michio. You were never this greedy before. You always gave up your tributes to the others. Why do you want so many now?" The kappa pulled the girl he had nestled next to him into his lap. "You better not take this one."

"Clearly, this discussion would be better saved for the morning, once you've all slept off the alcohol," Michio stated, disgust clear in his voice. "They're coming with me."

He quickly grabbed Tegan's hand and led her out of the room, Haruka and Noel following close behind. They swiftly made their way through a door on one side of the room and into a hallway, raucous laughter trailing behind them. Tegan stumbled a bit to keep up with Michio's long strides as he took them through a maze of corridors. His fury was so palpable that she couldn't even argue with him until they had all come to a stop outside of the majestic palace that stood where the broken temple once had. Or rather, the temple wasn't there because it was clear they were no longer anywhere that resembled the mountain they had just hiked up.

Michio let go of Tegan's hand once they had stopped and looked at her, fury glinting in his eyes until he seemed to realize she was a bit out of breath. The fury quickly faded to concern.

"Are you okay?" he asked Tegan sincerely. He then glanced at Haruka and Noel.

He got a nod from Haruka, who was also a little winded. Being the shortest of the group, she clearly had had to jog to keep up. Noel, who had fared much better, gave him a quick yes and focused his attention on Haruka.

"Are you going to explain yourself?" Tegan asked once she had finally caught her breath.

"Yes, but not here. We'll go to my place. Are you ready to walk?" Michio asked. "I'd fly you there, but I can't take all three of you at a time. Possibly you and Haruka, but Noel would be a handful."

After a short discussion in which Noel insisted Michio fly with Tegan and Haruka and Haruka protested because of her fear of heights, they finally decided to make the half-hour walk to Michio's home. If Tegan had been able to, she would have marveled over the small palace that Michio called home, surrounded by tall Japanese maples. There was no time, though. Whatever they were going to do, they needed to do it soon enough that they weren't stuck in this place, surrounded by yōkai who thought of them as playthings.

A tengu servant met them at the door, and with ebony wings fluttering, it immediately rushed them all off to bathe and change clothes. Tegan felt uncomfortable in the kimono she was then dressed in, as it was a bit too much like a dress for her taste. However, her other clothes were caked in dirt and sweat, and she was reluctant to put those back on. She didn't really have a choice anyway, as another servant tutted at the state of her clothes and took them to be thoroughly washed.

Impatiently, she waited in a large hall for the others to join her. She couldn't blame them for taking their time, not if they were even half as tired as she felt. Honestly, she would have encouraged them to slow down and even rest a bit. She wanted her friends fresh and ready to go. It was easy to be harder on herself, however, so she had wasted no time washing up quickly and cooperating the best she could with another one of Michio's servants, who had helped her dress due to her inexperience with wearing a kimono.

She paced the floor, watching as yet more servants set up a low table with plates of food. She may not have been familiar with wearing traditional Japanese clothing, but she was fond of Japanese cuisine, and the smells that greeted her made her stomach growl.

"You can get started if you're that hungry," Michio quipped, seemingly back to his normal sardonic state. He had entered the room so soundlessly that Tegan hadn't noticed.

Tegan wanted answers more than food, but it would be irresponsible to start asking questions of Michio before the others had arrived. She relied on them for their knowledge and expertise and considered them equal partners in this rescue mission. It would have been unwise to ask questions without their input. Instead, she sat down at the table and considered what questions to ask later. Michio sat near her and watched as she expertly used her chopsticks to serve herself.

"It's nice to see a Westerner who isn't afraid to try our cuisine and modes of dress," Michio observed.

"Considering my job, I have to be open-minded about things that most people don't even think of as actually existing. Trying food from another culture is child's play. I've certainly already eaten my fair share of Japanese food back in California. That, and my clothes were taken away, so it was either this or nothing."

Tegan focused on the food before her, trying to ignore how imposing Michio looked in his haori and hakama. He had seemed like an ordinary young man in modern clothes when she first met him. Now, there was something timeless about him, both ancient and young. Seeing him in his environment, it was clear that his sometimes smug and arrogant behavior really came from his position of power.

Noel soon joined them, followed quickly by Haruka. Both were also wearing traditional Japanese clothing. Tegan waited until they had eaten a bit and then began to ask questions.

"What is going on?" Tegan asked Michio. "Why didn't you tell us who you were? Why did you get involved? How are you involved in all of this? We need answers."

Michio sighed, then looked Tegan in the eyes. "First, I'm sorry I had to lie to you. There's a lot to explain, and hopefully I'll be able to help you understand everything."

"I hope so too because things aren't looking good for you right now," Tegan replied.

Michio gave a wry laugh and then began. "I'm a tengu . . . a bird demon. I've lived among this community of yōkai for several centuries now. As time went on, I found that many yōkai tended to foolishly hold themselves to the past, so I've made a point to go out among humans and learn about the modern world. I've been more aware than most that, over the centuries, we've become seen more as legend than real. Every time my people choose to abduct humans as tributes to make up for the lack of offerings, the humans have become more of a danger to us with their increasing developments in science and technology. While humans may have feared us in the past, they would now be more likely to see us as oddities to be studied. I'd rather not be kept and studied for science."

"That sounds reasonable," Noel replied. "Knowing the academic world as I do, some scientists might be more interested in their research than the impact that research has on those being studied, despite ethical obligations."

Michio nodded. "I've been wanting to stop this practice of abducting women in order to protect my kind. Also, I've always found it distasteful in general. These women are manipulated and seduced into thinking that being here is what they want. While I've always been due one of these women because of my position, I've always refused to accept them."

"That explains your conversation with Takumi and the joking comments about you being greedy," Haruka stated.

"Exactly," Michio said. "We don't really need offerings. We like offerings, but we have plenty of skill and magic to get what we want and need without humans giving us things. It's tradition, but many have mistaken simple tradition for obligation. Some get angry if we don't get enough offerings to suit their narcissistic pride. It's a waste of energy and time, but when one lives for centuries, creating unnecessary drama can be the only entertainment that keeps one going."

"So essentially, you're on our side, and you have been from the beginning?" Tegan wasn't sure she was willing to believe what he was saying.

"Well, when I first answered the advertisement from Ryutaro and Haruka a few months ago, my motivations weren't entirely altruistic. I wanted to see how much of a potential threat ISPIE might be. When it was clear that the goals of the organization were relatively reasonable, I stayed in contact."

Tegan nodded. "We aren't out to hunt and kill; we just want to keep people safe from potential threats. If the supernatural beings we investigate mean no harm, there's no reason to harm them. Sometimes we even try to help them."

"Yes," Michio replied. The relief at being understood was clear on his face.

Tegan debated how to proceed. Michio didn't seem to be lying to them now, and she kind of understood why he had kept his true identity hidden. She didn't want him to think they trusted him entirely, though. She couldn't always tell if a supernatural entity was being truly helpful. Then again, she couldn't always tell with regular people, either.

"Okay, let's say we work together. You clearly know more about these yōkai than we do. Do you have any ideas on how we should proceed?" Tegan asked.

"I do." Michio paused to sip some miso soup. "I showed you that knife-throwing grip on purpose."

"How will that help?" Haruka asked.

"Tomorrow, when we speak with a more sober council, I'll propose a test of skill. We can pit you against one of our skilled knife throwers. If we win, the women will be allowed to go home to their families," Michio explained. "The council will find this highly entertaining, as having a test of skill like this will be even more diverting than having a few women around who they'll eventually tire of."

"And if we lose?" Noel asked.

"They'll probably have you all stay to serve them."

"No. No, I won't risk my people that way," Tegan stated firmly.

"They won't agree to it if the risk isn't great for you," Michio explained.

"Then I'll be the one to stay. If I'm the one who will be doing this test, I'm the one who should be making the sacrifice." Tegan looked at her friends. She knew that if she had to be left behind, they'd work with Ryutaro to get her back.

Michio smiled approvingly. "I can't guarantee they'll agree, but we can try to negotiate that no matter the outcome, your friends will leave."

"Good." Tegan began to eat again, trying to hide her frayed nerves. The once-decadent food now tasted like ash in her mouth, but it was better for her to eat and be at her best for tomorrow than to give in to her worries.

The rest of the meal continued in silence, each person focusing on their own thoughts as the food gradually disappeared from their plates. When Tegan had eaten enough, she excused herself and was led by a servant to a guest room for the night.

A little while later, she heard a knock on the doorframe. She knew exactly who it was. With a sigh, she invited the person on the other side to enter.

"I know something's up," came Noel's rumbly voice. He entered the room smoothly and sat down next to her futon. "I know it's not just what's going to happen tomorrow, either."

"It's no use evading you, is it?" Tegan replied. This was not an uncommon occurrence. They'd been friends for so long that they both could easily read when the other needed a friendly ear and possibly a stern lecture. She had a feeling she was getting both tonight. She begrudgingly took a seat and spilled her guts . . . all the conflicting feelings she was experiencing over Michio, all her self-doubt, and how stupid she felt about the whole thing.

"Tegan, you are a brave woman," Noel began, "except when it comes to your heart. This has happened too many times. You like a guy, you convince yourself there's something wrong with him, and then you just continue on alone. Look, it seems like Michio had good reason to hold back on us. I would too if I thought the people I was working with might hunt me down for not being human. He opened up to us, though. He gave us a chance. I think we can trust him. Honestly, I think you can give him a chance too. Be brave. It's okay to give someone your heart."

"You really think so?" Tegan felt so small and vulnerable.

"Yeah. I do." Noel stood up. "Sleep well, kiddo. I know you'll make the right choice."

He exited the room, and Tegan laid down on the comfortable futon that had been set out for her. Her busy mind refused to cooperate with her, however. The thought of someone capturing her heart was scarier to her than the yōkai capturing the abducted women. After tossing and turning for a while, she left her bed in frustration and wandered among the halls until she found a porch to sit on. A gentle breeze blew along the back of her neck as she stared blearily at an exquisite garden.

"Your futon not to your liking?" Michio's voice came down to her from above.

Tegan looked up to see him perched on the roof over her. "No, the futon is fine. It's my brain that's a mess."

Michio jumped down and sat next to Tegan. "Your brain, a mess? That's hard to believe. You seem so together and in charge most of the time."

She gave him a bleary smile. "No, that's just the guise I put up. My brain runs a mile a minute most of the time."

"I might be able to solve that problem," Michio said.

Before Tegan's sleepy mind realized what was happening, she found herself held in Michio's arms as he ran and leaped for the sky. When it finally hit her that his large black wings were pumping them up into the air, she grabbed his neck as tightly as she dared. She felt, rather than heard, Michio laugh.

"You didn't prepare me for this!" Tegan exclaimed, her words lost in the wind.

Whether she wanted it or not, she was now wide awake. She glanced about, careful not to look down, and slowly started to relax with the regular rhythm of Michio's wings flapping as he flew them higher. He then glided for a bit, holding her tightly, until he landed among a grove of blossoming cherry trees. The full moon provided plenty of light to look upon the delicate pink flowers. Tegan gazed at the magical landscape before her.

"I've always been fond of this grove. I take a lot of photos here," Michio explained as he placed her on her feet again. "Before there were cameras, I'd paint."

"I can see why." Tegan took a few steps away from him and reached out to touch the blossoms on a nearby low-hanging branch. She heard a camera click as a few blossoms blew past her cheek.

"Do you really have to do that now?" Tegan asked, a little annoyed, though in reality she was probably far more annoyed with herself than with him.

Michio gazed into her eyes. "Yes, I do. You have no idea how beautiful you looked just now."

"With bed head and bleary eyes? That's hard to believe," Tegan replied, trying to sound tough and failing miserably.

"Here," Michio said. He showed her a photo of herself that surprised her. While the first photo he had shown her had captured her strength, this one had captured her vulnerability and curiosity. She usually didn't like others to see her like that, but she had to admit, the gentle kiss of blossoms that passed by her face as she touched the ones still on the branch was captivating.

"Is this . . ." Tegan stopped, her heart fluttering a bit. "Is this how you see me?"

"It's one way. I see you like this, and I see you the way you looked in the other photo. They're just different aspects of you." Michio took his camera from her hands.

Tegan took stock of the situation. Her heart was beating so fast; she wanted to believe it was just from the flight, but she knew it wasn't. He was standing close enough that he could easily reach out and touch her, but he seemed to be restraining himself.

"If things don't work out tomorrow," Michio began hesitantly, "I can . . . I can try to make sure that you can stay with me, if you prefer. I can still afford you more freedom than any of the others would. We'd have to make it seem like you're bound to me, but it would be in name only."

Tegan gave him a small nod. She hadn't wanted to think about what would happen if things went wrong, but the fact that Michio was thinking about it was strangely reassuring. "That doesn't sound entirely awful," she said softly.

His shoulders dropped a bit. "Good. I'm glad. You're the type of person who shouldn't be caged."

Hesitantly, he reached for her cheek and pushed a strand of hair behind her ear. It was unexpected. Tegan hadn't been treated so gently in a long time. Maybe it was exhaustion, maybe it was fear, and maybe it was just that he seemed to see her more clearly than anyone else had in a long time, but she tilted her face up slightly. Her gaze met his, and then his lips met hers, so softly that she could barely tell they were there. All the arguments she'd been having with herself about her attraction to him fell silent in that one moment. She couldn't get her thoughts to convince her feelings that this wasn't a good idea anymore. It startled her in a way she hadn't expected.

He pulled back and caressed her cheek with his thumb. The heat in his gaze made her blush, so she lowered her head.

"That's unlike you, to be so shy," Michio uttered, surprise coloring his tone.

Tegan glanced up and saw a smile on his face. Unlike his usual confident grin, it was tender and slightly fragile, almost like he was asking permission. For some reason she couldn't fathom, her own hesitance dropped instantly, and she closed the short distance between their bodies. Quickly, in contrast to the tame brush of lips from before, their kiss became passionate and warm. She felt like she was melting into him as the blossoms swirled around them.

It felt like the kiss could last forever, yet it ended all to quickly, and they reluctantly pulled themselves apart.

"You need rest. Let me take you back so you can sleep," Michio offered.

Tegan nodded, feeling strangely calm as she allowed him to pick her up and fly her the short distance back to his home. They walked through the halls in silence, fearful of breaking the spell. Upon reaching the door to her room, Tegan turned to face Michio once more.

"Sleep well." Michio gave her a gentle kiss on the forehead. He then turned away and walked down the hall, almost as if he was being blown along by a breeze.

Sleep greeted her quickly after she laid herself back down on the futon. Her last thoughts were that she felt changed somehow and she wasn't sure what to make of it.

The next morning in the great hall of the palace, they were met with a very different scene from the one they had experienced the night before. The council of yōkai were all seated around the room, quite sober and attentive. The abducted women sat to one side of the room. Tegan listened as Michio used his silver tongue persuasively to argue their case and propose the challenge. She noted something she hadn't the night before . . . she fully understood everything the yōkai were saying. Though it sounded like Japanese, it was as though a switch had been turned on in her head so that it translated everything into words she knew.

She glanced at Noel, then whispered into his ear, "You understand what they're saying too, right?"

"I noticed it last night but forgot to mention it," Noel whispered back. "Some sort of magic, perhaps?"

"We should note that for later reference," Tegan replied.

"Are you two done?" a voice boomed from the other side of the room. The bushy-tailed ōkami from the previous night glared at them.

Tegan wanted to respond sarcastically, but she didn't want to ruin their chances after Michio had been working so hard to argue their case.

"My apologies," Tegan said and offered a respectful bow.

There was a pregnant pause. The room felt heavy with anticipation. Tegan didn't even want to imagine what would happen if they said no.

"Get Shouta," the ōkami announced. Someone stood and darted quickly from the room.

The three humans looked over at Michio, unsure of what the ōkami's request meant. Michio joined them to explain.

"The good news is that they agreed. If you win, the women will be let go. If you lose, Tegan will stay. Nobody has dared such an attempt as far back as any of us can remember, so the idea was enticing. The bad news . . ." Michio pushed his hair back from his forehead.

Tegan sighed. "I was hoping there wouldn't be any bad news."

"The bad news is that you're competing against Shouta. He's the finest knife thrower we have. I trained him personally. Defeating him will be difficult, but the tendency of yōkai to pull pranks and manipulate things to their advantage could make it worse." Michio gave Tegan a pointed look. "You'll have to work twice as hard to be just as good."

"So she's Ginger Rogers to his Fred Astaire," Noel stated.

"I understand that reference. And yes, exactly."

Tegan allowed herself a moment of dread before she pulled herself together. "Then I'll be Ginger Rogers."

Haruka gave Tegan a hug. "You'll be better than Ginger Rogers."

They all sat together as they watched a servant bring in a stack of paper targets. Another couple of servants moved items around the room, while the council arranged themselves on the dais to watch the competition. They left an empty spot, and Michio guided Tegan, Noel, and Haruka to sit there. Anticipatory whispers added to the already charged atmosphere.

Momentarily, a wiry tengu entered the room. While on the slender side, it was clear that he moved with both grace and efficiency. He bowed to the council, then offered a bow specifically to Michio.

"Sensei," came a clear voice from the tengu's mouth. "I am honored to compete. I hope you will find my skills much improved."

"I am certain you will do well, Shouta," was Michio's unruffled reply.

Shouta glanced at Tegan. He looked at her as though she was something unpleasant that he had stepped in. Tegan refused to be intimidated and gave him a smirk back. He rolled his eyes and returned his attention to the council.

"Do you really believe a mere human is worthy competition for me?" he asked in a bored tone, checking his fingernails for dirt that wasn't there.

Takumi spoke up. "Of course not, that's why we chose you. If the girl wishes to be humiliated, then by all means, humiliate her as brutally as you can."

Shouta gave a sly smile, and then stood at the center of the room next to a waist-high table covered in throwing knives.

"Why are the targets just piled in front of him?" Tegan asked Michio.

"You'll see," Michio replied.

"You will have a hundred targets. You will be limited to one minute. The timer will start after the first throw. The number of targets hit and the location of the hits on the targets will determine the winner," Takumi explained. He gestured to a spirit, who rose from her spot on the dais and floated forward. "If you will?"

The spirit raised her hand. A hundred paper targets rose into the air and arranged themselves at various points around the room, away from the dais. "Ready," came her breathless whisper.

"Begin," announced Takumi.

The targets began moving quickly, almost as though they were caught in a whirlwind. It was dizzying to watch. Shouta stood quietly for a moment, as if trying to determine a pattern. He yawned inattentively and then suddenly burst into movement and began to throw his knives. His quick, graceful movements were deceptive, hiding the power behind his throws as he took down target after target. He hit his final target as it zipped mere inches over Tegan's head. The knife stuck the target to the wall, having hit the center perfectly.

Shouta smirked at Tegan. "Beat that."

A servant gathered all the targets and counted the hits. "Sixty-three hits, fifty-one in the center."

Tegan gulped. She'd practiced with moving targets before, but the speed of these targets and the varying distances were intimidating. She knew that the world record for throwing knives at a human target was a hundred and two knives in one minute, but that was nothing compared to the whirling mass of paper she was expected to hit . . . or maybe not expected to hit.

"Are you ready?" Takumi sneered at Tegan.

Tegan stood. Michio led her to the table in the middle of the room where the knives were set.

"He wasn't even trying. He just focused on showing off," Michio whispered into Tegan's ear. "That gives you an advantage."

"Some advantage," Tegan whispered back. "He was good, and I've never done anything like this before."

She thought back to their hike of the day before, when she had caught a glimpse of something out of the corner of her eye. She may not have hit the bird, but she had hit one of its feathers. She wasn't sure if she would hit enough targets in the center, but she was determined not to give up.

She walked to the center of the room and arranged the knives on the table next to her so they'd be easy to grab once she needed them.

"Ready," she heard the spirit say.

"Begin," came Takumi's voice.

The whirlwind of targets began to swirl around her. Tegan watched as some flew by faster and some moved more slowly. She closed her eyes and calmed her breathing and then picked up a knife for each hand and tried to come up with a game plan. While Shouta had thrown his knives at various targets around the room, showing off, she didn't have to follow suit. Enough would cross in front of her that she shouldn't have to move around as much as he had. Sometimes simpler was better.

"Are you going to start?" jeered Takumi from the dais.

She ignored his words and the tittering laughter that followed. They didn't think she could do it. She found her focus and decided to prove them wrong.

Her eyes spotted her first target, and she began the longest minute she'd ever experienced in her life. *Thunk.* The first knife hit the first target dead center and pinned it to the wall. She continued throwing with speed and precision, avoiding theatrics and keeping herself focused only on the task in front of her.

The spirit must have noticed Tegan's throwing pattern, because the number of targets passing through Tegan's line of sight decreased. She noted that—it was one of the tricks the yōkai had no doubt been planning to resort to, and it was likely a sign that she was doing better than they had expected.

Tegan softened her gaze and began to throw at targets that may not have been in her direct view but that she could still see from the corners of her eyes. They were harder to hit in the center, but she wasn't going to give up. The spirit must have noticed that Tegan wasn't stopping, because the targets began moving faster instead, once again passing in front of Tegan.

The knives and targets diminished as Tegan continued throwing, so completely focused that she just barely noticed when Takumi yelled at her to stop.

The room went utterly silent as the remaining paper targets fell to the floor around her. She turned slowly, as if everything had suddenly switched to slow motion, and looked at the dais. Everyone was staring at her, except for the servant who began to gather the targets.

She gave them a sarcastic curtsy and feigned an innocent smile. "Will that do?"

Haruka and Noel instantly ran to her.

"You did great, kid," Noel said, lifting her into a huge bear hug that crushed her lungs.

She had to catch her breath before Haruka gave her a hug as well. "We don't know the numbers yet, but that was impressive."

"I just hope it was enough," Tegan replied. She looked back at the dais to see Michio speaking with Takumi. It was clear that Takumi was not happy.

"The score is—what? Sixty-eight hits, fifty-five centered?" The ōkami quickly rifled through the targets, counting again.

"Let me see that!" bellowed Shouta. He grabbed the targets from the ōkami and counted them himself. He then screamed in rage and stomped out of the room.

Michio ran to Tegan and pulled her into his arms. "You did it!" He laughed. "You really did it!"

Tegan was so shocked, she couldn't even speak.

Takumi approached her and gave her a bow. "I don't think I've ever seen anything quite like that. You've given us something to talk about for quite some time and maybe even taught Shouta a lesson about not resting on his laurels."

"Will the women be released?" Tegan asked.

"As reluctant as we are to let them go, we gave our word and it would dishonor all of us if we didn't make good on our agreement." Takumi sighed as he glanced over at the abducted women.

"You'll take all spells off them, as promised?" Michio added.

"Yes, they're free to go, spells removed." Takumi waved a hand at the women, and their calm demeanors gave way to confusion. Haruka quickly approached them and began to explain what was happening, attempting to quell their fears. Two of them collapsed against each other in tears, while another completely passed out. Three of them were extremely agitated, ready to attack their captors until Noel approached them. They quickly became quiet once they saw him, no doubt intimidated by his immense size.

The hebi walked back to the dais as the tanuki shouted for sake to celebrate the worst humiliation in history. The group of yōkai quickly regained their cheer and began to carouse, completely ignoring the women they had stolen and the humans who had saved them.

"Let's get them out of here while they're distracted," Tegan said, nudging Michio's side with her elbow.

He grinned. "Good idea."

By that evening, all the women had been brought to the Maruyamas' home and were returned to their families. Tegan happily watched the tearful reunions.

"This really is the best part of the job," Noel remarked, sipping from a cup of tea.

Tegan giggled. "The tea or the families being brought together again?"

"Both." Noel smiled and then took another sip of tea. "This is fantastic tea, by the way. The Maruyamas gave me several packs of it to take home."

Tegan shook her head and left Noel as he attempted to speak to one of the no-longer-abducted women about proper tea ceremony etiquette in his broken Japanese. Haruka must have overheard the conversation because she quickly rushed over to help translate. Tegan stepped out the front door, hoping that the families would focus more on their returned daughters than on her for rescuing them.

"Everything good?" Michio asked, perched on the stairs leading up to the Maruyamas' front door.

Tegan sat down next to him and smiled. "It is. How about you?"

He stared out at the few scattered stars that were still visible despite the street lights. "I'm not sure."

"How's that?" she asked. She wrapped her arms around her knees and gazed at the stars along with him.

"Would you be bothered if I told you that I don't want you to leave?" Michio asked after a brief silence.

Tegan's heartbeat sped up. That kiss he had given her had been nothing like any kiss she'd ever had. She had been trying not to think about leaving, knowing that she might not see Michio again. She was grateful they hadn't gone further than kissing, because while she would have loved to stay and see how far a relationship with him could take them, she wasn't willing to give up her duty to ISPIE.

At least, she wasn't ready just yet.

She reached her hand out to him, and he took it in a warm grip. "Well, you could always join ISPIE since you know about us already and could offer some valuable insight."

He snickered. "I might just have to."

"I mean, who else is going to help me improve my knife

throwing to the point where I could hit a hundred moving targets in one minute?" Tegan teased.

"I could always send Shouta to you as punishment for disappointing his sensei," Michio proposed facetiously.

"Ew, no," Tegan replied, wrinkling her nose.

"Okay, now that was actually very cute," Michio teased back.

"I'm not cute!" Tegan exclaimed, giving Michio a playful slap on his shoulder.

Michio rubbed at the spot she had hit. "Hey, that hurt!"

"Oh, I'm sorry. I didn't mean to hit you that hard," Tegan apologized and started to rub the spot for him.

"You know, if you kiss it, I might feel better," Michio suggested nonchalantly, his face turned away from her.

Tegan began to laugh. "You'd like that, wouldn't y—"

Michio pulled her into his lap and gave her a passionate kiss. This time, she didn't feel anything holding her back at all. The maelstrom of arguments against getting close to him now seemed so far away, as though part of another life. This kiss didn't feel like a fleeting dream from a fairy tale. It felt real. It felt like something she could rely on—something she wanted to rely on.

When the kiss ended, she nestled into his shoulder, apprehensive about returning home the next day. "We'll meet again, right?"

"We will; it's a promise," Michio replied. He gently twirled a lock of her hair around his fingers as he smiled peacefully.

"It better be," Tegan quipped playfully. "I'll come hunt you down if I have to."

They both laughed and held each other close as they listened to the sounds of joy and relief that drifted out the windows behind them. She still felt a little hesitant about what this unexpected relationship might bring. At the same time, dropping her guard with him and allowing him to capture her heart had brought to light feelings she now found herself ready and yearning to explore.

FROM DEATH'S LIPS

YNES MALAKOVA

THE PRICE OF ADMISSION

La Grondaia.
    Ammorante.

The words are heavy in my mind.

I awaken with a shiver, nestled between a pair of balsam firs with branches that buckle under the weight of snow. I count the markings I have made in the sole of my boot. It has been seven days since General Grimstaad ambushed my *ammorante* and me, stalking us from afar, lying in wait as we crossed the threshold from the kingdom's border into the black mountains.

The wind bites into my skin, and my mind is seized by memories of my *ammorante*. I recall his eyes, gray upon waking, and how they would sparkle cerulean when he lifted them to the sun, his lips pulling into an easy, cavalier grin. The tips of his blond hair would brush my shoulders when he greeted me, the thick, wild curve of his words like the twined branches of a blackberry vine: his love-murmurs both succulent and abrading in my ears.

Whether he still lives or has perished, I do not know.

I shudder from the chill of the air upon my skin, goosebumps pockmarking my forearms as my mind reels beneath the memory of Grimstaad's cruelty. Cold frightening nights I spent, listening to the spirits-fueled rants of a madman—his eyes alight by campfire as he gleefully devised his methods to exact vengeance upon my *ammorante*. And his pledge. His pledge to me. For my love of my *ammorante*, he vowed to cleanse me of my iniquities and banish the wickedness that my *ammorante* had imparted unto me.

I touch my fingers to my cheeks, recalling the sting of frigid water, my lungs burning for want of breath while Grimstaad plunged my face into the depths of the river, again and again. My *ammorante* had howled in despair, thrashing against his own constraints while I fought in vain against Grimstaad's strength.

My stomach lurches and my breaths turn sharp, labored. I squeeze my eyes shut, blood rushing through my ears as I hear in my mind the dull thud of Grimstaad's boot against my *ammorante*'s ribs. I remember clearly, four days ago, sobs of relief racked my body as Grimstaad made the decision to separate us, taking me as his captive while tossing my *ammorante*, wrists and ankles bound, into a prison cart with his men.

Bound for *La Grondaia*.

The words chatter between my teeth as I shake the frost from my cloak and rise. Save what meager lessons I gleaned from my childhood studies in the *Accademia* about its origins as a mining quarry, I know little of *La Grondaia*. I have only learned, from my days as Grimstaad's prisoner, that it is an enormous, sprawling underground prison—and Grimstaad's greatest achievement. His voice had flushed with repletion, brimming with liquor and pride, when he spoke of his prisoners building this prison-tomb themselves, shovels clanking against stone and dirt to create its ceaseless tunnels. It is reserved for the most dangerous of the *banale*: brigand lords, assassins, treasonous men.

Men like my *ammorante*.

I am unable to shake from my imagination depictions of him stretched over a torture-stone in *La Grondaia*, deep purple lashes and dried blood spattered across his back.

My fingers reach for the hilt of the pistol holstered to my thigh, and I close my eyes, allowing the chill of the metal to penetrate my skin. The weapon glows crimson in the midmorning sun, a spray of fine golden leaves shimmering across its barrel.

The memory of Grimstaad's gruesome smile and throaty death-rattle flashes in my mind. I took his life with this weapon, veritable tool of annihilation.

It is the last vestige I have of my *ammorante*—his gift to me. His promise. As I clutch it in my palm, my breaths deepen and begin to steady. I draw the hood of my cloak overhead.

La Grondaia.

Ammorante.

I am coming for you.

Without Grimstaad to advise me, my *ammorante*'s whereabouts are lost. I know not under which range of mountains *La Grondaia* is situated nor how deeply its tunnels run.

For days, I inquire among smugglers and mercenaries and come up empty-handed. None of them possess knowledge of the whereabouts of the prison, let alone how to navigate its treachery. But my efforts are not wholly in vain: in my hunt for information, the same name rolls repeatedly off the tongues of these men.

Murphy Hawthorne.

For a few coins, I have no trouble convincing them to lead me to him.

Hawthorne's tent stands solo in a clearing by the river, a ten-minute walk from the Orchards of Eiroda; on a moonless night, it might be mistaken for an outcropping. But this is no such night; a fresh blanket of snow glistens in the silver rays of a waning moon. Whoever he may be, this man is foolish to believe he is shrouded from danger.

I poise myself by the flap of his tent, careful to quiet my footsteps. My hand slides through the folds of my skirt, reaching for the leather strap around my thigh.

The tarp rustles, and I draw my pistol.

"*Signore* Murphy Hawthorne?"

Long, tangled hair peeks from beneath a bandana and blends into a heavy overcoat. Where one begins and the other ends is impossible to discern. From his silhouette, his only truly marked feature is his beard, a tapestry of dark hairs peppered with streaks of silver.

He turns toward me, and the lines and angles of his face emerge in the moonlight. Light and shadow play on his forehead, his twisted locks of hair casting a solid block of shadow across half his face. An umber eye meets mine and I feel small, childlike. Within his iris is the quiddity of a man who should not be standing in my presence—one who should not be standing anywhere. He should have found his way to the tomb years earlier, yet he persists, though the dual scythes of time and peril perpetually whip at his heels.

When he moves, a burst of white stretches down his right cheek, and my gaze fixes on a thick wool patch covering the socket that should have housed his other eye. A wide, jagged scar begins just above his brow and drags straight down his cheek, thick and pink, with spines that climb atop one another like the strokes of an artist's pen gone awry.

My grip weakens on the pistol, and I feel my lips soften in deference. I draw a quick breath between my teeth. My fingers twitch, wanting to trace across this serpent of flesh.

I scowl at myself. *Focasi!* I pull free of my stupor and press the barrel of my weapon squarely against Hawthorne's forehead.

"*La Grondaia.*" My voice is firm and low. I press the steel deep into his skin. "Where is it, *Signore* Hawthorne?"

He grows quiet, and his single eye shifts, rolling like a marble. "So, you have finally arrived, little *filia.* I had expected you to come for me much sooner."

I snap my teeth together, my finger pulsing on the trigger. "Tell me what I wish to know, *dead man.*"

"You are looking to infiltrate *La Grondaia,* are you?" His lips flicker into something between a grimace and a scowl. "That is foolhardy, *filia*."

My mouth falls agape. My cheeks flush and I press my lips together. "My plans are of no concern to you!"

"Perhaps not," he replies. "But know this. You will not find another who has dwelled within the tunnels of *La Grondaia* and lived to speak of it. So you must decide. What do you seek from me: my life or my knowledge? I suggest you weigh your options carefully."

He chuckles softly to himself, and my eyebrows fold with ire. "Do you find death amusing, *Signore*—"

Before I am able to complete my thought, he swings his arm and knocks the pistol from my hand. I hear it hit the snow with a soft thud. I reach for the blade tucked within my cloak, but Hawthorne seizes me. I hiss and strike at him, but I am unable to wrench free. He presses me against him and locks my arms to my sides. He stands so close that I feel the warmth of his breath upon my nose. His glove wraps around my jaw, and he squeezes my chin between his thumb and forefinger.

"Take heed, *filia*. You have spoken too loosely of your plight. I advise you to exercise caution in the future."

He releases me, shoving my body from his. The force sends me stumbling backward, and I tumble into the frost. I feel the tail of his coat brush my arm as he whips around, lifting my pistol from the snow. He turns it over in his hands, gently stroking the barrel.

"The smugglers were kind enough to supply me with your description," he says. "'Watch for a girl with straw-colored hair and eyes like emeralds,' they said. 'She's thin as a wisp, but a scrapper. Speaks in a strange tongue. And she carries a *pistol*, of all things.'"

He cocks back the hammer, points the weapon at me, and squeezes the trigger. The weapon clicks with a quiet *tink*.

"I thought as much." He snaps the barrel open and rubs his fingers against bare metal, neither powder nor cap tucked within.

I taste fury and humiliation on my tongue, and my hands begin to shake. I curl them into fists, sinking my nails into my palms.

Hawthorne shakes his head. "Senseless, heedless woman. You

are going to get yourself killed." His dark eye rolls across my cloak, and he raises an eyebrow. "Perhaps we can strike a deal, though, and temper your appetite for blood. The smugglers tell me you can handle yourself with a blade."

I swallow hard, forcing my voice to hold steady. "What would you have me do?"

"I am one of the *banale* who live beyond the reach of the kingdom. Wintertime is harsh. Supplies are short. If you raid a few caravans and bring us food, in return I will supply you with the knowledge you seek."

"You are *banale*!" I narrow my eyes, my fingertips itching for my blade. "And you wish for me to become one of you?"

"You are already in trouble, are you not? And you say you need my help." The corner of his lips twitches up into a smirk. "They'll never see a little wraith like you coming."

The knot in my forehead begins to soften, and a smile threatens to appear upon my lips. Hawthorne extends his arm to me. I hesitate before squeezing his hand in agreement.

"Very well."

"Good. Now, there is one other matter to address." He snaps the pistol shut. "You understand, *filia*, information is my crop. My currency. This pistol . . . is your currency. Consider it the price of your admission."

"Admission to what?"

Hawthorne tucks my weapon deep into the folds of his jacket. "They call us Serpentine."

CADENCE OF NIGHT

In the beginning I work alone, until the fervor of my night raids grows among the members of the Serpentine camp. I only allow two to join me: Benji and Magdalene—a pair of siblings, with matching auburn hair and hazel eyes, whom I have befriended. They rival me in their youth, and in time, I come to share a tent with them.

When we conduct our raids, I order them always to release the merchants. The enforcers I kill with a light stroke of my blade. True to Hawthorne's prediction, I am a specter to them. But as more blood is spilled, my appearance becomes known and I begin to earn the infamy that vexed my *ammorante*. They know me only as Viper, and inns and taverns attach to their walls bulletins calling for my capture. The enforcers grow in number, with sharper blades and better senses, and it soon becomes clear that I cannot continue without exposing Benji and Magdalene to an early grave.

For this reason, I enlist Hawthorne's help.

I sit by his side at sunset, enveloped in the safety of his tent. We spread his maps before us and study the trade routes on hands and knees, marking points of attack. I follow the meticulous lines of his pen, adding my own airy numerals next to his.

Magdalene and Benji study the caravans from noon to sundown, and Hawthorne himself plots the night convoys. He trusts no one else with this task. I had once delegated the role to Benji and reported his findings with confidence, declaring his numbers boldly upon the parchment, until Hawthorne blotted ink over my writing, obliterating my finely penned twos in favor of his thick fours. This had incensed me, but at night, when I had counted the fallen, I turned my chagrin onto Benji, reprimanding him for his carelessness.

Hawthorne retires from our planning once the stars have spread across the sky like a scattering of dust. He wipes his pen, places it neatly beside a stack of parchment, and reaches for his coat. He tucks a fiddle beneath his arm and lingers by the flaps of his tent. He never speaks his invitation, but it hangs between us like the moon, a lullaby cradled between branches.

I strike my tinderbox and bow my head, scrawling in the margins of the map. The tarp rustles, and Hawthorne leaves me to work alone by candlelight. The wick burns low, and shadows lick at my writing. I rub my eyes. A roar of applause rises from center-camp, and for a moment I lower my pen. The lively pluck of Hawthorne's fiddle ignites the air, followed by a whoop and then laughter and the elevated voices of men and women spinning together. My toes drum against the tips of my boots. The scent of hickory and meat charring over fire wafts through the tent, causing my stomach to churn. I squeeze my lip between my teeth.

I work until the music turns soft and slow, the voices falling away as the Serpentine retire to their tents. Only when my plans are steadfast do I retire from Hawthorne's tent and return to my own, nestling between Magdalene and Benji's sleeping forms.

The raids take on a pulse of their own, a chaotic cadence like the quick tunes Hawthorne plays: The racket of wheels colliding with stone, the thump of boots flagellating the earth, the shouts of merchants and enforcers as we hold our blades to their throats. Then the shuffling of tarps, the scrape of crates, and a soft jangle of coins as we fumble through our captives' pockets.

Days roll into weeks, and the raids become indistinct from one another. The unyielding frenzy begins to take a toll on my health. My appetite waxes and wanes; my back aches as I hunch over the maps. One night, I succumb to sleep without my knowledge and startle awake in darkness, alone in Hawthorne's tent with my pen nestled between my fingers.

When I return to my tent that night, Magdalene offers me a concerned glance. I nod at her and smile. Her eyes dart to mine and then shift to the crack in our tent. She peels the flap back and cranes her neck before pulling the tarp shut.

"Viper, I must speak with you." Her lips are pulled taut, her eyebrows creased. A limp braid flops onto her shoulder, wild strands of crisscrossed hair peeking out like blades of grass. "Everyone has noticed how much time you and Murphy spend together. They believe you are . . . working more than maps."

My eyes widen at her bold words. I force them shut, counting my breaths to calm my countenance. "You would insinuate that I am lying with him?"

Lines of hesitation form on her face. "Yes."

"Magda—"

"Viper, please!"

I rub my forehead and sigh. "Cease your idle talk. We have many long nights ahead of us."

She shifts her weight from one leg to the other, teetering strangely. Her hazel eyes pool with fear, but behind them, I sense conviction.

"Murphy would not allow you to put yourself in peril," she mumbles, "if he knew you were with child."

We stare at each other in awkward, wide-eyed silence. My head begins to throb. With trembling lips, I knit my brows.

"Diche diabli!" I exclaim. "What rumors do you conjure while I am away?"

"No rumors, Viper. I've said nothing of your condition." She breathes out slowly, hesitating. "It won't be obvious for some time. But I can tell. I told you that Benji and I grew up on a farm . . . and while he worked the fields, I looked after the cows. I . . . got real good at picking out the ones that would have calves in the spring. My pappy and I used to bet on it, 'til I took all his coins one year. He yelled at me, and I tried to tell him, there's a trick to it. They just look different. But you have to have an eye for it. I'll show you what I mean."

She reaches for me, and I feel my lips pulling back into a snarl. *"Ficio*, Magda! I am no cow!" My hands are quivering. There is no hiding the flicker of fear in my voice.

Magdalene narrows her eyes. "Viper . . . you are not aware?"

I shake my head. It cannot be true. It cannot! Surely she is misguided! What chance is there that her work with farm animals could apply to people?

"This is rubbish!" I snap. "Magda, you are mistaken!"

Gently, she places her hand on my shoulder and guides me to a seated position.

"Lift your blouse, Viper. And be very still."

I untuck the hem of my shirt from my waist. Her palms are cold against my skin. She presses into my abdomen firmly with both hands against my flesh. I wince. And suddenly, from deep within, I feel my insides twist, a pressure expanding in my belly like a clenched fist unfurling, finger by finger.

She is not mistaken.

A wave of nausea sticks in my throat. I push her hands away and tug my blouse down.

"Murphy is a good man," Magdalene says. "He will do right by you."

I avoid her gaze, and her mouth grows slack.

"Viper," she says, "is he not—"

I lunge for her, clamping my hand over her mouth. The tent spins around me. I realize, in this moment, that I have been holding my breath. Magda brings my ear to her shoulder, and my body breaks into sobs.

Ammorante.

"Shhh." Magdalene runs her fingers through my hair. "No harm will come to you. You are in good care. We will cancel tonight's raid, you will rest, and in the morning—"

"No." I wipe my eyes on my sleeve, and my voice finds resolve. There is too much at stake.

"Our raids will continue as planned."

DANCE OF FRIENDSHIP

I smooth my hands over my protruding belly. When I am not leading a strike, I have chosen to spend my nights in Hawthorne's tent, tucked away from the clamor of the Serpentine's music and feasts in the center-camp. His black tarp has become my haven, a place of respite. Tonight he sits beside me, scratching his pen across parchment. I watch his lips move, though no sound pushes through them. He makes silent calculations, his beard entangled with the shade of night.

"*Signore* Hawthorne?"

"Hmm." He cocks his head, his gaze fixed on the map spread before him.

"I am . . . curious," I say. "How did you lose your eye?"

Hawthorne scoffs, his brow furrowing. "Do you think of us as friends?"

"Friends?"

"Yes, friends," he says. "That is a question you would only ask a friend."

He raises an eyebrow, and I prop myself upright.

"I disagree," I say, raising my chin in defiance. "I am sure Benji has asked you this question. Do you consider him a friend?"

"Hmph." Hawthorne presses his lips together and is silent. He lowers his pen and watches my fingers glide across my midsection. "It is a question that only a friend would *answer*."

A smile pulls at the corner of my lips. "Then it is I who must ask: do you consider me a friend?"

Friend. The word stands between us like a wishbone, each of us clutching one end. I pull at my sleeve, wondering which way it will break.

"I didn't lose my eye," Hawthorne growls. "It was taken from me."

"In *La Grondaia*?"

"It is late, and you are with child." He frowns and wipes the ink from his pen. "You should not be going on any more raids."

"So our friendship is confirmed," I say. "You do not wish to see me in harm's way. It is why you keep the location of *La Grondaia* hidden from me, though I have completed more than my share of the Serpentine's strikes."

"You have," he says. "So perhaps it is time to rest."

I rise, placing my hands on my hips. "*Murphy*, you must honor your end of our deal."

The gash in his cheek crawls away from his nose as his lips fold into a tight, grievous smile.

"Senseless, heedless woman. You truly do not know when to stop." He sighs, rubs his temples, and mutters a handful of words to himself that escape my ears. He folds his map and turns to me. "I will make you a new deal, Viper. Join me tonight in our camp. Eat with us. Dance with us. And rest. Do this for me, and I will draw your map to *La Grondaia*. You have my word."

The crackle of fire punctuates the night as oil drips from meat. Murphy has finished playing, and he rests his fiddle. I am seated beside the fire, and he lowers himself beside me. His chin brushes my shoulder, and I breathe in the hickory smoke clinging to his coat, mingled with the essence of his skin.

The low lull of guitar music fills the night, and Murphy's gaze grows glossy, distant, as if his thoughts swirl through the air with the music and smoke. He stands and extends his hand to me. I know what he asks, and the thrum of soft music, paired with his dark voice, holds me in its enchantment. Quietly, I give him my hand and rise.

He poises his palm flat against the small of my back, and my stomach brushes against his coat buttons. Our feet turn in a slow circle, and my skirts drag along the earth, stirring flecks of dust and ash around our ankles.

With a gentle press to my tailbone, he guides my hips to sway with him. I sigh softly, resting my ear on his shoulder.

"Friends do not dance like this," I say.

"If that is so," he murmurs, "then perhaps we are something else."

I peer past him and catch a glimpse of Benji craned over a group of women huddled by the fire. He nudges one of them and points at me. Magdalene swats at him, shooing him from the gaggle. I chuckle softly, squeeze Murphy's arm, and motion toward Benji and the Serpentine women.

"You know they are whispering about us."

"Yes."

"They think we are lovers."

"Do they?"

Even under the veil of darkness, I see his lips hold a soft smile. My feet glide with him, and his face becomes a charcoal portrait in flux, with fibers of black and gray etched around his mouth and a pop of light in the corner of his single eye. He spins me; Benji falls from my view. Murphy presses his cheek into my hair, and I feel his warm breath on my earlobe.

"We could allow their rumors to become truth."

I grin abruptly, flashing my teeth.

"*Signore* Hawthorne." I feel the flush of my cheeks. "You of all people know the boundary between rumor and truth is but the bend of a mirror."

He dusts my lips with a wisp of breath, and I touch my tongue to the corner of my mouth, sampling the tincture of his scent. His lips quietly reach for mine. With my pulse throbbing in my throat, I lock my mouth over his.

The fibers of his beard press into my chin. I had imagined they would be like twine and leave abrasions upon my skin, but like his lips, his hair is fluid, frictionless. I close my eyes. Shifting my chin, I sigh and roll my bottom lip over his. His palm glides up the side of my skirt, pausing when it reaches the circumference of my belly.

A swift thump thunders across my abdomen.

I gasp, breaking the seal between Murphy's lips and mine. My fingers slip from his grasp, and I step back, adding a gap between my body and his. I feel warm, too warm beneath my clothes. Sweat beads at the top of my brow. The light of the fire no longer bathes me with its calm incandescence but glares at me like the flickering eyes of a devil.

Murphy's brow furls, deep lines spreading across his forehead. He reaches for me, brushing his thumb across my cheek.

I turn away. I do not belong with him. I have no place in the Serpentine; I should not be frolicking among the levity of their melody and breathing in the aroma of tender meats on spits.

I belong back in the tent, studying the layout of *La Grondaia*.

I touch my fingertips to my cheek, hoping the redness that marked my skin has faded.

"Our dance is finished."

Murphy's eyebrow twitches, a bolt of pain cutting across his eye. "It does not need to end here."

"Do you forget? I am pregnant as a sow!" I lower my voice. "And this child is not yours."

"I am well aware of that." His nostrils flare, and he draws in a staggered breath. "And I do not need to look far to know that the father of your child is a fool."

"A fool?" My arm shoots to my hip. "What is it you believe you know, old man?"

"I know you still love him," he growls. "Which some would argue makes you just as foolish."

I draw my arm back and swing at him, striking him across the cheek.

"Viper." My name sends two quick pulses through his scar.

I turn and shuffle down the eastern trail, rustling branches as I cross into the trees.

Marked for Death

I hear him shout my name at my back, but I do not turn. I cannot not allow myself to see if Murphy's face holds bewilderment or anguish, or to glide my eyes over the crevices of the scar that enraptures me. I am confident he will not follow me outside the sphere of the camp. He would not dare. I have spoken my answer, and Serpentine know that to violate my privacy and defy my words is to incite my wrath.

The music of our encampment fades as I charge into the darkness. The trees in the valleys capture a dense fog, and with their tops blotting out the moonlight, I navigate by touch alone. My boots crush ferns and rocks, and I march on. The night's humid air gathers under my hair, welling up against the base of my neck.

I carry myself deeper into the woodland until my mouth becomes dry and perspiration clings to my collarbone, small droplets dragging down my neck and wetting the front of my dress. I hear a trickle of water a short distance away, the chatter of a brook grating against my eardrums, chiding me for heeding the succubus call of the moon. The soft press of Murphy's beard still lingers on my chin and cheek.

Avventata. How could you be so foolish?

I pause, panting, and double over, clutching my knees, catching my breath in short bursts. My tongue is like parchment—even in the humid night air—and the water of perspiration trickles down my dress, summer heat wetting my armpits and running down my thighs.

I rub my lips, smudging the impossible attraction between us. Yet my heart still hums to the chords of the Serpentine musician's guitar. I touch my tongue to the corner of my lip. A jitter of enthrallment mingles with the guilt that throbs in my temples. My emotions are a tangled wad of threads.

I right myself, spreading my toes against the tip of my boot to keep my body centered. I knead my thumbs into the small of my back as I move, listening to the crinkle of twigs and grass bending under my girth. The butt of my boot slaps the earth, and moisture penetrates my socks. I glance at the grass in bewilderment. The ground should not be wet. I am too far from the brook's bank.

I take another step forward, and a tremendous force cinches my belly, a band of pressure, like a serpent squeezing me. I gasp and flatten my hand against the gnarled knot of an oak. I bend forward at the waist, and in a flash, my senses go numb. The blood in my veins curdles.

Magdalene had warned me of the imminent signs of childbirth, but I had only registered them in a distant region of my mind, in the same manner I had heard of many lands when I was in the Damica, like Eiroda or Middleton. I had understood them only in a scholastic sense, never having sunk my teeth into the red flesh of orchard fruit or watched the merchants barter with wild motions and billowing sleeves.

The pressure in my midsection suddenly begins to ease, the belt of pain unthreading loop by loop. I sigh in relief, blowing a long breath between my lips.

I am fine. I straighten my spine and sweep my hands through my hair. *My mind is playing tricks on me.*

I shift my legs and take a step back. A pool of fluid is caught in the rub of my thighs, and it trickles down past my knees. I grab my skirts and clutch them between my fingers. They are damp with fluid.

The invisible belt slithers around my belly once more, constricting my abdomen with greater force.

This cannot be happening.

"Magdalene!" I shout as loud and as strong as my voice will carry. The lonesome chirp of a night bird twitters in response.

"MAGDA!" I push through limbs and leaves, lurching over rocks and stumps, back toward the Serpentine camp. A sharp pain twists in my back, and I bend to my knee, pressing my thumb deep into my flesh to relieve the pain.

I can hear the wild drumming of the Serpentine, barely audible through the trees. I stumble blindly through the darkness, shouting Magdalene's name again and again until my throat is raw. The pain in my midsection grows with each step, and I charge forward toward the music, my hoarse voice diminished by the looming trunks of oaks.

I feel a burst of fluid release from my body, warmer than before. I bite my lip and forge ahead, balling my skirts between my thighs. A pressure-spasm bites into my midsection, and I stumble, falling to my knees. A ribbon of moonlight peeks past the tops of the trees, and in its light, I see my fingers are coated in blood. I try to rise, but my strength is streaming from my body, staining my skirts and skin red. The scent of iron and grass mingle in my nose, my vision grows dim, and the world fades around me.

I awaken to the sound of wheels clattering over rocks and brush, a hard jolt lurching me against the side of a travel cart. I feel the firm press of a hand, and I am greeted by Magdalene. Her face is chiseled with worry lines that spread across her forehead and pool under her eyes.

"You're awake, Viper." Her lips pull into a tense smile. "Try to stay with us. Don't go back to sleep."

"We're almost there." A man speaks behind her, and I immediately recognize Benji's voice.

I blink in an attempt to clear the fog from my mind. Even this small gesture is painful.

"Almost where?"

Magdalene and Benji trade glances.

"You got lucky, Viper," Benji says. "I'd had my fill of spirits and stumbled onto you when I went into the trees to take a—"

Magdalene clears her throat and casts her brother a sharp look.

"Anyway." Benji shrugs. "I found you out there and went and got Madgalene. She took one look at you and turned white as a ghost. We picked you up and carried you back to camp, and Murphy told us to—"

"Murphy." I squeeze my eyes shut and sigh regretfully.

"He's on his way," Magdalene says. Her fingers comb through my hair. "Try not to think about that. Just breathe and stay with us."

"You'll get to tell him goodbye. I told you, you got lucky," Benji says. "Magda slowed the bleeding. But she said it's twins and it's a breach. We don't have the training to save you, or the tools, so—"

"Benji!"

"She has a right to know she's going to die, Magda!"

"She is not going to die! That's why we're taking her . . ." Magdalene's words trail into silence.

"Taking me where?"

Magdalene and Benji trade glances and do not answer. We continue to drive over bumps and curves at breakneck speed—and then the cart jumps and the road becomes smooth. I know immediately: we are crossing from the borderlands into the kingdom.

"Stop!" I cry. I cannot return to the kingdom. It would be better to die. To risk saving me would mean not only my own death; they would hunt Murphy and Madgalene and Benji and the driver of the cart, and any other Serpentine who has accompanied me on this trek. And if we fall, the Serpentine would be destroyed. The raids, the fire in the eyes of the once-downtrodden men and women—all of it would fade to dust. They would be crushed by the kingdom, with men like Grimstaad leading the charge. I writhe in Magdalene's grasp and try to break free. My efforts are in vain, though; the cart steers on, regardless.

The wheels finally come to a screeching halt in front of what looks to have once been a storefront, but it is dilapidated, abandoned, the scent of heavy dust stinging my eyes. Benji's familiar face greets me.

"Easy, Viper." He hoists my arm over his shoulder, and together, he and Magdalene lift me. I shake my head no and try to push them away, but my strength has abandoned me. I groan as we move, a ripple of pain squeezing my abdomen. My legs can no longer carry my weight; my feet drag, limp, as they push open the door. I see that the shop was once a forge; a large anvil stands in the center of the room, and a scatter of soot-covered tools are spread out on singed countertops. Magda lays a sheet overtop the anvil, and Benji rests me on it.

The driver of the cart is here, as are two women whose names I do not know. They murmur to each other, trading cryptic words, and I strain my ears to catch their conversation.

"We couldn't get him . . ."

". . . enforcers . . . in droves . . . lying in wait . . ."

"Lost three of ours . . ."

"Murphy thought they'd been counting . . ."

". . . knew we'd come with her . . ."

". . . we got the assistant, at least."

I hear the wheels of another cart, a shuffling, and shouts. The door thumps open, and two Serpentine men enter with a third pressed between them. He is a small man, frail, with an ashen tone to his skin. His glasses hang crooked on the bridge of his nose. A compression squeezes my body, and I gasp.

Pietro Fatagnia. Pietro! I know this man! We studied together in the *Accademia;* each day, we passed each other in the halls—he, heading for his studies in medicine and anatomy, and I, to my lessons in the Damica.

"Laurel."

My name hangs on his lips in disbelief. In the midst of my pain, it occurs to me that I have not heard a soul use my given name in months.

My abdomen loosens for a moment, and I can once again breathe. *"Dire niente,"* I gasp. *Tell no one.*

I feel my consciousness slipping away from me as my abdomen squeezes. I fight to keep my eyes open, but the corners are narrowing, darkness hovering over me like a vulture.

"Viper!" Benji, or one of the other Serpentine, calls out. It is the last word I hear before I fall into darkness.

When I come to, we are still in the forge. My body lies nude on the metal of the anvil, the thin sheet now draped over me. The cold bite of the iron shoots up my spine. I cannot stop shivering.

I turn my neck to take in my surroundings. My head throbs at the exertion, threatening to split in half. Lying next to me is a curved blade. Not a sword, but a weapon I have never seen before—a blade with no hilt, only a smooth, cylindrical bottom. A basin of crimson water lies on my other side beside a heap of bloodied rags.

I try to move and realize that my legs and torso are paralyzed. I press my arms into the metal and attempt to roll to my side. I am met with a sudden jolt—a slashing pain, as if I had been struck by a sword and my insides were spilling out. I clench my fists and cry out.

Instantly, I hear hurried footsteps, and I am met with Pietro's face: sharp spectacles over crow's feet eyes that study me, concerned.

He kneels beside me. "You are awake."

I reply with a grunt, my fingers curled, clutching at nothing.

"I thought we might have lost you," he says, reaching forward. He places the back of his hand against my forehead. "Do not try to move."

"Wh—" I try to speak, but my pain chokes the words.

"Do not speak. Rest," Pietro says. "Your body has been through trauma."

"Trauma?"

He cocks his neck to the side, leaning his ear toward me. He looks at me skeptically, as though in disbelief that I would question his words.

"Yes," he says quietly. "When the brigands brought you to me, you were in breach. There was no chance of a natural delivery. I tried to tell them, but they held their blades to my throat and threatened to dump my body at the base of the mountains. Fortunately, a woman-rogue stepped in. She assisted me with your Cesarean."

My eyes widen, and my hands immediately shoot to my belly. It is no longer bulging, but the flesh is still swollen; even the light press of my fingertips causes an ache deep inside my body. I withdraw my hands and find they are covered in mud. The scent of heal-all and lemongrass lingers in my nose—Magdalene's signature herbs for patching wounds after the night raids.

"The woman," I say to Pietro. "Where is she?"

"She is with the other *banale.*" He pauses and presses his lips together. "And your children."

"Children?"

"Twins," he says quickly. "A boy and a girl."

Pietro fetches a fresh cloth, dips it into the basin, and wrings out the excess water. He takes me by the wrist and gently wipes the mud from my fingers.

"What happened to you, Laurel?" he whispers. "How did you end up in the borderlands, with child, in the company of *banale*?" I taste his disgust when he speaks the word. "Did they take you captive as well? Force you into their beds and—"

"No," I whisper. "I am here of my own free will, Pietro."

He nods, and I watch his eyes fill with fear. It is clear to him now who I am and what I have done.

Pietro's fingers quiver as he begins to clean my other hand. "Did you know that I fancied you while we were in the *Accademia*?" he asks. He dabs at my fingers gently, taking care to wipe each crevice of my knuckles and the spaces beneath my fingernails. "You were different from the other Damica," he continues. "They glided about in their ribbons and jewels, talking about courtship, fashion, and of course, their gifts. Always comparing to each other, competing to have the finest dress or the youngest suitor. But you were not like them. You were studious. Always carrying your study tomes. You walked with an air of dignity. And now . . ." He sighs and reaches into the basin with the cloth. "How does one such as you choose to live in such wickedness?"

Wickedness.

The image of Grimstaad instantly flashes in my mind. I reach forward and grip Pietro by the wrist. "If you knew what the king and his men stood for, you would understand that my decision was not difficult."

Our gazes meet for a moment and lock in sadness. I feel a knot of guilt in my chest. Save for his ignorance, Pietro is a good man. I squeeze his hand, grieving for a fleeting moment all that is good that I have left behind in the kingdom—the flowers in my mother's garden, the towering shelves of books in the library at the *Accademia*, and Pietro—friends like Pietro. But I understand that we no longer belong to the same world.

He clears his throat and pulls back his hand. I hear a trickle of water as he rinses the last of the mud from the cloth. "Rest now . . . Viper. You have a long and arduous recovery in the weeks ahead."

I flash him a forlorn smile. "Thank you, Pietro."

In the evening, when my men come to greet me, I order them to release him unscathed.

GIVE AND TAKE

Six weeks into my recovery, and I have been laid flat on a travel cart twice. I was transported first to a nook in the mountains, and when I had regained my strength from that journey, I was taken back to camp, where I rest now in a private tent, tended to by Magdalene.

Her requests to bring me my children are turning into demands. She continues to ask with a mousy countenance, fearful that I have regained the strength to strike her down for her persistence. I must admit, I have been tempted, but Benji is far more grating. He is obstinate about it. He tells me it is unnatural for a mother to dismiss time with her children with nothing more than the flick of her wrist.

Today I am able to stand, and I examine my body with a handheld mirror. Besides my shrunken belly, I do not look any different. The same green eyes stare back at me, though with a few sleep-starved wrinkles bunching underneath them. I run my finger down my cheek. My skin is still taut; my face feels the same. My hair is still the same: long braided cords like rope, slung over my shoulders. The only evidence of motherhood is the rigid scar that runs from my pelvis to my midsection, and even with that, the pain has subsided and it feels invisible. My fever broke weeks ago, and each morning I regain more strength. By the end of my second week, I could once again sit up; today I stand, and perhaps tomorrow I will even be able to pull back the tarp of my tent.

For the first time since I arrived back at camp, Murphy has come to visit. He rouses me from my slumber but, thankfully, says nothing of my children when he enters my tent, nor does he speak to the rumors he has undoubtedly heard about my refusal to see them. This is one of the few times I am grateful for his callous disposition. He has come neither to congratulate me nor to question me. He stuffs his hands into his jacket pockets, shuffles his feet, and paces. He is unsettled—the twitch in the corner of his cheek pulls his scar and belies his calm air. He holds in his hands the map for our next siege against the kingdom.

"How many are there?" I ask.

"Twelve," he replies. I press my elbows into the blankets and sit up to listen.

"Twelve enforcers," I say. "And how many of ours do they expect will come?"

"Six," Murphy grunts, staring past me at the back of the tent. Perhaps he is considering whether my mind has been addled by the countless salts and numbing herbs that have been forced into my blood, that I will not be ready to coordinate an attack during my convalescence.

"We should strike at noon," I tell him. "They will be expecting us to come at night."

He stands as still and unwavering as a statue, not meeting my gaze. His expression is blank; I cannot read him. I fidget with the seam of my sheet, permitting the silence to pass between us.

"We should send one or two men tonight," Murphy says finally. "They will serve to distract the enforcers."

I nod. It is a smart move to throw them off. It is also a dangerous tactic, as the men we send will almost certainly be captured or killed.

I raise my chin. "I'll go," I say to Murphy.

His eyes comb over my body, and he raises an incredulous eyebrow. "Don't be foolish," he scoffs. "Magdalene will go."

"Magda?" I protest. "But she is watching—"

"I will make other arrangements for the children."

I furrow my brow. "Other arrangements? What does that mean?"

He frowns, his scar dragging down his face, writhing like a centipede with its many legs. "What does it matter, Viper? Your friends all say you have no interest in motherhood."

I bite my lip. There it is, the dreaded topic. I was confident Murphy would stay silent, but alas, the bitter rumors escape even from his tongue. I cross my arms in defiance. "And what does that matter to you, old man?"

His eye flickers wide for a moment. His nostrils flare. I do not care that I have caused him pain, for the pain of his words is far worse than any poison I may inflict upon him. He says nothing but approaches the side of my makeshift bed. His coat rustles gently, and he lowers himself so that he and I sit at eye level.

"Do you recall our dance?"

"Yes," I huff. My arms remain crossed. "How could I forget? A dead man . . . dancing with a dead woman . . . in the dead of night."

"You are more than a dead woman, Viper."

"Hardly," I reply. "My legs are barely able to carry their own weight."

"Tell me this, Viper: would the dead be capable of carrying life?"

"Life. Ha!" I scoff. Here is this detestable word. It is a peculiar one to be falling from his lips. "What does a scarred, one-eyed man know of life?"

"I know it is precious," Murphy says. "It must be preserved. That is why I brought you to the forge. So you could give life instead of taking it."

"You mean, so I could birth my children," I correct him. "Children who will be marked for death once it is known that their mother is the Viper."

"Hmph." Murphy's lips twitch and his scar writhes up his face. "You know, you are far too cynical for a *filia*."

I scowl at him. "Perhaps it is because I am not one."

"Children are resilient," he continues without acknowledging my words. "They will find their way." He leans in close to me so that I feel his breath on my ear. I hear a secret on his lips, both chiding and ominous. "Or did they not teach you anything about children in the Damica, besides how to conceive them?"

My mouth falls open, but I am able to catch my breath in my throat before it leaves my body as a gasp. Damica! He knows! He always seems to know—his single, discerning eye unearthing my secrets, always with appalling precision.

My pulse surges, wild with questions. I hide my surprise by turning my focus to my bed linens, pinching the crisscross of uneven threads between my thumb and forefinger. I furl my lips and say quietly, "And what would Murphy Hawthorne know of children?"

"I have three of my own," he says briskly. "Two daughters. One son. My eldest will be fourteen years of age this spring."

"Murphy!" I gasp. "How could you have not told me?"

He raises his chin. "You didn't ask."

I can do nothing but stare at him, wide-eyed in surprise.

"I don't just take information, Viper. I give back. I give it freely to people, when the time is right." He removes his gloves and flashes me his left hand, fanning his fingers before me. They are absent any jewels or gold. "Heed my words, Viper. I have learned this lesson:

you can do more than you believe is possible. Even with a broken heart and a bounty on your head, you can still give life to these children."

An uncomfortable silence lingers between us. So many questions hang on my tongue, but my eyelids feel heavy, my body too tired to ask.

Murphy pats my shoulder. "Get some rest. Magdalene will be in shortly to clean your incision."

"Wait." I curl my hand around his wrist. "Before you go . . ."

"What is it, Viper?"

"How did you know I was Damica?"

"You mean, other than your polished gait, your posture when you sit, your awkward language, and utterly perplexing behavior?" He breathes in deeply and sighs. "There are bulletins with your likeness appearing throughout the western region of the kingdom. It turns out that the doctor whose release you ordered had a loose tongue, *Damica Laurel Aleandri.*"

I squeeze my eyes shut and bury my face in my hands. Pietro! A spur of betrayal needles at my heart. This is how he has chosen to repay me for sparing his life?

"They all know! They know, Murphy!" My nails bite into his wrist. "What should I do? What can I do? And what will happen to Pietro?"

His hand sweeps across his forearm, and he loosens my grip on him.

"I will handle it. I have already sent Benji with four men to take care of Pietro. You know what has to happen," he says. "Listen to me, *Laurel.* Whether it's over your name or your children, despair over the inevitable does no good."

I sigh and fold my hands into my lap. My heart is raw, threads of sorrow's web woven through it and knotted at the ends. "What of the children, Murphy? You have heard what the Serpentine say . . ."

He flashes me one of his scoff-smiles. "You made up your mind weeks ago about what must happen." His lips soften, and his dark eye brightens with compassion. "It's for the best. You've made the right decision. You are of far better service to us as Viper this way."

I find myself tearfully returning his half-smile. He knows he has solved the riddle that has perplexed Benji and Magdalene and so many others. It is love, not disdain, that keeps me from my children: love of my *ammorante*, love of the Serpentine. The moment I lay those babes upon my chest, they would explore my body with their chubby fingers, their tiny eyes gazing like marbles upon my face—and it would be over. I would not be able to bring myself to lead another strike. My courage would falter; the thought of death would strike fear in my heart and reverberate through each decision I make henceforth.

I would no longer be Viper. I would be something else.

WHISPER OF LIFE

Six months have passed since the birth of my twins—three months since Murphy arranged for their transfer—and I have come to befriend Kalim, the *clericus* instrumental in persuading the council to accept the children into the Order's care. I learned he had once known my father, and I grew fond of him quickly, making weekly trips to the mausoleum just outside the gates of the Order to visit him. He brings fresh juice, coffee, and rhubarb tarts—my favorite from my childhood—and we sit by the tombs, sharing stories while the wind carries the hum of the Order's hymns to our ears.

Kalim tells me of the past, days that he and Murphy shared in *La Grondaia*, harrowing tales of Grimstaad's men and their cruelty—and how Murphy led them to their escape. I dab at my eyes as Kalim shares the names of others in captivity—some *clericii* like himself, who have done no wrong but are the victims of baseless inquisitions. He receives frequent reports of their well-being from Murphy, who monitors the prison closely. After we have dined together many times, I hold Kalim's hand and divulge to him the name of my *ammorante*. He reports no news, and I am shattered.

Kalim seems to sense the trouble of my heart, and he pours

coffee into my cup, asking me of my childhood. I tell him tales, old tales, like my father once read to me from his tomes: stories of my mother's passing, my tutelage under the Headmistress, memories of my dear Suzette, how she coaxed me to depart the *Accademia* quickly following my betrothal to the Head *Signore* of Tenuta d'Exley. Kalim is troubled by the Exley name. I learn from him that they were once benefactors of the Order and that he believes their name has since been usurped by practitioners of the dark arts.

I shed tears during the telling of my journey, and Kalim soothes me. He tells me his belief: that with no reports from *La Grondaia* of my *ammorante*, he is not there but in pursuit of me at the Tenuta d'Exley.

He also believes that with no means to combat the dark arts of Exley, my *ammorante* will find only his death.

There is no time to waste; I must depart tonight. There is no opportunity to bid farewell to Magdalene and Benji; I shed tears of regret as I toss the last of my items into my satchel and steal into the forest.

The evening sun spreads across the horizon, and soon the final streaks of yellow and pink shrink into the trees. The soles of my boots patter lightly on the early frosts of night. The moon has risen by the time I reach the river, and my path forks in two. To the east, I will find the trail back to the mountains, back to the kingdom . . . and back to the Tenuta d'Exley. And should I head west, the Orchards of Eiroda will greet me, rows of trees with slender trunks tipping their heads at my arrival.

Though my map coaxes me east, my feet insist that I turn west. I will find Murphy in the orchard. Some nights, I have spied him from afar, perched on a rock precipice with ink and parchment at his side, watching merchant caravans that seek to avoid the dangers of the main roads. On this night, I spot his thick coat veiled among a grouping of trees. He sits with his back curved over a low fire, his gloves wrapped around a bottle of spirits.

I approach him, removing my hood. "*Bellenagta*, my friend."

The bottle slips from his grasp and rolls on its side. "Viper!"

"Did I frighten you?" I retrieve his drink and pass it to him.

"Always." His lips curve up into a smile.

The bitter winds of late autumn cheat me of warmth, and I take a seat beside his fire, drawing my cloak to my body. "Is that so?"

"Hmph." He grunts, takes a long swig from his bottle, and hands it to me. "Drink. It's a cold night."

I swirl the spirits, and my tongue burns with their astringent taste. I lean back and sigh, releasing my breath into the sky.

"Murphy, will you play your fiddle for me tonight?"

He raises his eyebrow. "For what reason?"

I smile wistfully and ruefully at him, watching the contortions of his scar. I feel the sway of the moon overhead; its rays bathe his face in light and darkness.

"I have come to bid you farewell."

Murphy's posture turns rigid and raw. "You are going to *La Grondaia?*"

"Hmm."

"You believe you may die tonight."

"I believe I may perish every night," I say. "There is a saying in my native tongue: *Dolce sussurro della vita, dallelabbra di morte.*"

He frowns, and I bring the rim of the bottle back to my lips.

"What do those words mean to you?" he asks.

"Sweet whisper of life," I reply. "From—"

"Death's lips," Murphy completes the phrase brusquely. "I didn't ask for a translation. I asked what the words meant to *you.*"

The spirits ignite my palate once more, and I blink, handing the bottle back to him. He swallows the remaining liquid and tosses it aside. My head is beginning to feel heavy; I struggle to stay alert. I watch flecks of snow twirl from low-hanging clouds, catching in Murphy's hair, bleeding into his jacket.

My eyes flutter closed. "My mother taught them to me so I would cease to mourn when her illness claimed her." I sigh and listen to the crackle of the snow falling on the fire.

"When she passed," Murphy asks, "did her words bring you comfort?"

"There is no comfort in death."

"Then why do you chase it?"

I blink and dab at my forehead with my sleeve. The spirits are causing my skin to swelter, and I slip my cloak from my shoulders. I wish to brush my lips against his cheek, to feel the warmth of his guidance and protection one last time.

"Because death has chosen me."

I catch Murphy's eye roll across my bare throat. "You should choose life."

Life. Ha! I wish to remind him we have traversed this road at every pass, only to arrive at death's doorstep, always! I feel wisps of snow beginning to catch between my lashes. I have stayed too long. I reach for my cloak, and Murphy seizes my wrist.

"Choose life, Laurel."

Is such a decision still possible?

I glance past him at the bare trees grasping at the sky. The world lurches around me, heaving my thoughts across my skull until they are a mash. His command simmers in my blood.

Choose life.

Life?

The question trembles in my loins. I turn my eyes to the moon, and she smiles in my favor. My pulse is torrent and my breasts harden, for she stirs desire within my heart. I am awoken to the yearnings I abandoned the night of my dance with Murphy.

My breath is shallow. The pledge to my *ammorante* is heaved about, a hapless ship upon the moon's silver-crested waves. I wrestle against her bidding, but the strength of her pull I know well. She knows I need to thank Murphy, to say goodbye—and she beckons me to do so in a language he will understand.

"Murphy," I gasp. "Will you have me this night?"

He thrusts his lips against mine, and I taste the fiery whip of his spirits. There is no more talk of life and death. I break the seal between our mouths with the prod of my tongue, eager to explore the tips of his teeth.

His hands curve over my breasts, and he slips his fingers under the hooks of my blouse, tearing it from my body. As he fumbles with the last clasp, I plant my foot on his chest, launching him backward. I hear his back thump into the frost, and a peal of laughter escapes from my lips. It is the laughter of my childhood, long before I carried the burden of choice. The bliss comes from days my mother tended her garden while I sang hymns on the porch with my father.

My laughter awakens madness within him. He charges at me and pushes my back into the earth. I curl my legs around his torso and lock his body over mine. He tears the final clasp of my shirt and his hands trail up my body. The vagary of our deep kisses mingles with my giggles, and as his lips trail from my lips to my throat, I thrust my hips to the side with all my might, rolling him onto his back. He curses in surprise, and I straddle him, my shirt billowing triumphantly, hanging from my shoulders.

"Perhaps it is I who will have you."

He flashes me a grin, and his arm clamps around my waist. I squeal and claw at the dirt, frozen grass crunching beneath me as he flips me onto my back. He peels my skirts crudely down my hips. I arch my back and my blouse and hair spill across the ground, strewn with grit and snow. His belt clinks and drops into the grass. My skirts are still tangled around my ankles when I feel his palms spreading apart my thighs.

I groan at the pressure of his phallus entering my body, but my abdomen soon swells to his cadence: firm, modest strokes that stretch me slowly, evenly, until the tension in my brow melts like frost. I smile softly and release a sigh. A fleck of snow is nestled in Murphy's beard. I reach to brush it away, and he catches my hand, lacing his fingers through mine.

Murphy's lips curve upon my breasts, and his fingers tighten around mine. He quickens his pace, and the blood in my cheeks blazes. My breaths turn to spasms, and my loins—their pulse, their life. It's all I feel. All I know.

I howl with pleasure, and the moon blankets me in her white smile. Anxiety and euphoria flood my body, and I writhe in ecstasy. I nuzzle my cheek against Murphy's silver-stained scar, pinpricks of love's light tingling through my thighs. He is nepenthe and I am reverie; he gives seed and I give mirth.

We have, together, denied the whispers of death.

We are flesh. We are life.

SWEET DECEIVER

I awaken with crickets buzzing in my ears and a gentle frost blanketing my hair. My cheek is nestled between Murphy's bicep and breast. I watch his chest rise and fall. He is at peace. His lips lie tender, black as the night's sky. His scarred cheek appears soft—it has lost its menace and is no longer a spine but a ravine, dried and cracked from age.

My blouse is scattered across the grass like a frightened sheet. I catch the outline of my cloak nearby, the hood folded neatly.

Satisfied, the moon has released her hold on me.

It is time.

My lips brush the whiskers on Murphy's cheek. "*Arrivederci, sweet deceiver.*"

I will carry him in my memory, always.

As the morning sun rises, I tear at a knob of channa root with my teeth to purge Murphy's seed from my body. My face sours as its fibers catch in my teeth, bitter milk spreading across my palate. Murphy will be waking soon. Perhaps he has already risen and knows I am gone.

I hope he will come to understand: I could not make this trek without saying goodbye. I hope that in time, he will forgive me.

Ammorante.

I am coming for you.

GREY DAWN BREAKING

Nyri Bakkalian

ONE

She was trouble from the beginning: That, I can tell you right now. Trouble with a capital *T*. And it didn't help one bit that I got *dragged* into that fateful assignment in the first place, just on account of being the token trans woman on staff. But these things happen, and that's how I met Chloe Shaw.

Let me back up and bring you up to speed.

For about ten years now—seven and a half, when I met Chloe—the past has been leaking into the present.

We're not entirely sure when or where it started. We don't have a way of stopping it. But the government first got wind of this about ten years ago, and in its typical clunky, haphazard way, it got to work. A haphazard effort consisting of personnel borrowed from half a dozen agencies eventually formed what became JTIC, the Joint Temporal Integrity Commission, which operates under the shared purview of the Department of Defense and the National Archives and Records Administration, and . . . oh hell, I'm losing you, aren't I?

Long story short: I work for JTIC Philadelphia, where we monitor and contain temporal ruptures across a broad swath of southeastern Pennsylvania and the tristate area beyond. And when people from the past wander through these ruptures—as they often do—we resettle them and help them slowly acclimate to and integrate into life here in 2020.

Some of them—hell, *most* of them—have done well. Others aren't interested in playing by the rules, and that makes for trouble. And like I already said, Chloe Shaw was trouble with a capital *T*.

I was coming off shift in the evening that day, when Martha Stavridis found me in the locker room.

"Hunter! Hey, Hunter!" She poked her head around the long row of lockers. "Oh, there you are. Good thing I found you before you got out."

I looked up from the bench while I laced up my tanker boots. "Lookin' to grab a drink when you're done for the day, Stav?"

"Change of plans." She shook her head. "You're being preempted: the boss wants to see you in her office on the double."

Speechless? Yeah, I was speechless. "Voluntold," they used to call it in the Army. Sure, I'd live, whatever it was my superiors wanted, but *c'mon!* I had plans for the night and the weekend.

"Not to grouse," I remarked, slowly collecting myself and grousing anyway, "but I'm off-rotation for the next forty-eight hours. Couldn't Gareau find anyone else?"

Stav leaned against the lockers. "She asked for you by name, Hunter."

Sonofabitch, here we go. Clearly, I was at least going to get some kind of harangue over a fuckup and maybe even get shitcanned. Either way, getting called into the head office couldn't possibly be good.

So, bag shouldered and street shoes on, I straightened up and took a deep breath. "Let's go, Stav. Might as well get this over with. Sooner the better."

Ten minutes later, I was standing in the office of JTIC Philadelphia Director Nora Gareau, shaking her hand across a cluttered desk.

"Sergeant Hunter," she said, in deference to my old military rank. "Thanks for coming in so quickly—I understand you were scheduled to rotate off-duty for a couple days."

Probably not a shitcanning, I thought. *The commanding officer doesn't start one of those with 'Thanks.'*

"Not a problem at all, ma'am," I replied, my old military habits kicking in.

"Let me get right to the point," Gareau said, leaning back in her chair. "We're in need of a rather unique skillset of yours."

"Forgive my lack of clarity, ma'am, but which skill do you mean?" *That* was honest enough: I had *plenty* of skills after a decade in the Army.

"Lived experience as a trans woman," the director clarified. "You're public about your sexual orientation and gender identity, and in this case, those will be assets."

Fuck. I was being roped in—ticking off the "diversity" box on the checklist. No, no, no.

"Ma'am, much as I'm glad to have the Commission's support as an out trans lesbian—"

"We need you," Gareau sharply interjected. "One of our refugees is a problem you are uniquely positioned to address in a manner acceptable to all parties concerned."

Translation from corporatese: you've been *voluntold*, Hunter.

Slowly, I relaxed my arms from their reflexive "parade rest" clasp behind my back. Gareau gestured to a seat opposite the desk. When we were both seated, I folded my arms and subtly tilted my head back. "Who's our 'problem,' ma'am?"

"Name's Chloe Shaw," Gareau replied. "Private, F Company, Seventeenth Pennsylvania Cavalry, here from the aftermath of Gettysburg."

At *Gettysburg*. I winced. That was a case I'd heard about, but only just a bit.

"How am *I* suited to help Private Shaw, ma'am?"

"She keeps escaping our secure housing in Delaware County. Been butting heads with the other refugees ever since she arrived too. Things are good for LGBTQ people today, but people from the late eighteenth and early-to-mid-nineteenth century aren't quite as understanding."

Things are good. I had to fight hard to not roll my eyes right out of my head at that. Good? With the number of trans people murdered every year around the world and with anti-gay legislation still popping up like the plague despite every ounce of good progress?

"And I'm going to be involved in shepherding her because I'm lesbian and trans."

"Lesbian, trans, *and* a combat veteran," Gareau added. "To oversee a nineteenth-century lesbian combat veteran. Who better positioned for the role than you, Hunter?"

I nodded slowly. "Compliance on the part of displaced persons is essential to our mission of safe resettlement and temporal integration, and the good private is proving . . . noncompliant, then?"

Gareau suddenly leaned forward to gesture pointedly with the tip of her stylus. "A horse soldier from 1863 on the streets of 2020 Philadelphia is a *liability*, Hunter," she spat. "We just brought her back from her third attempted breakout, and luckily she didn't attract much attention. Our mission, our facilities, the temporal rifts that bring people like Private Shaw to the present—all of it is classified for the public's safety and peace of mind. So we—*you*—need to ensure that this woman gets with the program. For her sake and for all our sakes."

Translation from corporatese: she's *your* problem now, Hunter.

"I'm going to forward the relevant files to you immediately," Gareau concluded. "You're to take custody of Private Shaw immediately: Conference Room Four, B Level. Be aware that she's currently under guard."

Custody. My head spun. "Excuse me, ma'am? *Custody?*"

"Yes, Hunter, you're taking custody of Private Shaw. If she wants the present, she can have it, as long as she's under your direct, 'round-the-clock supervision. Consider all other present duties superseded. As of this moment, Chloe Shaw is your assignment."

The director dismissed me then. It's a good thing she did; I wasn't happy. Not one bit. I glanced at the relevant documentation on my work tablet as I made my way to B Level. Twenty-eight years old, survivor of some of the Civil War's worst fighting, now a refugee in a strange time. Everybody she ever knew, dead.

How would *I* feel if I'd gotten thrown forward 150 years while I was in Syria, fighting in Raqqa, or riding a shotgun on a Stryker down the southwestern MSR out of Qamishli, sole survivor of the Tenth Mountain Division in some godforsaken future time?

Maybe by then, I mused, *society would've gotten its shit together about being a little better when it comes to people like me.*

I got my first look at my horse soldier when I came into the conference room. She hurried to her feet as the door opened. She couldn't have been more than five foot three inches, but God, her gaze was like *fire.* And in those suspendered riding pants and that flannel? I think I felt a little weak.

Butch women, dude. Tellin' ya.

"I'll be outside if you need me," said the sentry who'd let me in. Then he turned, nodded quietly, and excused himself.

We were alone and eyeing each other silently. Words eluded me. I was still flustered and reeling from the sudden change of assignment.

"That's an infantry horn." Quiet surprise spread over her face. "W-what?"

"Your arm. Those are quite a few tattoos, but you've got an infantry horn." A sly grin warmed her face. "Waiting on a soldier?"

With the early summer weather getting hot, I'd tried to wear short sleeves with my work clothes as often as I could, as much to show off my full-sleeve tattoos as to keep cool.

"N-no." I shook my head with a sheepish chuckle. "I *was* a soldier. A sharpshooter—Regular Army. I was in for ten years."

Her eyebrows rose. "Without getting caught?"

That's complicated, I thought. Then, in the interest of simplicity, I nodded slowly. "The Army doesn't really care what you are anymore so long as you're healthy, can shoulder a rifle, and can do your duty." I paused, as much to collect my thoughts as for emphasis. "I'd say 'a lot's changed,' but you've probably been hearing that a lot."

She rolled her eyes and nodded slowly. "Every time I bone something."

Bone something. You have no idea how hard it was to keep myself from cracking up. English has changed since the fighting at Gettysburg.

'Boning'? How the fuck am I gonna survive this assignment without cracking up at all the wrong times?

"I'd be glad to swap stories if you'd like. Seems we're going to be seeing a lot of each other."

Her smile faded. "So you're here to take me back to the village."

"No." I shook my head. "No, Private, I'm here to take you to Philadelphia. The Commission, in its infinite wisdom, has seen fit to release you into my custody and entrust *me* with your acclimation to this time period." At that, I chuckled. "May God have mercy on us both."

I offered her a hand to shake. "Sergeant First Class Leigh Hunter. Pleased to meet you."

She eyed my hand in suspicion and briefly wrinkled her nose, as if in disgust. Then, taking it in her own hand, she gave it a firm squeeze just as our eyes met.

"Chloe Shaw," she said. The fire was back in her eyes, as if to say, *You can't have me.*

Like I said: trouble with a capital *T.*

Little did I know that, in time, she'd have *me.*

TWO

She was right to chafe as much as she did under Commission supervision: they—*we*—had fucked her over. When the Commission picked her up, Chloe was still under the male alias with which she'd joined the Army in 1861.

There were a lot of people who joined the Union Army. To my eyes, as a trans woman, some of the ones who historians like to call women were clearly trans men: people assigned female at birth who saw an opportunity to be seen as who they truly were, seized it, and never let it go. Albert D. J. Cashier is probably my favorite example: he lived his entire life from the Civil War onward as Albert D. J. Cashier. So who the hell are we to say, "No, this person was really a woman"?

But then there were others, people like Chloe Shaw, who were women that assumed a male alias because that was the only way they'd be able to go to war. This came with the higher level of privilege afforded a man, even outside the Army.

Among other temporally displaced people living under Commission supervision, having that alias voided instantly made Chloe's life harder. Under the stress of being displaced, the strain of discrimination she'd blissfully escaped for two years in the Union Army, and the pressure of having her movements restricted, was it any wonder that she'd escaped so many times? As a woman who, according to the files from Gareau, was clearly attracted to other women among the displaced people she'd lived with, she ran into a further layer of bullshit from her nominal peers.

And now *I* had her and was charged with the single-handed mission of making things right. If she'd been screwed that many times over, how could I really make things right? How could I convince her that she was going to be okay? How on earth was I going to manage *that*? And I mean, the present was no utopia either, though at least *some* things had changed. But where the hell was I supposed to even *begin*?

The first few days passed quietly enough. We mostly kept to my apartment in south Philly. While I couldn't know what it meant to be thrown out of my own time, she and I were soldiers alike. And in the wake of a hard-fought battle, sometimes the best and most precious thing is finding some utter peace and quiet.

We talked a bit, sure, but on the whole, she was almost as wary of me as she was of stepping outside the door. That many times getting her ass hauled back in when she so much as attempted to get into the city, and now she was squarely *in* it. From her perspective, the hesitance was understandable: surely there had to have been *some* hidden catch. So I took the opportunity to get some remote work done: paperwork, overdue reports, things of that sort. I'd know if she slipped out, so I let her have free rein of the place and otherwise tried to get on with life while we both caught our breath and adjusted to the new normal.

I think it was the third day when she asked the burning question about the flag that hung from the living room wall. I'd been working on a secure laptop from my perch on the edge of the beat-up old sofa when she brought it up. There were a couple, so I assumed she'd asked about the military ones.

"Well, I mean, the Army flag is obvious, but the guidon's from my last unit: Second Battalion, Fourteenth Infantry Regiment." I pointed to the little blue swallow-tailed guidon with its white numbers and crossed rifles.

She shook her head. "The other one—this one." She was pointing at the rainbow flag.

"Ah. *That* one. Yeah." I pinched the bridge of my nose and sighed. *Shit, here we go.*

Language by which we express things as complicated as gender, sexual orientation, and sexuality have changed a lot. But with that in mind, I tried in that moment to sum it up: the banner that represented the broad range of gender identity and sexual orientation; a banner that was only a couple decades older than me.

When I finished, she tapped at her chin and eyed me pensively.

"And you hang this here flag because . . ." A glimmer of realization appeared. *"Oh!"*

"And that, Private," I said, "is why you've been entrusted to my care."

She seemed to relax at that, at least a little. And in the days and weeks that followed, she grew on me pretty quickly as she needed minimal guidance as her acclimation to the present continued.

She knew how to take care of herself, first of all, and generated neither bullshit nor drama. Maybe it was her no-nonsense nineteenth century sensibility, maybe it was the military background and discipline that she and I had in common, but at any rate I found it incredibly refreshing. She'd already settled a bit into the twenty-first-century basics—stuff like showers and coffee machines—and whatever else of the myriad things that were new to her, she could handle amazingly well. No nonsense, no hemming and hawing—some frustration, sure, but otherwise she got right to business.

We found we had a hell of a lot in common, apart from the gay thing and the now-ended Army career. I was from Millbourne—a short El ride right over the city line—and she was from Norristown—just a bit farther northwest on the light rail out of Sixty-Ninth Street. I didn't have to explain what a *train* was, obviously, but the first time we rode the El was, as it were, a *trip*.

Memo to self, I scrawled in my note-keeping app that night. *Point out where automated announcements are likely going to happen. Gareau isn't going to be happy if your high-value asset dies of shock.*

We each had a complicated relationship with the city too. To me, it's been ever-present and easy to get to; back before I joined the Army, it was literally just down the hill along Market Street, big and loud and smelly and strange, yet somehow utterly compelling too. For her, it was a bit farther off, in a time before rapid mass transit and cars, but a focal point all the same: home, *ish*, but not quite.

Now, 150 years out of time, Chloe was faced with an unenviable conundrum: the city she'd thought she'd known wasn't the same anymore. I would always have an awkward situation on my hands when I came back from a tour of duty, but this was worse. The streets didn't run the same way, the blocks didn't smell the same way, the gas lights were gone, there were subways—and all that was just the tip of the iceberg. Somehow, though, she never gave up.

I tried to maintain at least *some* modicum of professional detachment. But like I said, she'd been growing on me. And as she slowly, steadily, caught up on a century and a half, I found that the gulf was narrowing.

Finally, there came a day I'll never forget, when the gulf between us started to close. We were in Washington Square Park, in the shade under the tall trees. We'd tended to be formal up 'til then—Sergeant Hunter, Private Shaw. She certainly hadn't objected: maybe the military formality was more comfortable among the utter loss of footing in an era and world so unknown. But it was starting to grate on *me*.

You have to understand; it's not that I'm at all ashamed. I came of age during my decade in the Army. I made a whole lot of friends for life there, and by the end, I'd done more, seen more, and experienced more than I could've imagined when I first joined, for better and for worse.

To be called *Sergeant* for this long again, though. It took me back to my final days in uniform—and not in a good way. Those were the days when my gender dysphoria was in overdrive and I'd gotten to the point where I just plain couldn't ignore it anymore. And it took me to my last tour, to the fighting in Syria and the Kurdish women I'd fought alongside—and the ones I hadn't been able to safely guide home.

One way or another, I hadn't made my peace with *Sergeant* yet. And after that much time in such close quarters, I felt like I could finally put my foot down. So I stopped her. Gently, with just a raised hand and as calm an expression on my face as I could muster.

"Leigh," I said to her gently, almost breathily, careful not to slip into my rougher "staff NCO" voice. "Just Leigh. Please."

"Excuse me?"

"There really isn't any sense in . . . I mean, there shouldn't be any need for us to . . . fuck, please don't feel obligated to call me *Sergeant* anymore, is what I mean." I paused, leaned back against the park bench, and rubbed the bridge of my nose. "I haven't been in the Army for a good three years, and besides . . . it feels wrong now coming from you. So . . . call me Leigh. No *Agent* or *Miss*, either, please; that's a little too formal for my taste. Just call me Leigh. Please?"

Much to my chagrin, I was actually *blushing*. My eyeline had dropped to my knees, and my hands fidgeted with the sleeve of my rapidly cooling coffee cup.

"A-all right," she replied. "So long as I can return the favor, Leigh."

She was smiling. I think that was the first time she made my heart melt.

"You've got yourself a deal, Chloe."

THREE

Things went smoothly for a while. She was staying in her lane, and I was doing well guiding her with a relatively gentle hand through all the little intricacies of integration. Then there came a day when I had to go and fuck it all up.

All because we went to a *bar*. And well, all because of *me*.

So. Little by little, I'd tried to ease her into the realities of life in the present for a woman attracted to other women. I did what I could to explain the good and the bad things: yes, two women could be a lot more open about romance, could even get married, but no, it's not utopia by a longshot. There's a long way to go yet before we have anything that resembles real equality. I told her about some of the history of the past half-century too: about the Dewey's Lunch Counter Sit-In and about the brave black trans women who'd fought back at the Stonewall Inn in New York and started a movement that continues today.

But that trans stuff in particular was the sticking point, for me. I was too chickenshit to really go much further than the perfunctory little bit I'd mentioned along the way. And I certainly hadn't told her that *I myself* was trans. It wasn't even *her*, mind you—it was my policy with most people. Contrary to what some scum would have you believe, a person is under no more obligation to tell anyone that they're trans than that they're gay. It's their own story to tell. And after ten years in the Army, I've learned to trust my gut when it comes to watching my own back. Inasmuch as I was out at work, beyond that I tended to keep a low profile about my transness.

Every time I see a trans person for whom it's a nonissue, a trans person who is just out and proud and thinks nothing of it, I'm thrilled—really, I am. That's the world I want to be living in. But that's not the world I've seen firsthand, and it sure isn't the strange and unfamiliar new future world into which people like Chloe keep wandering.

You need to understand this. This is *why* things fell apart as badly as they did the night at the bar. Because I was too chickenshit.

I was the one who suggested it first. Things were going so well, I decided to throw caution to the wind and offer the possibility of something new, something maybe a little risky but which offered the opportunity for good things. *Immersive education*, my teacher friends call it.

"Let's go to a dyke bar," is what I said. At her puzzled head tilt, I hurriedly added, "No, uh . . . no dikes like with the little Dutch boy. This is more or less a regular bar but focused especially for lesbians."

She perked up at *that*.

It's a funny thing, that word. *Lesbian*, in its modern meaning, was only first used in the 1870s. She missed its origins by *that* much.

Anyway, it was all good, that night at Le Chat Noir, up on Twelfth and Walnut. She was kind of breathless at first but seemed to take to it rather well after a little while.

It wasn't until we were heading back that shit hit the fan.

We moseyed on home at a leisurely pace, taking in the warm summer evening air as we made our way southward. There were a lot of bars and other little watering holes along the way. Not all of them were queer-friendly, and many of them had tables out in the summer and partygoers who lingered outside and harassed passersby.

That's when it happened.

"Hey . . . hey . . . it's a girl?"

"Nah. That ain't a girl."

"Hey! Hey!"

My feet were moving fast now, my hand clamped around Chloe's shoulder. We couldn't have this talk now, but if I could move her along, we could at least get out of harm's way.

"HEY! SIR!" I didn't turn my head, but I could hear the footsteps hurrying behind me.

"Leigh," Chloe protested. "What's happening? Slow down!"

"Shut up and walk," I growled, stomach heaving. We veered into an alley. "They're after me."

"Why are they calling you *sir?*"

"They've clocked me." Fuck, I was slipping: how the hell did I explain *clocked* when I might get my ass and *hers* killed? How could I explain these things in a rush in a Philadelphia alley in the midst of what was supposed to be a pleasantly tipsy stroll back?

"Hey, *tranny*, I'm talking—"

My memory gives out then. Chloe says they closed the gap, tried to grab for me, and a scuffle turned into a fight. It was all instinct after that, old habits born from combat. I remember blurs of motion, flashes of fear and panic, fists striking flesh, and the sudden, familiar tang of blood in my nostrils. There was a distant bloodcurdling scream; only after the fact did I find out that it was my own.

The fuckers ran. They were lucky they did.

The police never showed up, and honestly it was better they didn't. Close though we'd gotten, Chloe was still my *mission*. And what the hell was that going to mean to a city cop, especially with my blood alcohol level as high as it probably was?

I can't remember messaging for assistance, but apparently I did somewhere along the way because an unmarked JTIC vehicle came to get us. We were hauled off to the Commission offices under Franklin Institute, separated for a good long while, treated, debriefed extensively, and finally dumped unceremoniously into the very conference room where we'd met.

She came in after I did, under guard. I had my head in my hands, certain already that this hangover was going to be a bitch, in more ways than usual.

"I don't understand you, Leigh Hunter," she finally said. "You come from an incredible world, you're a fascinating woman, you give me every reason to connect with you, and then you fail to trust me when it counts the most?"

When I looked up, she was standing beside me.

"Look . . ."

"Stop," she said. "Stop talking."

The words died on my lips as she pulled out the seat beside me and sat.

"I may not understand everything, but I'd have thought by now I'd proved to you that at least I was essaying to do so."

Any words I might've had evaporated at that.

"Do you truly believe," she asked, quieter now, "that I'd think any less of you for the circumstances of your birth?"

It took me a while to meet her gaze.

"No. This world is cruel, and I've had to learn to protect this part of me, but . . . no."

"Then," she said, "let's start from there."

FOUR

It isn't easy to face your ghosts, whatever form they may take. I can tell you that right now. And as combat veterans, Chloe and I both have our share of ghosts. Hers live in the hills of Virginia and the fields of Maryland and central Pennsylvania, mine live along asphalt tracks through the Syrian desert and in the quiet little corners of mountain hamlets in Afghanistan, but we both have them. Not everyone can, or even should, go face their ghosts *in situ.*

But it was a few weeks after the post-bar fight that she suddenly told me one day, when we were out for a run at Penn's Landing, that she wanted to do it.

"I want to see Gettysburg," she said.

Somehow, I felt obligated to talk her out of it. I mean, come on, revisiting the site of a trauma is tough enough, but when that trauma is the Battle of *Gettysburg*? That takes a special kind of nerve.

"Are you *sure*?" I asked finally. We'd paused to catch our breath, sitting perched on the concrete seawall that overlooked the Delaware. Across the river on the New Jersey side, at anchor in Camden, was the battleship *New Jersey.*

"I think I'm ready. I think it's finally come time."

In the weeks since the fight, the Commission had been keeping a closer eye on us, but surely if we kept a low profile, things would be okay. I checked in with Gareau over a morning vid call the next day—I got a tongue-lashing and a "For god's sake, Hunter, don't get into any fights" but otherwise met with no opposition when I asked for permission. So. We packed our shit, got into my Subaru, and hauled ass westward from Philly's urban sprawl and on into the rolling greens of central Pennsylvania, where the terrain starts to rise abruptly toward the peaks of the Appalachian Range.

Even on my own, I've always enjoyed driving through my home state. There's just so damn much to see. And some people think of Pennsylvania as one entity, but to me, they're mistaken. Whoever says that probably hasn't lived here; if they've visited, they've probably only blown through Center City in Philly.

If anything, Pennsylvania is really a mishmash of five different things in one: Southeastern Pennsylvania and the Philly area, Northeastern Pennsylvania (which, let's be honest, is really an extension of New York City), Northern Pennsylvania (sorry, Coudersport, but if the nearest big city is Olean, New York, does anybody *really* live there?), Pittsburgh and Western Pennsylvania (which includes parts of West Virginia and Ohio, in a way), and Central Pennsylvania. And—sorry, California and Texas, but I'm allowed to bitch—it's *big*.

So as much as I *like* Gettysburg, it's always a little odd being in Central Pennsylvania after the long drive west through Lancaster and Harrisburg and then south into Adams County. *This,* I have to remind myself, *is still the same damn huge-ass state.*

There wasn't much room for those kinds of lovingly distasteful reflections this time, though. Chloe was on my mind, and whenever she wasn't asleep or taking in the landscape with wide-eyed wonder, she was asking questions or offering running commentary. Think about it: for someone from an era of horses and carriages, when even the country's rail network was still growing, the idea of this massive highway for cars utterly boggled the mind. And yet here it was, stretching out for-seemingly-ever and ever to the western horizon and far beyond.

I have to admit, though: somewhere around Lancaster, I found myself musing about the look on her face if we did a coast-to-coast drive. It would be a hell of a thing seeing the look on her face at the sight of the Mississippi River or upon hitting the Pacific Coast and swimming in the waters of Big Sur at the end of the trip. Sure beats having to sail around Cape Horn or take a train across the Isthmus of Panama or whatever they did in her time.

We stopped to stretch our legs at a rest station along the way, somewhere short of Harrisburg. I waited a little longer than I should have before I intervened to help her work a soda fountain in the turnpike rest stop. As good as she was getting, *that* kind of fight with technology was just too damn funny, and I was done fighting my feeling that, gods, this girl—who I'd begun in moments of idle fancy to think of as *my* girl—was just too damn cute.

After four hours or so on the road from Philly, lots of conversation, a hastily downed bag of chips, and a soda disaster averted by wet wipes and a metric fuck-ton of napkins, we finally got clear of Harrisburg and maneuvered around Chambersburg. At last, we were finally over the backroads of Adams County and hurrying down the Chambersburg Pike into Gettysburg.

As we started to crest the rise past the little municipal airport, I glanced at Chloe again to find the curiosity and wonder replaced by a quiet, ashen stare. I had to remind myself: for her, it's been no time at all. When she left, the fires of war were still smoldering, and the wounded were still on or near the field. Now here we were, passing Buford's statue on the Chambersburg Pike, and there were statues and historical buildings and crass touristy junkshops with increasing frequency as we came into town.

How would you *feel?* I asked myself as I had off and on in all the time we'd been together. *How would you feel if you skipped over the next 150 years and some strange future soldier took you on a tour of Raqqa?*

I parked the car in the huge, rambling lot of the Gettysburg National Military Park's visitor center. Any humor was gone now. Though only one of us had actually *been* there, we both knew— though in vastly different ways—what it meant to be there now. We both knew the pain the earth here carried and the ghosts, literal or otherwise, that lingered.

Without undoing my seatbelt, I leaned against the steering wheel and turned to meet her gaze. "You're sure you want to do this?" I asked her gently. "We don't have to do anything you don't want to. You just say the word and we can leave anytime. There's plenty of other shit to do around here, after all."

For a moment she was quiet. "No, no," she finally said. "I, uh . . . I was there. I was there. I know how terrible it was. And if it's become this important to what the Union became, I need to see this place for myself, as it is now. So um, I, uh . . . I need to know."

Shit, I couldn't look her in the eye at that. My eyes were on the battle scars tracing dark lines around my hands.

"Yeah," I said quietly. "It was no Gettysburg, but I've been there. And I'd feel the same in your position."

"Rock, uh . . . *Raqqa*," she said, tripping over the syllables of the name of my personal hell. "Wasn't it?"

I nodded quietly. "Raqqa."

I don't open up about my last tour of duty to just anyone. Yet at the beginning, perhaps out of a sense of obligation to showing her just what we had in common as soldiers, I'd filled her in on not only the past century and a half of American military history in general but my own career in particular. It was bits and pieces, dribs and drabs at first, but somehow, once I started talking about it, I couldn't stop. A little here, a little there, and now a veteran of Brandy Station and Gettysburg knew the story of a veteran of Kobani and Raqqa.

As guilty as I constantly felt for daring to compare my pain to hers, we'd bonded over it.

"War is war," she offered. "Doesn't matter where. After what you saw in Syria? You know that as well as I do."

"Yeah, and war is all hell," I added, almost reflexively.

"General Sherman," she answered, recognizing the words of one of her era's greatest soldiers without missing a beat. "Right?"

I nodded. "The man knew what he was talking about."

In the end, we wound up leaving the visitor center rather quickly. This, too, was my fault; I figured rather than go for the slick multimedia crap, let's start with the Cyclorama, the wraparound painting of the battle at its height. At least *that*, in its original form, dated back to her century.

The place is supposed to leave an impression, sure, but to someone for whom—before coming unstuck in time—the battle was just three days before, it was a little too much too fast.

"Leigh. *Leigh!*" She tugged at my sleeve with increasing urgency. "I can't. I have to . . . we have to go!"

There's still a part of me that pales at the idea that I can compare what I went through to someone who fought at fuckin' *Gettysburg*. I mean, how on Earth could I ever show that kind of nerve? *Please!*

But war is war, and war is all hell. Or . . . hell, General Joshua Chamberlain fits better here: "war is destruction, word and deed." It doesn't matter if it's on the killing-fields of Gettysburg or in house-to-house fighting in fucking Raqqa. The fact of the matter is that battle is terrible.

So I took her by the hand and led her out until we got to the car and she could breathe again.

Eventually, she calmed enough to speak.

"I don't know if I can handle this museum. I'm sorry, Leigh . . . I don't know if I can handle this. Not now. Not yet."

I simply nodded. Then, despite myself, I didn't hold my tongue.

"I get it."

She cocked her head, turning to look up at me. "You what?"

"I, uh . . . I understand." I sighed. "At least, I think I understand. Honestly, I don't know if I could go to Raqqa anytime in the foreseeable future myself, and it's been *years* for me. But . . . but then it's not the same. It's not here. It's not American on American. And as terrible as it was, it just doesn't—"

"What was it you said," she interjected. "Sherman's words?"

"War is all hell," I murmured, looking away in embarrassment.

"Leigh. *Leigh*," she said insistently. "I think you *do* understand."

Honestly? I was relieved by the affirmation.

"You, ah . . . you have no idea," I stammered, voice starting to choke up, "just how much respect I have for you. Even for being here at all."

I was relieved. And what's more, I was blushing.

Her hand was on my shoulder.

We had an early dinner in one of the restaurants in central Gettysburg, surrounded by Civil War kitsch and the inane banter of tourists: just the two of us, women brought together beyond time, survivors alike, each haunted by our share of ghosts. After the brief visit to the visitor center, we'd ambled around town for a while. Now, we sat with the enormity of it all, of the battle and the past and the 150 years we were still trying to bridge, though we'd managed, somehow, to grow close in spite of them.

Sometimes we talked, but more often we ate in silence. And that was just fine—no bullshit, just like we both preferred.

"I had a thought," Chloe finally said over the last potatoey remnants of what had been a hearty dish of colcannon.

I looked up from a sadly-too-shitty glass of some new IPA from some sadly-too-shitty new hipster-infested brewery out near Pittsburgh. "Hm?"

"All these unit statues and general statues." She gestured out the window at the Chambersburg Pike with a spoon. "They built one to ours, right?"

I had to look it up on my phone, but I found it. "Yeah, there it is. Seventeenth Pennsylvania Cav. Big ol' granite slab just north up the road a bit."

Fifteen minutes later, we were there on Buford Avenue, just off the Mummasburg Road, with cars zipping past mere feet away as we looked up at the mighty stone-carved sentinel overlooking the long-silent battlefield.

"Seventeenth Pennsylvania Cavalry," I murmured, as my eyes

passed over the chiseled inscription. "Second Brigade, First Division, Cavalry Corps, Army of the Potomac."

"Sarn't Ferree," Chloe said in recognition of the granite bas-relief cavalry sergeant. "They . . . they got his nose wrong." She chuckled. "Somehow, I am *not* surprised."

Crickets chirred as we paced around the granite slab.

"The regiment," she read from the obverse inscription, "in whole or in part participated in fifty-five engagements, among which were the following: Gettysburg, Chancellorsville, Mine Run, Wilderness, Todd's Tavern, Sheridan's First Expedition, Cold Harbor, Trevillian Raid, Deep Bottom, Fishers Hill, Winchester, Gordonsville, Goochland C.H., Five Forks, Sailor's Creek, Appomattox."

Then she circled back to stand beside me.

"I . . . I should've been there." She sighed. "Riding right alongside 'em. I should've seen that through to the end."

She was still my charge then—my mission. So in hindsight, while we'd certainly become friends, I'm still not entirely sure when exactly it was that we became a couple. But then, is there ever a real, hard-and-fast date for something like that? I guess, from the vantage point of two and a half years on—with her released from Commission oversight with the blessing of the Powers That Be and with us living together as partners—it doesn't much matter in the grand scheme of things. But if you were to ask me to point to a date, I think we both knew, right there and then, on that evening on the side of the Mummasburg Road, that we'd become something more.

How did I know?

Because my heart was full and my eyes were wet.

Because I felt her hand close around mine and *squeeze*.

Because there was *something* in her suddenly tearful voice when she finally spoke again that made it so obvious.

"I'm glad you're here," she said simply. "You understand."

"Hey," I murmured around the tears. "There's nowhere I'd rather be."

I knew then because—for what must've been the longest time, crying together there in the monument's shadow, surrounded by our shared ghosts, near and far—we held each other in the Gettysburg fields as the darkness gathered around tall grasses and distant trees standing their decades-long sentinel.

Mission be damned. From that moment on, I was *hers*.

VOICES AND VISIONS

K.A. FOX

ASH

I let myself hang limp over Langer's shoulder, ignoring the urge to tense or wince every time he purposely banged a dangling part of me into first the walls and then the stair railing. I kept my breaths deep and even, the peace of the unconscious. I didn't flinch when his wandering hands grabbed my ass, but I promised myself he'd get a taste of Messer when this was finished. One bite for every unwelcome touch.

I was keeping count. For justice.

I didn't react when I heard the metal-on-metal grinding of a key in a lock or even peek through my lashes when a door creaked in response. My body hit the stone floor hard, but still I focused on my breathing. And the count running in my head. Langer had worked himself up to thirteen by the time the door clanged shut behind him.

He laughed, taunting me from his place of safety. "Enjoy the dark, Chara. He'll be coming for you."

I waited, still and silent, as he plodded his way back up the stairs, joking with the men who'd followed him down. I waited even after I heard the cellar door slam and the lock twist. I opened my eyes slowly as quiet filled the space around me, not twitching a muscle until I was sure they were gone.

I was right where I wanted to be. In this cage, they wouldn't consider me a threat.

I rolled to my side, ignoring the aches that nagged at me. Slowly, I scanned the cage I was in, letting my eyes adjust to the darkness. For now, I could just make out vague shapes as I eased back against the wall. My fingers brushed what felt like an old sheepskin, but I couldn't bear to touch it further to confirm. Athair above only knew what it might really be. Or what might be living on it.

Silence pressed down on me. This was the hardest part of the job: waiting. Patience was one of the virtues I never had been able to learn very well, though the Sisters had fought that battle as if my very soul depended on it. Waiting made me itchy underneath my very skin, an itch that was hard not to scratch. Not understanding the importance of waiting when required to led one to make bad decisions. I'd made plenty of those.

Even just thinking of the Sisters conjured their voices in my head. *"You're stubborn, girl. Not stupid. You can learn."* Those had been hard lessons. This waiting would be especially painful if I had to listen to them the whole time.

A sigh escaped me. I was surprised when it was answered by a snore. I froze in place, waiting for any other sound. There was a brief rustling off to my right, then another snore. Then nothing. Silence reigned again. I crawled along the wall, careful, my hand out to feel ahead. When my fingers brushed metal bars, I relaxed. Whatever, or whoever, was sleeping down here was outside my cage. For now, I was safe.

I tucked myself into the farthest corner, my head against the chill stone. More silence. It grew heavier as the minutes passed, weighing me down. I closed my eyes, whispering old rhymes to myself, my low voice cutting through the quiet. When the rhymes could no longer defeat the silence and the voices inside my head rose in volume, demanding my attention, I sang.

Softly, I sang an old lullaby first, then a song of the Sisters, and finally an ancient Shelta Cant. Over and over and over, I sang until the melodies soothed me and the voices eased. Calmness settled itself into my bones, and I rested.

It was the scratching that woke me. Repeatedly, something brushed over the stone, a harsh, rhythmic sound. A sound I recognized, like knives being sharpened.

I waited, letting my vision readjust to the daylight of the dungeon. Instead of black, now there were varying shades of gray. Small chinks in the wall allowed some airflow high above me, and a dim light trickled in. I began searching the pockets of lighter gray, until it came again. That sound. Next to my cage.

I tensed, looking immediately to the bars that separated me from whatever had been sleeping on the other side. And my breath stopped.

"Oh my." It wasn't the Sisters whispering to me this time. It was another voice, younger, sadder. Rose, she'd said her name was. *"Such pretty eyes watching you. Run away. Far away."*

I snorted. Running away wasn't an option, and I'd been shit at it all my life. But I couldn't disagree. Those eyes were pretty. And they were definitely watching me. Intently.

"So, ya're the singer, then." The voice that belonged to the eyes was rough, like it wasn't used often, and very deep. The sharpening sound came again, even though the eyes didn't move from me.

"So, you're the snorer, then," I answered back from my corner. One of the voices in my head whispered cautions about poking at dragons, but I ignored it.

His laugh was warm and sudden, like he couldn't contain it. I relaxed a fraction but didn't allow myself to move any closer.

"Snorin'? Didn't realize I did that." When I didn't say anything, his head cocked to the side, the eyes studying me from a different angle now. "Chara, huh? Interestin' name."

"It's not my name. Langer just said that to dig at me. See if I would respond."

"He's an arse, that one. Can't wait to have my chance at him."

I agreed but had to stake my claim. "You can have a go at him when I'm done. He's got thirteen bites owed me."

"Bites? Sounds like he racked up quite a debt."

"Aye."

We stayed where we were, surveying each other, with nothing else to say. And the silence began to press in. I held out as long as I could, but soon the voices inside began to clamor and I was forced to start reciting rhymes again. Under my breath, the barest sound was just enough to break through the stillness. Enough to ease them back down so I could concentrate.

"Ya aren't good with quiet, are ya?" His voice was smoother this time, like our minuscule conversation had rubbed some of the edges off.

I stiffened. Admitting weakness was something I didn't do. And admitting a large one to a man I didn't know couldn't happen. Shouldn't happen. No matter how pretty his eyes might be.

I could feel him watching me when I didn't answer, but I was still surprised when he spoke again. "It's the darkness that gets me. Makes it hard not to see things. It's taken me a long time to get used to the visions. Darkness seems to bring them on more. Harder to pretend they aren't happenin'."

I rested against the wall, shocked at how easily he'd offered up that bit of himself. Grateful that he didn't push me to do the same. So I gave in to honesty. I had no idea how long I'd be down here waiting. I might as well get it over with.

"Silence is . . ." I paused, searching my mind for the right words. "It's too much sometimes. The voices inside my head get so loud, I can't focus." I waited for a comment, but none came. "If I can break up the silence, the voices quiet down."

"Ya know, that's a very reasonable explanation from a woman what says she hears voices. Makes perfect sense to me." There was no tease in his words, no laughter. Just thoughtful consideration.

I sighed. "Pretty sure you're the first person to ever consider my explanation reasonable. Most people just assume I'm crazy and leave me be."

Now that made him laugh. "Most people are too afraid to admit we've all got a bit of crazy in us. I'm not one of those people."

"My thanks, then. I'm glad we can be crazy in this hole together."

Another laugh, which I was surprised to find I truly enjoyed the sound of. "Excellent. But if we're both goin' to be crazy, we should at least know who we're bein' crazy with. Since Chara is not your name, what shall I call ya?"

"What's your name?" Names were important. If he was willing to share his, I'd consider sharing mine.

"Fair enough. I'll go first." His face drew even closer to the bars, enough that I could make out fair skin and thick stubble under those pretty eyes. "I'm Ry." He stuck his hand through the bars to my side, his palm up, open to reveal there was nothing hidden. It was an invitation. Or maybe a test.

I left my safe corner and moved carefully toward where he waited. He made no sudden moves, didn't say anything else. He just smiled as he let me come to him. Like a hunter would let his prey draw close before the killing shot.

"Oh my. Such a beautiful smile. Run away. Now." Rose's voice was almost ringing inside my skull. *"It's never safe when they're so lovely."* Other voices rose to join hers, their words of warning becoming a chorus inside my head. Even the Sisters tried to make themselves heard.

I refused to listen, intent on the man in front of me. "Fair enough," I mimicked. "I'm Ash."

I slid my hand into his. He squeezed mine gently, his large fingers dwarfing my smaller ones. His calloused palm brushed mine and my skin grew warm against his.

He didn't comment on my name, just squeezed my hand again and then released it. He rested himself against the bars, no doubt waiting to see if I would retreat back to my corner. I stayed where I was, within what I knew was grabbing distance if he was so inclined. I'm not without my defenses. He'd tested me. Now I was testing him.

I leaned in. He was easier to see now, the light having brightened a bit above our heads. "Your accent. It's familiar. Like you're from here. Or nearby. But not quite right."

"Ya got a good ear. Must be the musical part of ya." Ry paused, taking a deep breath. "I've been gone a while. Too long, maybe."

"Why'd you come back?" I found myself a little desperate for an answer, another glimpse into who this man was.

"Family business."

That was it. I waited, hoping he'd add to it, but he didn't. So I tried again. "Is it the family business that landed you in this hole?"

A sad smile crossed his face. "Aye. Shouldn't have left it so long. But I'd spent so much time on my own that when I realized it was time to come home, it was almost too late. Might still be." Something in his voice struck me, a feeling in my gut. I'd heard it before. Felt it before. Yearning.

Before I could say anything more, he turned it all around. "I should be askin' ya these questions. How did ya get yourself thrown in here?"

I gave my answer some thought. Then, carefully, "It's just part of the job."

"Your job is to get yourself thrown into a cage? Might want to reconsider your employment." His voice teased me, tempting me to smile at him. I didn't.

"Gotta do what the work requires. And right now, what I'm looking for requires me to be stuck here, waiting."

"Ah, ya're lookin' for somethin'?" His voice told me he was pleased with this bit of information. I didn't say anything, refusing to look at him. "Or maybe, is it a someone?"

I fixed my gaze on the stones above his head. Sound was starting to make its way down to where we sat. People were moving around outside now. Langer and his crew would likely be here soon. I needed to be ready.

"Ash," he whispered. "Are ya with me?"

I closed my eyes for a moment, listening for the voices that were always lending me their opinions, wanted or not. But this time, they were quiet. It was such a rare occurrence, the quiet inside my head, that I wondered if something was wrong. Was this the turning point; was my mind truly scuttered now?

He called my name again. "Ash, darlin'. Are ya with me?"

I turned to him, opening my eyes. "They'll be coming for me soon."

He nodded. "Did the voices tell ya that?"

"No. It's strange. Usually, they're falling all over themselves when I'm on a job, helping me find what I'm looking for. But they're quiet now."

"Ya miss them?"

That made me smile. "No. I just wonder if this is what it's like at the end. When my mind breaks away and there are too many pieces for me to put back together."

"How can I help?"

It was a simple question that stupidly made me feel warm all over. "I don't think you can. It's my job to do. Mine to finish."

Another nod from his side of the bars. "What is it ya're lookin' for? Maybe I've heard somethin' about it."

The opening of the upstairs door interrupted anything I would have said. Light flooded in, and I was finally able to see the man I'd been talking with. Really see him. I caught my breath. A flare of almost recognition lit through me. I'd never seen him before, I was sure. But I was just as sure that this was the man I'd always hoped to see. Wanted to see. His eyes weren't just pretty, they were haunted and kind. His hands, which had been so gentle, now gripped the bars between us with such strength that I expected to see the metal bend beneath them. From the bulk of him kneeling on the cold ground, I knew that if he was able to rise up to his full height, he would tower over me.

The thought didn't frighten me.

"Goodbye, Ry." I couldn't hide the trickle of sadness in my words, and I watched understanding spread across his face. "It's been lovely."

The door to my cage swung open. Rough hands grabbed me, dragging me along the stone and onto my feet. I turned away from the one man I didn't want to leave behind and faced what waited for me upstairs.

As I was led up the stairs, I could feel something, almost like a thread, connecting me to Ry, even as I got farther away. When the door slammed shut behind me, I felt that connection sever deep inside, a painful hit to my gut, and I fought the urge to cry out. The voices, which had been quiet, rushed in to fill the void, scrambling over one another, demanding to be heard. I pushed them down, forcing them to a manageable level. This was it; I couldn't let myself be distracted.

Verbrech shoved me along the passageway ahead of him, toward the end, where I could see Langer standing outside a door.

"You shouldn't have come here, you know. He warned you." Verbrech's words made little difference to me. I'd made my choice. It was this or lose myself more, bit by bit.

The smirk on Langer's face as I was marched up to him made my stomach turn. He loomed over me, leaning down to sniff at my hair. To breathe an oily whisper into my ear. "You're nothing but filth now, Chara. He'll be done with you. Then it's my turn."

I twisted my neck so I could look up at him, my gaze intent on the raised scars that marked the side of his face, just outside the corner of his eye. "So good to see you still have what I left you that last night. I didn't kill you then. Even though I should've."

He flinched, and then anger flashed across his face. He grabbed my hair and pushed me through the door, into the office of the man I'd truly come here to see. The one who'd told me never to come back.

Drake leaned back in his chair, his dusty boots resting on the shiny wood of the desk. He watched as Langer positioned me very specifically into the place I was sure he'd been instructed to. Drake always liked his drama. We stood like that, Langer's fingers twisted into my hair, pulling until an ache began to pulse at the end of each strand. Drake was going through a pile of items on the desk, pretending disinterest in what was happening in front of him. It was a game I'd seen him play before.

As he picked up the sheath from beneath the papers he'd left on top of it, I saw a flicker of something. A twitch in the muscle on the left side of his mouth. He knew what the sheath held. He was surprised I had it. He was even more surprised I'd brought it here.

Finally, he raised his eyes to mine. At a quick wave of his hand, Langer suddenly let go of me, leaving me off balance and about to fall forward. I felt the minute change in the air as he raised his arm to hit me, and I just let my awkward momentum carry me down to the ground.

He swung through suddenly empty air, a grunt of surprise erupting as I swept his legs out from under him. He hit the floor hard, unprepared to cushion his fall, and I was on him. When I'd let myself be taken, I knew he wouldn't be able to resist lifting my knife and claiming it for himself. It hung on his belt, exactly where I'd known he would display it. He'd once taunted me about naming it; I'd warned him that a named weapon would always serve you better because naming it meant you loved it. He'd just laughed and called me crazy.

Now, as Messer pulled free, it rang with a high, bright note and the voices in my head rose in accompaniment. I let them loose as I tore into Langer, Messer finding all the open soft spots. I didn't need to see anymore; a thin sheen of red covered everything as he thrashed and I held on. When he stopped moving beneath me, my vision cleared and the voices inside were triumphant. Open eyes stared up at me, blood staining Langer around the thirteen holes I'd made.

Debt paid.

I staggered to my feet, sure I was covered in blood and not caring. Drake stood there watching but he hadn't interfered. When

Verbrech ran into the room, Drake held up his hand, a simple command to stop. I stood between them, poised and ready to move as the need arose.

"Bring a cloth for the lady, Verbrech. And warm water. She needs some cleaning up." Drake's voice sounded exactly the way I remembered it. Cultured, educated. And still just as cruel.

"But sir, Langer . . ." Verbrech hesitated. "She did this to him . . . so fast."

"It was his own fault. He didn't tie her hands. He treated her like she was weak. He knew better." When Verbrech started to say something else, Drake continued. "And you know better than to defy me when I give you an order. Do it. Now."

I didn't look away from Drake as Verbrech backed out of the room. He still held the sheath in his hands, waiting until it was just the two of us before he set it down on the desk. He came toward me, a twisted smile on his face. "Oh, Chara, how I have missed you."

"You don't get to call me that." I spat the words at him before I could stop myself. "I'm not that person anymore."

He shook his head, laughter spilling out. "This is what I've always loved about you. So delusional. Grasping for a normal you could never have. I was very disappointed when you left me."

Now it was my turn to laugh. "We shouldn't lie to each other." I wiped the blood from Messer's blade on my pant leg, cleaning it almost unconsciously. "You used me. When I left, you were just disappointed you couldn't use me anymore."

He shrugged, an almost agreement. "And yet here you are, Chara. Returned home. To me. Where you belong." He took another step forward, arranging his face into what I knew he considered a charming expression. "We can be good again, you and I."

"No, I'm here for the things you stole. I'll take them and I will leave." At his mocking expression, I couldn't resist the urge to add, "You won't be able to stop me."

"But, Chara, you're as much a thief as I am. You know that's the truth. Those voices in your head, they were our guides, leading us to the greatest treasures. You're the reason I became the man I am."

I hated it, but there was truth in his words. Not the whole truth, but truth all the same. "You used me." I ground the words out, refusing to give in to him. "I was scared, afraid I was going crazy. You told me following the voices would help. Then I find out you're the one killing these people in the first place."

I didn't expect to see remorse on him, and I was right. Now his smile was just contemptuous. "Took you long enough. Imagine my surprise the first time I realized that the man I'd killed the day before was one of the new voices you'd started to hear. And that suddenly you knew where he'd hidden his gold."

The voices inside screamed at this, and the force of their rage battered my skull. I swayed on my feet. I was tired, hungry. I didn't have much time left. My eyes dropped to the sheath Drake had left on the desk. He saw and grimaced. He reached for the leather, lifting it up as if he would offer it to me.

"Was this your plan? Return this to me and I'd give you whatever you asked for?"

It was my turn to shrug. "Seemed as good an idea as any."

"And if I didn't agree to that?"

"Then I'd kill you and take what I wanted anyway."

He roared at that. "Oh my, my. Now there's the spirit I've missed."

I squared my shoulders. Verbrech would be back soon, and I needed this done before he got back. "No more games, Drake. You've taken what you shouldn't, and I'm here to take it all back."

He stepped around me, over Langer's body still sprawled on the floor. Between me and the door. There was a sound in the hall outside, a scuff that could have been a step. Verbrech back to clean me up.

"Come and take it, then, Chara. If you can."

I had tensed myself to move, my muscles bunching in readiness, when the door burst open behind Drake. Verbrech fell through the door, a shard of white protruding from between his ribs and red foam at his lips. He reached for Drake as he staggered, dying.

Drake jumped away, realizing too late the danger that put him in.

He twisted back toward me, bringing his arms up to defend himself, but Messer was already buried hilt deep in his stomach. His eyes locked onto mine, the voices inside me screaming their vengeance, and I believed in that moment he could hear them as clearly as I could.

As he slipped down to the floor, I whispered to him, "I told you not to call me that."

I supported myself on the desk as the room started to spin. Already, I could hear Langer's voice screaming inside me, Verbrech's right behind him. I could manage them, could lose them in the midst of all the others crowded inside my head.

The worst, I knew, was still to come, and I braced myself.

When Drake's voice exploded, I was as prepared as I could be. Every horrible thing he'd ever said to me began again, amplified by my skull. I threw a wall up; this was my mind and I was in control. I forced him into a corner, caging him as he'd caged me before. He raged against the bonds I crafted, trying to break away, but I refused to let him go. He would tell me what I needed to know.

It wasn't until his voice was ragged, sobbing, that he broke. Gave me the location of what he'd stashed away. I found the keys, hidden where he'd said they'd be. Scribbled down the directions onto a scrap of paper. Time was running out. I had to get this to someone who could help, and I was empty. I'd used all my energy. Drake's voice was starting to surface again, louder by the second. In the end, I knew he'd win and I would shatter. But the sacrifice would be worth it.

I didn't expect hands to grab me from the darkness of the hall. I didn't expect the callouses on them to feel so good, so warm. I didn't expect to see those pretty eyes, checking me over intently. Searching me. I didn't expect the sudden silence inside me, the silence that opened up as soon as his skin touched mine. It was divine. The knowledge that it had been Ry that had stopped Verbrech—had taken out one of the threats so I didn't have to—left me giddy. Because of him, I'd been able to end it all.

"Ash, are ya with me?" His voice made me ache inside, it was so gentle. "I got some men here now, to help us. Are ya with me?"

I grasped his shirt, pulling him close so I could whisper in his ear. "He has them hidden. Tell the people. They have to find the women he took." I shoved the note into his hand, a soft kiss grazing his cheek as my legs gave out.

I let the darkness take me.

When I woke, it was to the sound of running water and a man humming a melody I knew. It was the Shelta Cant I'd sung to calm the voices before, and it worked its magic on me now. I opened my eyes to see Ry beside me, the worry on his face chased away as he smiled.

"We've gotta get ya cleaned up now. Ya're a right mess."

I didn't fight him as he undressed me, every movement he made slow and easy. He kept the melody going until it seemed to fill the space around us. He lowered me into the water and washed me clean, until nothing was left of what had happened. By the time he was done, I was floating, luxuriating in how new I felt.

He pulled me up. I leaned into him, using him for support as he wrapped a towel around me. As he chafed my arms, trying to soak up the water, I tipped my head back. His lips were there, and I took advantage. The kiss I gave him wasn't chaste or timid. It was everything I felt inside given life. Gratefulness, passion, and even the fear that he'd be gone when this was over poured into that kiss. A kiss he returned.

At some point, he carried me from the bath and laid me on a bed. He tried to cover me with a blanket and step away, but I refused to let him go. I pulled him down beside me until I could remove his clothes, needing to feel all his skin against mine. He tried to protest that I was too tired, but I laughed it away. Settling on top of him, I waited until his pretty eyes burned with an intensity I desperately wanted to see before I let him fill me up.

Those moments were everything I needed to feel whole again. With him, nothing intruded, nothing broke our connection. It was the two of us, aching for each other and offering solace. Peace.

After we were both left gasping, fingers entwined, it was the most natural thing to rest beside him, his arms around me. There was nothing in my head but my own thoughts and the sound of his breathing layered with mine. The silence in the room stretched on, and for once, I didn't feel the need to break it.

But he did. "Is it better now?" he asked. "For ya, the voices?"

I mumbled an aye as I burrowed deeper against his side, loving the feel of him around me. His arms tightened, holding me even closer.

"For me too, darlin'. Ya ease the visions. I don't see them when ya're near."

I sighed happily, glad there was a reason he might want to stay. But there was something I had to ask, afraid the reminder of it might be enough to drive him away. "Your family business. Do you still need to attend to that?" I worked to hide the tremor in my voice.

"It's done. The visions showed me Drake had somethin' of mine. All taken care of now."

"You found it, then?" I fought against it, but I was slipping into sleep. Still, I heard his answer.

"Aye, darlin'. It was you."

Ry

I dozed holding her, but every movement she made jolted me back to wakefulness, alert for any threat. I'd finally found her, and now, actually having her in my arms, I was terrified of losing her.

"Shouldn't have waited so long, ya eejit." I muttered the words under my breath. All the visions of the last few years had been telling me to come home, but I'd continued on my way, running from what

I knew was true. How much harm had I done by not returning? How many people had died?

Ash moaned and twisted in my embrace, her eyes fluttering open and fixing on me. I braced for her fear, for her questions. Instead, a lazy grin drifted across her face. She carefully reached up, brushing her fingers across my rough cheek. I caught myself worrying that the stubble I needed to shave might hurt her.

"You're still here." Her words were quiet, whispered like she was afraid of breaking a spell.

"Aye. Didn't want to leave ya." I'd already learned this woman needed truth in her life. Even if it set me at a disadvantage, I'd give that to her.

Her fingers drifted to my hair, tangling in the dark curls. She tested the texture, stroking it, and I relaxed into her touch. She traced lightly along the rim of my ear and down the back of my neck, making me shiver a bit. It felt so very good, her exploration; I was afraid to interrupt it. I kept my grip on her light, pliable. She could stay or she could go. Her choice.

She shifted up onto her knees in front of me, the bedclothes sliding off her, and my breath caught. Last night, we'd both been craving connection and comfort. It had been wonderful, but too fast. This morning felt different.

Ash leaned in, her breasts swaying, but it was her eyes that held me. Such beautiful eyes. Deep blue with flashes of the sea as the light changed around us. Fierce pride and an aching pain warred in those eyes as she ran her fingers across the ridges of the scar on my bare chest. I leaned back, just enjoying the feel of her, and when she brushed her lips across that sensitive arc of skin, I fought to maintain control. I didn't want to frighten her away.

"Ry," she whispered. "Look at me. Please."

Those words were my undoing, a simple command wrapped in a request. I nodded, meeting her gaze with my own, not hiding the stark desire that wound through me.

"Again."

That was all she said before sealing her lips to mine. She opened her mouth, and all my restraint vanished. I pulled her against me, tasting her as we rolled, careful as I could be not to crush her. I felt her smile as my lips moved to her neck and then down, carefully seeking those spots that made her cry out. I forced myself to wait and learn every bit of her, teasing her bit by bit, until she called my name again and rolled her hips up to me. The sweetest offering. I took my time here too, savoring the flavor of her.

Finally, I felt her shiver beneath my tongue and fingers, a sated moan escaping her that fanned the flames inside me. She guided me up the length of her body, wrapping her legs around my hips once we were face to face.

"Now," she demanded. Her eyes closed in undeniable pleasure as I obeyed and pressed slowly into her, filling her up. She set our rhythm at first, rocking with me until she cried out and I felt her release surround me. Then I let myself go, no more holding back. She clung to me as my climax hit and the waves carried us away.

Afterward, there was no awkwardness. With her head on my chest as I trailed my fingers across her back, she told me a little. The Sisters had raised her, cloistered away with other orphaned children. They'd been the first to realize she heard voices, to caution her against telling anyone.

When sickness had come to their hidden world, it had been my Ash who'd cared for those who couldn't fight it. Who'd held their hands as they died. Who'd carried their voices within her after their bodies were gone.

She pressed a sweet kiss to my chest, and I felt the tears on her cheeks.

"Did no one ever try to help ya with this burden?" I asked, careful with this subject but aching for her loneliness. It was a hurt I knew all too well.

She shrugged against me, and I felt a distance start to spread between us. Before, I would have released her, but this moment needed more tending. I sat up, bringing her with me. I let her see me, the pain I felt for her and how much I wished to aid her now. I cupped her face, my thumbs brushing away the tears. I offered the only thing of value I had to give.

"If ya would have me, I will help carry this."

She gasped, a flush creeping through her skin. I brushed my lips along her hairline, kneaded the tight muscles of her shoulders, and waited. It was her decision to make. Her choice.

"You would do that for me?" Ash's voice quavered, hope a tenuous thing.

"Aye. If ya want me."

My answer pulled a laugh out of her, true joy this time. Her eyes flashed at me. "Clearly, wanting you is no hardship."

I grinned, mischief brewing. "I have other scars for ya to find. If ya're so inclined."

She tilted her head to the side, evaluating me, russet waves falling over one breast. "I'll save that for later," she promised. "Now, we both need food. For the next time."

She gave me a wink as she playfully pushed me away, and my heart sped while I watched her hips roll as she moved from the bed. Already I was dreaming of our next time.

The damage Drake and his crew had done to my family's home was already harder to see. My father's office had been cleaned, the bodies removed and the floors scrubbed until all traces of blood were washed away. The townspeople were just as eager to forget what had happened here as I was.

And grateful that they could move on. Ash and I had found plenty of food to pick from when we tore ourselves away from each other. Someone had even brought us clean clothes. People could be generous.

"Finally found your way home, eh?" came a voice from behind me.

I stiffened. People could also be fecking spanners when they wanted to be. Especially this one.

"Can't face me, can ya? Even after all these years."

No other way to end this than head on. I turned. "Shae. Not really much of a welcome."

"Ya don't deserve one. Leavin' the way ya did. Dishonorin' my sister." Shae fisted his hands, the tendons in his arms standing out. "Now gallivantin' all night with your woman up there. Shameful."

I held up a warning hand and kept my voice level. He needed to stop before he said anything else, or he'd suffer for it.

"Shannon's honor was never questioned. She chose, just like the old ways required. She just didn't choose me." He started to cut in, but I pressed on. "That woman upstairs is owed your respect after what she did for the people here. Her name is Ash. She killed the men responsible for stealin' your women. For killin' my father and brother. Ya will watch your words when ya speak of her. It'd be an honor to be chosen by a woman such as her. Remember that. I'll give no other warnin's."

"That's right. Start orderin' people around just as soon as ya step foot here. Thinkin' ya can take over. We won't all give in just because ya are Ryland MacTire."

I growled, crossing the distance between us, and he stumbled back, a look of shock registering on his face. Things had changed since we'd last seen each other. I was different. By the time his feet were solid underneath him again, I held him in place against the wall, my forearm a bar across his throat.

Baring my teeth, I stopped fighting the rage that coiled inside me. "Did ya give this same speech to that bastard Drake when he rounded ya all up outside, when he killed my father and my kid brother in front of ya? Or did ya just stand there and watch?"

Shae's mouth gaped, but no sound came out. He struggled, but I refused to let him go.

"Carefully, Shae. I've already seen what happened. I watched them die while ya stood by and said nothin'. Lyin' won't help ya now. I already know ya for the coward ya are."

I shoved away, disgusted by his presence. He scrambled for the door but pulled up short, surprise and fear dancing across his face. Ash leaned against the jamb, examining Messer's gleaming blade like she was making sure all the blood had been erased. When she was satisfied, she slid it into the sheath she'd strapped around her thigh and patted it contentedly as it slid home.

She turned her examination to Shae, and I worked to hide a smile. Such a tiny woman, standing there in the doorway, and Shae was too terrified to pass her. When she took a step into the room, he backed away, glancing to me as if to gauge which one of us was the lesser threat. I'd have assured him Ash was the more dangerous, but he didn't ask. Instead, he gave her a wide berth until she reached my side, her allegiance in this conflict clear.

He raced to the door, the way now clear. When he'd separated himself from us enough, he sneered as we stood aligned against him.

"The stakes will be raised, Ryland. For the likes of her, the stakes will come, and they will be raised. She will burn." With those words, he turned and ran.

ASH

Ry didn't say anything to me. His fingers just rested next to mine as we leaned against the desk, listening to the gutless arse run away. I gave him a few minutes to recover before forcing anything.

"I'd say there are some things you need to be explaining to me."

Ry sighed, nodding. "Aye, darlin', there are."

I settled myself into a chair so large that I sank back, my toes just brushing the floor. "Best get to talking."

I thought he'd choose to have the desk between us, but instead he pulled a chair over to where I waited. He folded down, his elbows on his knees, hands clasped. He whispered something I didn't catch before he met my eyes.

"I know what ya are."

Such simple words, but they hit hard enough to drive the breath right out of me. A part of me wanted to beg him to stop, but I couldn't. I needed the truth. His fingers wound around mine, joining us. He would tell me, but he wouldn't abandon me to hear it. I could feel the strength in him just from that scant touch. He was here. As long as I asked him to be. I sucked in air, steeling myself.

"Ash, ya're special in this world. A Soul Catcher. Ya don't just hear the voices of the dead. Ya carry their souls within ya." When I didn't say anything in response, he continued on. "Someone should've been around to help, to teach ya all this. So ya weren't left all alone."

He paused, giving me time to think on what he'd said. But there was a piece missing.

"I'm not the only one who's special here. You know what I am. But you haven't told me what you are. So? Explain."

He looked at our twined fingers, then back to me. When he spoke again, his voice was soft. "I'm what they call a Dreamer. A True Seer. Visions come to me, of things that are goin' to happen. Ya hear the dead. I see them die."

Ah, we were such a pair. Still, I knew he had more to tell. "Ry, what did he mean about the stakes?"

He flinched and tried to pull away from me, but I held on, wrapping my other hand around his. When I didn't let him go, he swallowed and pressed on.

"There was a time. The Burnings." He paused, gathering himself. "Soul Catchers were taken, tied to stakes, and burned in the town centers. Their people, friends and neighbors even, came out to cheer their deaths." His voice shook, and I felt his hands tremble.

I imagined it, the stench of burning flesh, the screams. The jeers of the crowd. Nausea swamped me, it was so vivid. My throat closed up, but I managed to speak anyway. "Why?"

Something dark and feral flashed in Ry's eyes as he answered. "Jealousy. Power. Fear." His whole body was shaking now. "Soul Catchers and their Dreamers were revered; they were leaders. But others were jealous and wanted to lead, so they set about with lies. Corruptin' the people. Athair above, Ash. Fear can be a terrible thing when it's unleashed."

Listening to him, I couldn't miss the deep pain underlying his words. This wasn't a history lesson. It was personal. Close.

"You saw this happen?" I asked.

He didn't answer right away, just lifted grieving amber eyes shining with unshed tears. When he was ready, he said, "It was my first vision. Woke me screamin'. I was ten."

My heart ached. My Ry, a young boy, seeing people burned alive. Again, I wanted to retch. All my life, I'd always just thought I was crazy. But how much more painful did it have to be to see those deaths? To know they would come true? As a child?

"Did your family do nothing for you?"

"My father and mother listened and realized what had happened. My mother went to warn our Soul Catcher and his Dreamer. She sent them away, hopin' they would be safe. My father rallied everyone here, turnin' away the mob when they came. Shae's father was the only one who argued against him."

Bad blood always runs true. That was something I'd learned quickly. "So there were no burnings here?"

He shook his head. "My father wouldn't allow it." He straightened up, the spirit I'd already begun to love coming back to him. "The stakes were not raised here. They will not be now."

"So this is why Shae hates you? Because you're a Dreamer."

Now his eyes were fierce, and I was happy to see that haunted look driven away. "He hates me because his family had plans for his sister Shannon and I to marry. When that didn't happen, they lost any chance at the position they had hoped to gain."

"Why did it not happen?" I waited, expecting something about a young man's inability to be true. The answer surprised me.

"We follow the old ways here. It was Shannon's choice to make. She didn't choose me."

Stupid git. That's what I thought of her choice, but since it left Ry for me, I couldn't fault her much. "And the old ways say she doesn't have to marry you if she doesn't want to?"

He gave a gentle laugh. "The old ways require it to be her choice. It was always said that men want but women know. So women are the ones who choose. Because they don't let their wantin' interfere with their knowin'.""

"Your old ones were wise." I smiled. "But did you love her? Want her?"

He considered the question before answering. "I enjoyed our times together. I wanted to make my family happy. To try. But she knew we weren't a match. She chose well."

A good answer. Still, I needed to know more. "Can you explain what's happening? This connection I feel, even when you're not with me? Like we're tied together somehow."

His eyes turned serious, but I saw a tiny hint of fear hidden in them as well. He turned to a shelf and picked through the dusty books, his fingers finally lingering on one volume. "Catchers were meant to hold the souls of those who died, to guide them on their way and release them. Young ones were taught to do this by those who came before. There used to be enough that none of them had to carry too many. They could purify the souls and release them to Athair when the time was right. Dreamers saw what was to happen and could try to change it. To warn their people and help them if they could. Both could be heavy loads to bear."

He handed me the book, and I opened the cover, running my fingers over the gilded letters on the old page. There was a carefully drawn image of two people curved together, two halves of a whole.

"Dreamers and Catchers are meant to ease the burden for each other. To be together gives peace, respite from the visions and voices. To be alone . . ." Here his voice faltered, and he took a deep breath. "Just believe me when I promise ya that most don't manage well alone."

Ah, there it was. "So what we feel, it's because of what we're meant to do?" I asked.

He shook his head. "No. It's not just that." He sat down across from me again, leaning forward so he was within reach if I wanted. "I saw ya, so many times. I'd be walkin' on a road somewhere, and suddenly your face would be there in front of me. I'd hear ya singin' or your laugh. Then, I saw ya here. That's what finally brought me home."

My heart twisted with his confession, even as hope rose up. He had come here for me. "But you said you saw your father's death. Didn't you come here for revenge?"

"No. My father and brother died, but I couldn't have gotten here in time. I still had to watch them die, over and over." His voice broke, a ragged, hurting sound. He took a deep breath, then focused on me again. "When I saw ya in this house, though, I knew I needed to come back. I had to be here."

I leaned into him, my hands cupping his stubbled jaw, and brought his eyes to mine. "Ry," I whispered. "We can't save them all. Even if we want to, we won't be able to. But we will try." I laid a gentle kiss on his lips, the spicy scent of him filling me. "I choose you."

The joy that bloomed across his face undid me, and our next kiss was not gentle. It singed me, left me gasping for air, and he pulled me out of my chair and into his arms. I yanked at his shirt, greedy for his warmth and unwilling to wait even a second. He lifted me up as he stood, obviously intending to take me back to bed, but I had other ideas. I wrapped my legs around his waist and slid my hand down the smooth muscles of his stomach. His quick breath made me grin, and I closed my fingers around the silk of him. He stumbled, fighting for balance with me in his arms.

"Wall," I growled at him. And that was all it took. With the cool wood at my back, we ripped our clothes away, not caring that someone could walk in. Not caring that anyone on the street might hear. Just us.

When he slid into me, I opened my eyes to his, pupils dilated as he drank me in. I soared as our rhythms joined, my heart pounding in time. I hung on, my nails carving into his back as the splinters did to mine, relishing every fiery slice that made my blood run even hotter. At the top of the cliff, I couldn't help but scream his name. He roared mine in return as he poured himself out inside me.

He cradled me as we caught our breath, enjoying the feeling of being joined together. I thought of that picture, two halves of one whole. Complete. By the time my feet finally slid to the floor, the shakiness had eased from my muscles and I could support myself again. He held me to him, lending me his warmth one more time before helping me into my clothes with care.

I felt light. My choice was made, and I no longer felt like something was missing. He tried to smooth my hair, but I laughed and pushed his hand away, kissing his fingers as they brushed past my mouth. The worry had left his eyes, and now they just gleamed, a happy amber glow that made me glad.

"I am pleased to see that smile on your face, darlin'," Ry said. "Makes me feel I did my job well."

"Aye. No one will ever hear me say otherwise." I winked at him. "Will it always be like this? No more visions, no more voices?"

He thought before answering. "I've heard stories that it could be turned off and on as partners needed. It took time, but they were able to learn. Are ya needin' the voices?"

I shook my head. "No, I'm enjoying the quiet, having nothing that interferes when I'm with you." I saw a flush creep across his face at that. "But if this is what we're meant to do, we have to be open when the need arises."

He nodded. "I think distance plays a part. When ya touched me the first time, the voices were quiet until they took ya away?"

I remembered the tearing pain I had felt when the cellar door closed, the sensation that I'd been cut loose from him. "Could be. We should test that."

"Now? Ya want to test this now?"

I could tell he was surprised, but I felt strong, ready to explore what all this might mean. "Aye. We need to. You stay here, and I'll go for a walk. We should both feel it if the connection between us breaks."

He looked worried. "I don't much like the idea of ya walkin' around out there alone. The people here don't know ya yet. They're grateful for what ya did, but that doesn't mean there won't be some who are afraid."

I agreed with him, but I couldn't let myself hide here. I'd come so far; it was time to stop hiding. This was a first step.

"You stay here. I'll walk around and see how far away I get before the connection breaks. When you feel it, come find me." Based on the way I'd been able to keep track of his location in the house earlier, he should at least have a sense of what direction I'd gone. "We won't know how this works if we don't try."

He finally nodded, and I pulled on my boots. Messer rested comfortably against the side of my leg, always ready. With one last kiss for Ry, I left to face my new world.

The town was much like others I'd been to through the years. This one was cleaner, the people less starved looking than some I'd seen. I was surprised that even a few smiles came my way. I followed the main street through the center of town, where shops were clustered and the bustle of the day was more noticeable.

At different places, I would stop and feel for Ry. Now that I understood more about what we were, I could sense a bit of him within me, shining and pulsing. The longer I was away, the farther I walked, the more the feeling of him dimmed. It was just on the outskirts, where the trees pressed in and more brush crowded the way, that I felt our connection snap. The impact of it drove me to my knees, and it hurt to breathe. I stumbled off the road and into the woods, hoping to regain myself away from the prying eyes of the town.

The voices I'd been without were suddenly there again, crowding the space inside my mind and crying for my attention. I gave them time to sort themselves out, breathing deep and even as they battled. Ry would come soon, and the voices would be quiet again.

The Sisters won out. *"Now you see, child. What we hoped to protect you from."*

I didn't answer them. I didn't have to. They would already know my hurt, my anger at being kept ignorant. They would also know that I understood. Their intentions had been good.

Drake's oily voice overtook the Sisters all too quickly. *"These people won't let you stay. They will hate you, curse you, and leave you to rot."* Purging him from my mind would be a welcome thing, once I learned how. Sending him where he belonged would be justice.

Another voice rose up, a quiet one that rarely spoke and had been with me for so long I couldn't remember not hearing it. Was it the first? I never knew. But now, Ara's voice overcame all the others. *"He is coming. He will hurt you. Prepare."*

I staggered to my feet, unsure but keeping the solid trunk of a large tree at my back. The woods had grown quiet, so the sound of footsteps crunching their way toward me were easy to pick out. I turned my attention that direction and slid Messer free, as ready as I could be.

The man who broke through the green brush in front of me was not the man I'd been waiting for. Shae barreled through, three men following him. They all stopped at the sight of me, taking in the knife in my hands. One of them carried a lantern, the flame burning bright even in the daylight.

There was no doubt in me. Shae had followed when I left the house, gathering his thugs along the way. He would win this war with Ry; he would burn me and tear out his opponent's heart in the process. I didn't need the voices to tell me that. It was written on his face.

I acknowledged his presence with a single nod. I secured my grip on Messer's handle, drawing strength from the carved bone I knew so well. This would be my hand.

"Come on, then, boys. Let's end this." I howled as they launched themselves at me.

RY

When Ash walked out the door, I followed her to the street. I watched her stride away, never looking back for me, as if she knew I was here and didn't need to reassure herself further. When she was out of sight, I leaned against the outside of the home I'd grown up in, waiting for that moment to come. The separation.

It seemed to take forever. But when it came, the pain doubled me over and I fought to stay upright. I stumbled away from the wall in the direction she'd gone, but I hadn't taken two steps before the vision hit.

Ash faced four men, her hair wild and that knife she carried a bright beacon. I recognized Shae, and my heart clenched, freezing in fear at what he would do to her. I saw them charge her as she screamed, and then it was gone. The vision left me, and I struggled to regain my senses, remembering where I'd last felt her.

I ran—past people who knew me and called my name, dodging around carts that threatened to block my way. I sucked in air, pushing myself to go harder and faster, anything to reach her before it was too late.

When I broke through the trees, I slid to a stop, stunned. Three men I didn't know were slumped on the ground. One tried to staunch the blood flowing from a gaping wound on his thigh, his face pale and agonized. Another lay motionless. The third was trying to crawl away, like a wounded animal.

A lantern had been dropped, its flame flickering. I picked it up, snuffing out the danger it presented. I knew why Shae had brought it here.

Ash was glorious, her skin marked with red streaks, her own blood mingling with that she'd pulled from her attackers. She prowled around Shae, striking fast and then dashing away before he could latch onto her. A fierce smile crowned her face as she danced, while Shae panted. She was wearing him down, and that knowledge lent her even more power.

One final time she moved in, her knife connecting with the back of Shae's knee. His leg crumpled, and he collapsed onto the ground. She stood above him, and I made no move to stop her.

"Justice," she whispered coldly before turning to the other men she'd already beaten. Her voice rose, strong and sure. "Justice. You are all called for justice. I could take it here, let your blood bear witness. But I will not. Your people will see you for what you are."

She turned to stride away, but her eyes found me. Shyness and shame crept onto her face, but then she stood straight, her hands out to her sides, refusing to hide from me. I was struck with awe. This woman had chosen me. I only hoped to be worthy.

I reached for her, my hands open and welcoming. I heard the people from town filling in behind me, having followed my mad run. I heard gasps as they saw the four men downed by this one woman and her knife. They'd hoped to make an example of her. Instead, they had become the example.

She stepped into my embrace, her knife disappearing safely into its sheath. She breathed me in, leaning against my chest as if she needed to share in my strength.

"Ry," she said, her voice low and just for me. "I'm sorry for this. I didn't intend . . ."

I stopped her. I tipped her chin up so she could see my eyes, the pride I would not hide. I pitched my voice so everyone around us would hear the old words I spoke. My voice was formal, no accent creeping in.

"I accept your choice. I am honored by your choice. And I claim you in return."

I kissed her fiercely. This was public, as it should be, so all would know. The rest we would deal with as it came. *This* was for us.

THE SAINT AND TRAVELER

SARAH WINDSOR

The clinic was always busy, but it was worst in the last hours before dawn, when the clubs closed and everyone who wasn't already passed out or dead poured into the streets of New London looking for further trouble. There was a blood trail on the blue plastic floor, and Peacock tried not to drag Yuri's bare feet in it as he stumbled through the doors. They smeared a matched trail beside it. There was nowhere to sit in the small bleach-reeking lobby, and he wasn't sure how much longer he could stand under Yuri's deadweight.

"How can a half-starved twink be so fucking heavy?" he complained to no one in particular. Certainly not to Yuri. The poor kid had been out since Peacock found him tied up in an unnecessary amount of black silk rope, suspended over a mirrored table in a private event room at the Goring Hotel.

Peacock shifted his grip on the slick ropes, propping Yuri against the wall. He scanned the lobby, looking for Mara, for anyone in scrubs. No one offered to help him or even noticed him. Mara's clinic was the kind of place where no one looked twice at a skinny black whore in holomakeup and six-inch heels carrying a bloody boy in nothing but bad shibari.

The doors to the inner clinic hissed open, and Mara stepped out just far enough to yell, "Who's dying? You're next."

"Someone's fuckin' dying, how're they gonna answer you?" he said. Mara was at his side and helping him with Yuri before he finished complaining.

"Peacock! JesusMary . . . What did you get into?"

They carried Yuri to the first open room and laid him on the table. Glowing info feeds showed his vitals as soon as he touched it. "Not good," Mara said.

Peacock was surprised by the twist in his gut. It wasn't like he and Yuri were close. The kid was a cocky little shit. But he couldn't be older than sixteen.

Mara slipped gloves on and shoved another pair at Peacock. "The fuck?"

"Make yourself useful. He's your friend, isn't he?" She grabbed a scalpel and freed Yuri of his bonds.

"Not really," Peacock said, pulling on the gloves.

Mara thrust a nozzled can into his hand. "Spray this anywhere he's bleeding."

Easy enough. He started where the bleeding was worst, spraying Newskin—or the clinic's knockoff version—liberally into each gash. The good stuff was Bio. This wasn't. It smelled like chemicals, looked like cum, and dried like clingfilm, but it was doing the job.

Mara had just finished hooking Yuri up to an IV when the door hissed open and a man stormed through it. "Out! Wait your damn tur—" Mara cut off when the stranger pointed a crossbow at her.

Peacock wondered what spraying Newskin into someone's eyes would do. He lifted the can, but two things stopped him. The first, and fucking shallow, reason was that the man was shockingly handsome—filthy, but he made even that look good. Within that stunned second—held by pale eyes, full lips, and a soot-smeared bare chest that looked like something from a CK ad—Peacock rethought startling a man with his finger on a trigger.

The man looked as confused to see them as they did to see him. "Where is he?" He glanced down at a clunky device in his not-crossbow-brandishing hand. He took three steps forward to the biohazard bin in the corner and then pocketed the device, shouldered the crossbow, and began rifling through the bin.

"Woah, woah, don't *do* that!" Peacock didn't even want to think about the man's hands rummaging around in all those sharp edges and body fluids. Fuck it, he couldn't watch this. He dropped the Newskin and ran over, dragging at the man's bare arm—the only clothing on his upper body was a leather vest and weapon straps. "That bin's got more diseases than every whore in Shoreditch."

The man fished out a broken shaft with a bloodied, barbed metal tip and scowled at it. Beneath the gore, a green light flickered. All at once, he gave in to Peacock's tugging, and Peacock stumbled back on his heels. The man caught him by the small of his back, steadying Peacock against himself. Peacock swallowed, not ready to be pressed against that much hot skin and hard muscle. This guy either had a fever or he'd been running.

He lifted the metal barb between them. "The man you pulled this out of." His voice was so deep, Peacock felt it in his stomach. "Where is he?"

Before Peacock could gather his wits to answer, there was a soft hiss. The iron abs at his front and arm at his back relaxed, falling away. Pale eyes fluttered. The stranger slumped to the floor, and Peacock found himself facing Mara with a spent tranq in her hand.

Peacock breathed. "Cheers."

Mara plucked the broken crossbow bolt from the floor where it had fallen and tossed it into the biohazard bin, along with the spent tranq. "Get him out of my clinic." She went back to work on Yuri.

How many men did he have to haul around in one night? This guy was at least twice Yuri's weight. It was all he could do to drag him by his arms.

He was exhausted by the time they were outside. He peeled off the latex gloves and sat on the curb, panting. Glitchy holo ads danced in front of the convenience store across the street. A red-cheeked Beefeater poured beer into a giant glass, froth spilling over the edge, over and over.

If he left this guy lying in the gutter for even the time it took to buy a cold drink and a pack of cigarettes, he'd be stripped by the time Peacock got back. That vest might be dirty and stink like the rest of him, but it still looked spendy. It had leather panels decorated with Celtic knotwork and lined with russet fur, with a big ruff at the neck and shoulders. Peacock ran his fingers through the ruff, goosebumps racing up his arms at how soft it was. Shit, that had to be real. He didn't know animals well enough to say what kind it was supposed to be, but it didn't matter. Only rich fucks wore real fur.

Never trust anything with cufflinks. That was the first advice he'd given Yuri. People who could afford expensive whores only came looking for cheap ones when they wanted someone single-use. Your corpse couldn't spend their credits, so Peacock didn't see the temptation. The little shit had given Peacock a smug smile over his shoulder as he ducked into a long white car. They passed so close, Peacock could see a gloved driver through the tinted windows. What a dumb fuck. Someone rich and weird enough to have a *human* driving them around, and Yuri thought, sure, magic, why not?

Who was the dumb fuck now?

Peacock left his hand in the fur ruff and let himself look. Unconscious, the man had a sweet face, those sharp eyes closed and dark under a black line of makeup, or soot, that painted his lids and the bridge of his nose. He was smooth-cheeked, but he looked to be at least in his twenties, maybe older than Peacock. His full lips were parted. His hair was short at the sides and a tousled mess on top. It looked soft as the fur under Peacock's hand and a similar color. He was all lean muscle and miles of gorgeous stomach. Low-slung leather pants stretched over legs that looked like he did nothing but run.

Any rich kid could dress up like a badass and get dirty for the fun of it. Plenty of them did, acting out simgame fantasies in real life, fighting each other in pits at Valhalla or hunting people in the slums. But the Valhalla crowd was all flash and flaunt: crazy armor, tall hair, big weapons. There was an underlying softness to them that armor couldn't hide.

There was nothing soft about this man. Other than his vest . . . and probably his hair.

Still, he'd put a bolt in someone and chased them to the clinic. That was a sick game like one of Valhalla's "warriors" would play. But alone? On foot? They always hunted in packs, riding around in souped-up, weaponized buggies. Damn, he was curious, but it wasn't worth the risk to stay. Peacock could imagine what some blood-sport junkie with a wounded ego might do to someone like him.

He was about to get up when he realized the man's eyes were open and watching him. His face was still gentle, a little confused. Peacock held his breath, not daring to move, even to take his hand away. He waited for the man to snap out of it and turn violent.

Instead, his expression softened into wonder. He reached up as if he would touch Peacock's cheek. Peacock flinched, and the man drew his hand back, breaking the dreamlike stillness between them. Peacock scrambled to his feet as the man sat up with a groan. He found his crossbow first, then patted a drawstring bag at his hip.

"Thank you, I think," he said.

Peacock backed away slowly, heart thudding in his ears. A full dose of tranq should have downed him for at least an hour.

The man held up both palms. "Wait. Please."

"Why should I?"

"You work here, right? At this place? I need to know about the man you helped."

"Do I look like a nurse to you?"

The man looked over Peacock's green thigh-high boots, his neon lace panties under clear plastic shorts, his bare midriff and loose crop top. He swallowed. "I don't know. So you didn't see him?"

"No. And don't you go marching back in there to ask Mara. She'll do worse than tranq you."

The man let his hands fall, arms resting loosely on his knees. "I need to know if he died."

"If you finished him, you mean."

"Yes."

"The fuck did he do to you?"

"Not me. My friend." He drew in a shuddering breath. "They killed my friend. They did . . . terrible things to her."

"Who they?"

The man shrugged, miserable. "I don't know who they were or how to find them here. There were seven. I killed three when I came on them and shot a fourth as they fled. Aoife wasn't dead yet, so I stayed with her rather than chase after. Not till the end. What they did . . . who would do something like that?"

"People are shit," Peacock said, tone gentler than his words. He found himself sitting on the curb again, just out of reach.

"I tracked them for days. They were riding, I was running, but they stopped each night to camp. I can't be far behind them. The blood on that bolt hadn't dried." He scruffed a hand through his hair so half of it stood up. "It doesn't matter. They could be ten steps gone and I wouldn't find them. I can't read any signs here. It's all cement. Light and noise. There are so many people." He curled up with his face hidden and his arms around his knees.

Days? It didn't take more than a day to cross New London, even if you were too daft to use public transportation. "You saying you've been running 'round the wasteland after some bleeding maniacs?" The pieces were there, but the idea was so unbelievable that it took him a while to put them together. "Hang on . . . you're from there, aren't you? Bloody fucking hell."

The man nodded into his knees.

People living in the wasteland was the stuff of B-horror sims, cannibals and mutants and shit like that. Most of the world was underwater, and everything that wasn't was either a city or a toxic hellscape. At least, that was what he'd always thought. Maybe cheap sims weren't the best guide to reality. If this was what the cannibal mutants looked like, the wasteland couldn't be so bad.

Still, he could only think of one kind of person who'd go joyriding there.

"So, the people killed your mate, what'd they look like?"

The eyes the man lifted were fierce. "They wore spiked armor. Some had colorful hair like yours." He gestured to Peacock's iridescent green nap and short white mohawk. "But . . . more. They painted their skin with her blood."

"Was their ride loud and covered in spikes and shit too?"

"Yes. It spat flames. They burned a path through the bracken I could have followed blind. I felt foolish for wasting a tracking bolt until I reached the city. Here, it was my only hope."

"Nah, I know where your blokes are."

"You know them?" He went still in a way Peacock didn't like at all.

"Hey, easy." Peacock bristled with a bravado he didn't feel. "You even think about pulling that crossbow again and we're done. No, these assholes are not my bloody mates. If you knew shit, you'd know a whore like me wouldn't go within miles of Valhalla. They'd rape me and hang me like a fucking banner in the longhall."

"Valhalla."

"Yeah. That's the place they all go to drink and fight and brag. I hear there's a tally board."

"How do I get there?"

"Castle Line to Blackbridge," he said, figuring it would be nonsense to the man but wanting to buy time. A smartcab would take him right there. Peacock had jumped the gun, thinking he'd help, and now he realized he didn't want to be responsible for sending this man to a bad death.

"I'll pay you to take me there."

"Fuck no."

"Please. Just within sight of it. Here." He undid the drawstring bag and emptied it into his hand—a pile of credit chips, each shining a full charge. Well, that was a surprise. His people might not live in the city, but they must buy things sometimes if he had that kind of money. Peacock leaned closer and picked up a chip to inspect it. The tiny blue number at the top read *100K*. This poor sot was offering him something like a million credits to take him four tube stops down.

Peacock could live for a year on that. More if he was canny. He held out his hand, and the man poured the chips into it.

"Tell me this isn't all your money."

"I doubt I'll survive. I'd rather you have it than they do."

At least he wasn't suffering any delusions. Peacock hefted the chips, a clattering handful of blue light. "Look, this is revenge, not a rescue. What's the rush? You've been running for *days*? Don't you want a drink and a shower and a fuckin' rest? I do. I've had *a night*. I'm done with cute, suicidal men. You want my help, we do this my way. You want to die, find someone else." He held the chips at arm's length and looked away. He couldn't watch himself give them back.

Two warm, calloused hands closed around his fist.

His flat was only a block away, but he never took anyone there. Instead, they went to the Saint and Traveler, a nearby pub with clean rooms and an owner he trusted. She looked up from cleaning the bar and paused, impressed with his catch. He wondered if it was the dirt or the pretty face.

"Rose Room free?"

"Sure. How many hours?"

"Eight, at least."

She raised an eyebrow and gave Peacock's companion another appraising look. Peacock fished in his bag and offered one of the chips for her to scan. She grunted at the denomination on the reader and then charged him for a full twenty-four hours. He didn't complain. Anyway, he felt like he could sleep for a week.

"Tea or a pint, then?"

"Two gallons of water. And two pints, sure."

"All that?" she called after them as they climbed the narrow stairs by the bar. "If you're hostin' the bloody Olympics, keep it down."

Everything in the room was rose patterned, but Peacock liked it because it had a king-size bed and a huge shower. The wastelander stood awkwardly in the middle of the space.

Peacock sat on the edge of the bed and unzipped his boots, moaning with relief. The man watched as Peacock massaged his arches. He picked up a boot by its heel, shaking his head. Then he went to one knee on the pink carpet. "Let me." He cupped Peacock's foot.

"Oh . . ." Peacock was so surprised, he let him. His next "Oh" was considerably dirtier.

"Why do you wear those?"

"They make my—ah . . . calves look—fuck . . ."

The man nodded agreement, then went to work on Peacock's calf as well.

By the time he'd finished both legs, Peacock was sprawled on his back, too relaxed to move. He expected those hands to keep going and was regretting letting them start. He was so tired.

But the man just laid his legs gently on the bed and headed downstairs. It was at once a relief and a bit insulting.

He came back with their tray of drinks.

"Water's for you," Peacock said, forcing himself to sit up.

They lifted pint glass and water jug in tandem, drinking with slow, steady relish. Peacock downed both beers before the man finished his first gallon.

"Rowan," the man said, setting the empty jug aside.

"Huh?"

"My name is Rowan. Caorthann in the old tongue. A sign of protection and divination." He gave a bitter huff. "I have not worn it well. Still, if I live and ever you need protection or a guide, I am yours."

"Caorthann." It rolled over Peacock's tongue, richer than the stout. How to follow such formality and sweetness? He didn't like gifts he hadn't earned. "I'm Peacock. Just Peacock." He laughed with a facetious tilt of his head and a hand to his chest. "A sign of male beauty."

"A good name," Rowan said, shy and serious.

"I'm joking, mate."

"I'm not."

"Look, I'm sorry. I'm exhausted."

Rowan's brows furrowed, though in confusion, not anger.

Peacock had never met a man who'd take being blown off so calmly after a million credits, a foot massage, and a cheesy come-on.

Rowan's face smoothed with understanding. "Don't apologize. I can take first watch."

"Watch?"

"I'll watch while you sleep."

That was some kinky shit. To each his own. Peacock rolled over and made himself comfortable on the rose-print pillows. He heard Rowan investigating the faucets in the bathroom, and eventually the sound of a shower running and leather thunking to the floor.

Peacock peeked over his shoulder. Rowan stood with his hands against the shower glass, head tilted back in ecstasy as hot water cut paths through soot and grime. Peacock rolled over for a better view, but Rowan didn't seem to notice that he was watching. Somehow, it made it better that he wasn't self-conscious or putting on a show.

Peacock's eyes were drifting shut on a view of taut, pale skin revealed. A shock of red hair curled around a thick, uncut cock. Rowan turned, and gray water traced a course over his back muscles. God, his ass!

Peacock's dreams picked up where his waking thoughts left off.

He woke hard and aching, not sure how long it had been. Long enough that Rowan's hair had dried to bright copper. He lay next to Peacock, head propped on one arm, watching him. The black stripe still ran from temple to temple across his eyelids and the bridge of his nose, a tattoo. Dirt no longer hid the freckles on his cheeks and shoulders.

Rowan reached out and brushed a fingertip over Peacock's cheekbone, the gesture he'd aborted when he woke before. "How did you paint yourself with light?"

Ah, the holomakeup. Peacock had forgotten about it. He'd set it to shifting mandalas, intricate lines that bloomed from white to gold to indigo. He liked how it framed his dark skin and eyes.

Rowan was transfixed.

Rather than answer, Peacock caught a fingertip lightly between his teeth, then drew it into his mouth. Rowan breathed in sharply, watching Peacock's mouth rather than his makeup now. He had such distinct callouses; Peacock laved his tongue over each ridge. He pulled off slowly, letting spit trail from his lips, then licked them. Rowan made a low, needy sound.

"I'm game if you are," Peacock said.

Rowan kissed him like he'd been waiting to. He smelled like roses, which made Peacock laugh into his mouth. Then Rowan's weight was on him, a hard thigh between his legs. They parted only to gasp breaths, then met again, hands everywhere.

Leather and plastic creaked as they ground against each other. Peacock's shorts were uncomfortably tight, tighter still when Rowan slipped both hands underneath them, over Peacock's ass, gripping hard. Peacock swore, breaking off their kiss to fumble his shorts open. Rowan slid them off and tossed them aside. He seemed to like the neon lace, leaving it on and askew. It wasn't covering much at this point anyway. He pinned Peacock's hips with his hands and swallowed him to the hilt.

Peacock gave a surprised cry, then another at how good it felt. He fisted a hand into hair just as soft as he'd hoped. Rowan was merciless, drawing hard and driving Peacock against the back of his mouth and throat. He'd definitely done this before. Peacock was fleetingly curious about his life in the wasteland, but he couldn't hold the thought. He braced a foot against Rowan's thigh, arching as sensation built.

"Rowan." Peacock tugged on his hair, but Rowan didn't heed the warning. It was too late. Rowan gave a deep happy sound, swallowing around him. He sat back, smug, and wiped his mouth. Then he reached down to milk the last spasms out of him with a slow, firm hand.

"Cheeky," Peacock said, panting. When he could, he rolled over and stalked toward Rowan on all fours. "My turn."

Rowan laughed. "You make it sound like a threat."

"Mm . . ." Peacock shoved him back, peeling those tight leather pants off him. He was as patient as Rowan had been hasty. He liked having a foreskin to play with. He liked Rowan's thickness and flush. He used every trick he knew.

Rowan's encouragement soon gave way to sounds of desperation, but Peacock didn't let up. When he slid a spit-slick finger into Rowan's ass, he had to squeeze him hard with his other hand to keep him from losing it right there. The veins stood out in Rowan's beautiful forearms as he clutched the hideous comforter.

"Please. No. Please, I can't."

Peacock looked up through his eyelashes, savoring a view of stark abs, a heaving chest, and Rowan's flushed, panicked face. He pulled off and scooted back, looking around for his discarded bag.

"Oh, I didn't mean to stop." Rowan's alarm was adorable.

"Who said anything about stopping?" Peacock rummaged for his lube, found it. Rowan hissed at the cool slide on his hot, tender flesh.

Rowan's eyes went wide—Were they gray or green? Peacock couldn't decide—as Peacock straddled him. He gripped Peacock's hips, gently at first. God, he was big. Peacock breathed deep, tilting his head back at the pleasure-pain of it. Pressure, and pressure, and pressure, and then the head of him slipped past tight muscles. Rowan gave a hoarse yell and bucked. A slick of burning heat. Peacock could feel every inch moving in him. It was too much for Rowan. His grip turned bruising, his hips snapping as if no speed or friction could be enough.

"Fuck yes!" Peacock shouted.

It was short, violent, and wonderful. Rowan collapsed back onto the bed, staring at the ceiling and gulping breaths. Peacock sat triumphant over his kill, feeling Rowan go soft inside him. Rowan whimpered when he slid free.

Peacock stretched out on top of him, watching Rowan fight off sleep. "Glad to see you're human after all." He'd been a bit worried at the stamina Rowan had shown so far, never mind brushing off a tranq like that.

"Will you keep watch?" Rowan asked. His earlier words clicked into place. Peacock was a little disappointed it wasn't a fetish.

"Yeah. I've got you."

Rowan was gone. He didn't move after that, even when Peacock cleaned him up with a pink washcloth and wrapped the blanket over him, or while Peacock took a long shower, or when Peacock slipped downstairs to order food. Peacock wanted to pop over to his flat to get a change of clothes. He wanted to stop by the clinic to see if Yuri had lived. But Rowan's trust held him there.

It was night again by the time Rowan woke, but the pub was still serving. Peacock bought him dinner since he had all his money. Rowan wolfed down his meal as if it would be his last. Then he ordered another. Peacock knocked back a pint, just watching, imagining that focus and appetite in other settings.

It was a shame to come to business.

"If they only got back yesterday, they'll be at Valhalla tonight for sure," he said when Rowan had finished.

"I need to walk this off before I fight anyone," Rowan said.

"You won't be fighting anyone till we follow them *away* from Valhalla. No charging in. Promise me." He pointed across the table.

Rowan nodded, thoughtful. After a pause, he asked, "Who was the other cute, suicidal man?" His tone mingled pleasure, as if glad to be included in the first category, and some hesitance that Peacock couldn't place.

"The bloke bleeding out on the table when you busted in."

Rowan frowned at his flippant tone. It took him a moment to press on. "Were you . . . friends?"

"Are you asking if we were fucking?" Peacock laughed, then laughed again at the blush covering Rowan's cheeks. What was this? It didn't make any sense. If they survived, Rowan would be headed back to the wasteland as soon as his revenge quest was over.

Looking at him now, Rowan out for blood made even less sense.

"You really wanna do this?" Peacock asked, not bothering to answer about Yuri. "The killing, I mean."

Rowan went from blushing to pale. He breathed like someone sorry he'd just eaten. Peacock imagined he was picturing whatever had happened to Aoife.

"She's past caring. What'll it help? You can kill these assholes, but you can't stop it happening again. Try to make an example, you'll just inspire the others. They dream of war."

"I care. Her family cares. How could I face them if I didn't try?"

Peacock winced at *family*. He wasn't sure if the pang was pity or jealousy, having the sort of life where your death had that weight.

He pushed away from the table. "Best get on it, then."

It was the worst night of his life, and it wasn't over yet. Events kept replaying in his head: Stopping by the clinic to bribe a can of Newskin off Mara and finding out that Yuri had died. Avoiding Rowan's awkward sympathy. Making him wait outside the flat while he changed. Stashing the credit chips—*Our lives are worth more than this.* Climbing into a smartcab and saying, "Valhalla."

Now they waited in a far corner of the dark lot, near a warbuggy Rowan thought he recognized. Hours of numb tension crept by, credit by credit on the smartcab's meter, as they listened to the roar of the crowd in the longhall swell and fade. Peacock had never stood on the shores of the rising sea, but he imagined it sounded just like that, something restless and hungry and merciless. He kept thinking about Yuri's cocky grin as he ducked into the white car and how heavy and limp he'd been in Peacock's arms when he cut him down just hours later, his golden skin bled pale. It was that easy to die.

Flush against his side in the close cab interior, Rowan smelled like sweaty fur and faint roses. He still smelled like sex. He was the most vital thing Peacock could imagine, all coiled energy and heat. Peacock couldn't bear the thought of watching him die. He'd thought he could save him, like he'd thought he could save Yuri. But he couldn't. Two men couldn't take on the roaring beast in that longhall.

He needed to go. Why couldn't he make himself go? Was it because Rowan trusted him in a way no one had before? Was it his odd gentleness? The way he looked at him, eyes full of wonder that turned lust into . . . something else?

"This isn't worth it," he said, low and urgent by Rowan's ear, as if whispering would help hide them.

"Those were all the credits I had," Rowan said, voice tight.

"I don't mean the bleeding credits."

Laughter and an off-key guild chant carried across the lot. Drunk warriors were wending their way toward them. Peacock's ear was near enough Rowan's cheek to hear his teeth creak. His pale eyes followed them—a lot more than the four he'd said were left to kill— as they piled onto a nearby buggy. Peacock had lost him.

The buggy roared to life and spread wings of fire. Metal-studded tires squealed and sparked as they careened past.

"That's them. Follow them!" Rowan yelled.

"Please specify a target vehicle," the cab replied in a pleasant monotone.

"That fucking buggy," Peacock hissed.

"Request not understood."

"Just go! Uh . . . west. Bollocks! They're headed toward bloody Blackbridge. Smartcab my arse, come on!"

"Would you like to go to Blackbridge Station?"

"Yes, thanks. It's an *emergency*!" That overrode the cab's speed limitations. He and Rowan were thrown back together into the plush seat as it accelerated from the lot.

The buggy was a torch blazing ahead of them, lighting the buildings to either side. They were gaining. No . . . it was slowing. It was stopping. It wheeled around, warriors whooping and leaning out the sides. It headed straight for them.

"Shit."

The cab's alarm chimed insistently and was cut short by the bang and screech of metal.

Smoke and blood in his mouth and eyes. Asphalt against his cheek. Pain. Hooting laughter. Peacock forced his eyes open. A polished armored boot toed his cheek till he was looking up. Figures were silhouetted against flames, spiked shoulders and hair and weapons.

"Rowan," he groaned. Where was he? Had they killed him already?

"Morning, lovely. You wouldn't want to miss this." A drunken croon. Someone straddled him, pulling at his belt.

Panic woke Peacock's muscles, and he struggled backward. The boot moved to his throat. Every time he squirmed, it pressed down harder. Rough hands yanked down his pants. *No, no, no.* His pulse thundered in his ears, echoes of that swelling roar. The beast had caught him. What came next was always bad, but with these men, it would be worse.

"Caorthann." He pushed the name past the crushing pressure. He couldn't breathe in.

Someone was choking, and it wasn't him. The weight on his throat lifted as the warrior stumbled backward. The man who'd been pawing him bellowed and stood, dragging at the hilt of an oversized sword at his back. He didn't have time to unsheathe it before he died.

Rowan crouched over him, hair and ruff singed and bloody. He had a knife in each hand. "Not him." He snarled at the others as they charged.

Peacock kicked the dead warrior off his legs and pulled up his pants. His hands shook as he fastened his belt. He was free. He should run.

Instead of running, he found himself hauling at that stupid sword. The tip sang along the pavement as he walked.

Not him.

It was hard to parse the chaos of light and shadow. There were the warriors, their backs to him as they circled warily through drifting smoke. They jerked and feinted like glitching avatars, attacking nothing. No, that was Rowan. He cut through them as if they were no more than holos and he the only solid body among them. He was so swift, so efficient, it took Peacock a while to understand as they fell.

Rowan still took a spiked bat to the side.

Peacock didn't remember how he'd gotten them back to his flat or why he'd gone there instead of the clinic. He'd emptied the can of Newskin over both of them, and the flat stank of plastic. They lay naked and tangled on the futon, not speaking or kissing. It was comfort, not sex.

And then it was sex. Gentle, clumsy sex, wordless and intense. They looked ridiculous, covered in milky film as they were, but Peacock didn't care. Rowan propped himself over him with his good arm and ground against him, tender flesh to tender flesh, holding his gaze the entire time. It was possessive in a way that should have pissed him off. Peacock hated protective men. Protectiveness had always come with a side of fists. It was just another name for someone's desire to control him.

This wasn't like that. It wasn't like that at all.

After they were spent, Rowan lay on him, trembling, hiding his face against Peacock's neck until he fell asleep. Peacock counted Rowan's rattling breaths through the hours, asking himself why he couldn't sleep for the need to hear each one. It was more than weariness of death and violence.

A man could only lie awake in silence for so long and keep lying to himself. He wanted to keep him.

"You were right," was the first thing Rowan said. It had been at least a day.

"Usually am." Relief thinned Peacock's voice. "About what?"

"It isn't any easier. It wasn't worth it. You could have died."

He spoke the last with a dangerous rawness. Peacock turned away and busied himself with the fridge. His flat was so small, nothing was out of arm's reach. He pulled out an Aquarius and handed it to Rowan without meeting his eyes. Rowan drank it to the bottom.

When Rowan reached for his pants, Peacock said, "The fuck you think you're doing?"

"I have to tell her family. It's the first thing I should have done. I was just too angry, too afraid to face them."

"It's all now or never with you." It was madness for Rowan to go now, when he was just on his feet. But Peacock couldn't tell him to stay and keep the truth from his voice.

Instead, he watched him don his vest and battered boots, his belts and weapons. There was just enough space for him to stand. He took up the entire room. All the space in Peacock's chest.

Then the asshole bent to kiss him goodbye. Peacock pushed his face away. "Off with you, then."

Rowan flinched and straightened. He only had to turn to be at the door. Maybe he was leaving like this for the same reason Peacock wasn't stopping him.

He looked back, just a pale eye and freckled cheekbone visible over the vest's singed ruff. "Would you mind if I came back?"

Silence stretched until hope shuttered in that beautiful eye. Rowan's face fell. He reached for the door.

"As if you could find the place."

Peacock stood slowly. He plucked a bolt from the quiver at Rowan's hip as Rowan turned to face him. A step forward backed Rowan against the door, skin against leather. Rowan's lips parted, either to speak or to kiss. Peacock held the bladed tip between their faces. The green light at its core pulsed like a heartbeat.

He tossed it onto the pillow.

ABOUT THE AUTHORS

Nyri A. Bakkalian, PhD, is a queer Armenian American by birth and a military historian by training. She is proud to have called both the American and Japanese Northeasts her home. Her writing, art, and photography have appeared in venues like *Gutsy Broads*, *Metropolis Japan*, *The Raven Chronicles*, *Gods and Radicals*, *Inklette*, and *QueerPGH*. Her essay "Curtains in the Breeze" won first place in *The Fountain Magazine*'s 2017 essay contest. What's her secret, you ask? Garlic and Turkish coffee. But really, mostly Turkish coffee. Follow her blog at sparrowdreams.com, support her writing at shiogamawaves.com, and come say hello to her on Twitter at @riversidewings.

Charleigh Brennan lives on a sheep farm in Vermont with permission of her dragon overlords. A San Francisco native, she is whimsical, pragmatic, and a chronic overthinker. She has studied folklore through extensive reading and her travels around the world. She writes about characters with diverse backgrounds who tend to be more than they appear. When she's not waiting for the sheep to quiet down so she can sleep or consulting her dragons on Very Important Matters, you can find her watching international movies with her Carl Jung action figure. Follow her on Facebook at Charleigh Brennan - Author.

Celosia Crane is a vintage maven by day and a romance author by night. She is a whiskey-loving lady with a passion for classic American muscle cars and a penchant for hair flowers, crinolines, and lipstick.

Weaving together themes of connection and second chances, her works include novella *Cardinals in the Snow* and *Whiskey Punch: A Vintage Hearts Novel*, published as a serial at www.patreon.com/celosiacrane. You can follow her antics at facebook.com/celosiacraneauthor, on Twitter at @CelosiaCrane, and on her lifestyle blog, celosiacrane.wordpress.com.

K.A. Fox is a proud military brat who has lived all over the world but now calls the Midwest home. She's a speculative fiction author who loves all things fantasy and science fiction, and a steamy bit of romance is always welcome.

She uses her psychological training daily to convince her husband and three sons that she's always right. She's looking forward to the day when her first novel, *The Devil's Own*, is available to all her readers.

When not writing, she can usually be found hiding somewhere with a book and a piece of chocolate or chasing after her adorable Hell Hound. You can connect with her at imkafox.com.

Patrisha Harrigan is a farm girl through and through. She plays in the dirt, deals with all manner of crap, and you rarely see her without a ball cap. She is a wife, mother, and aunt with a tendency to take in strays—human and animal.

She learned to create her own worlds at a young age as an escape from bullying and hopes to inspire others who suffer the same fate to do the same. Her husband is her high school sweetheart, and she firmly believes that there is someone out there for everyone.

When Patrisha is not wrangling critters, or kids, she visits the coffee shop in her head, where her characters gather to talk smack about her. You can follow her on Facebook at @PHarriganAuthor and on Twitter at @PatrishaHarrig2.

Ynes Malakova holds a deep reverence for the beauty found in darkness. With intense imagery and lyrical prose, she celebrates life, death, and the specter-like boundary between them. Her debut novel, *Viper*, is quickly nearing completion.

Ynes is known for her gothic elegance and has a closet full of sugar skulls, roses, and lace. Follow her at facebook.com/Ynes Malakova.

Dorothy Tinker grew up dreaming of fantastical worlds and creatures, of plots in space, and of strange new cultures. After studying mathematics in university, she rediscovered her true passion and rededicated herself to her literary dreams.

Since then, Dorothy has published an ongoing series of young adult spiritual/fantasy novels, *Peace of Evon*, *Gift of War*, and *Lost King*. Her short stories and poetry have appeared in anthologies by HWG Press, Inklings Publishing, Writespace, and OWS Ink.

You can follow her on Facebook at @DorothyTinkerAuthor and on Twitter at @dorothy_tinker, and you can support her writing at patreon.com/DorothyTinker.

Sarah Windsor is an emerging author of queer romance, cyberpunk, and fantasy. Reading fantasy novels with queer heroes gave her the courage to realize her own bisexuality, and she writes to share that courage and solace with others. Her queer protagonists find love and tenderness in hard worlds, happy endings they never would have imagined for themselves.

Sarah has a BA in fiction writing from the University of Pittsburgh and an MA in East Asian studies from Duke. But she truly learned storytelling through years of play-by-post roleplaying. She has lived in England and Japan and currently lives in Pittsburgh, which makes her cyberpunk heart sing with its rusty bridges, self-driving cabs, and tech conglomerates rising from the husks of old steel mills.

You can read her serialized fiction at windsorwritesblog.word press.com. Find her on Twitter at @Windsor_Writes and on Facebook at @CyberpunkAndUnicorns.

BALANCE OF SEVEN

Balance of Seven is an intersection of authors, literary network, publishing house, and author services. Though we focus on speculative fiction in all its forms, we love to support authors in all their literary endeavors. Whether that support takes the form of publishing their story in our biannual anthology, adding them to our list of associated authors, sharing their work in our online bookstore, or providing them with the contacts and services they need, we strive to provide quality assistance in any area they might need.

To learn more, visit our website at www.balanceofseven.com.

CREATIVE CENTRAL

Creative Central with Debbie Burns is a gathering place for kickass lady fiction writers who want belonging—people invested in us and us in them—and a *safe space* to grow our art. (Safe even from whiners, blamers, complainers, and unkind-ers.)

Uplifting, positive, supportive, kind—it's our very own Grand Central Station, where writers-of-all-walks meet, crossing lines as we travel our own unique journeys. Deb created this group so like-minded fiction writers (emerging, re-emerging, or otherwise) could ask questions, build relationships, celebrate wins, support fellow writers, and step boldly onto the path of career writing. We are all at different stages in developing our craft and careers, but in this group, we are all here for the same reason: to take our writing to the next level through collaboration, community, and education.

When a new lady fiction writer joins Creative Central, she embarks on the journey of living outside her comfort zone, practicing courage, reaching for her dreams, and following her Soul Song.

If this speaks to your own journey, come join us at www.creativecentral.me and share insights, chat experiences, ask questions, unravel writer's block, and find breakthroughs! Or just hang with the tribe and get your write on with other awesomesauce ladies like you.

Magic happens when we sing our Soul Songs.

And, girl, it's time for you to sing.

www.ingramcontent.com/pod-product-compliance
Lightning Source LLC
Chambersburg PA
CBHW070919190726
48292CB00004B/1024